I0524629

Whispers Of Betrayal

Amanda Burrows

Published by A.S.HUNT PUBLISHING, 2025.

WHISPERS OF BETRAYAL

First edition. January 30, 2025.

Copyright © 2025 Amanda Burrows.

ISBN: 978-1763848610

Written by Amanda Burrows.

Chapter 1: John's Suburban Life

John Hawthorne stepped through the threshold of his home, the early rays of the sun casting a golden glow over his well-groomed features. He inhaled the crispness of the suburban morning, filled with the scent of dew on manicured lawns and the distant aroma of jasmine from Mrs. Donnelly's trellis. With deft fingers, he adjusted the silk tie at his throat, a choice made by Sophie for its understated elegance, in a hue that mirrored the tranquil sky above.

The world around him hummed with the quiet symphony of routine. Leaves rustled gently in the whispering wind, casting shadows that danced on John's face, as if hinting at a life less ordinary. Deep down, he longed to be swayed by this silent melody and to break free from the invisible bars of predictability. Yet, here he was, preparing for another day, cocooned in the familiarity of schedules and deadlines.

As John stepped down from his porch, feeling the cool concrete beneath his polished shoes, he noticed his neighbour, Mr. Jenkins, walking down the sidewalk with his aging Golden Retriever, Buster. Mr. Jenkins smiled in recognition, and Buster wagged his tail in slow, lazy arcs.

"It's a beautiful day, isn't it?" Mr. Jenkins called out, a statement so common that it felt almost rehearsed.

"Indeed," John replied, the corners of his mouth lifting easily. "Though I suspect the flowers might start demanding a pay raise for working overtime in this sunshine."

Mr. Jenkins chuckled, the sound echoing through the air like the comforting rumble of distant thunder—safe and expected, yet still hinting at something more. John watched as the man continued on his way, the dog plodding obediently beside him. It was a scene of suburban contentment, but beneath the surface, John felt the undercurrents of restlessness tugging at him with unseen hands.

Holding the newspaper firmly in his hand, John turned back towards the house. The black ink on the white paper stood out sharply against the vibrant colours of his front garden. As his eyes scanned the headlines, his mind wandered, caught in the tide of what-ifs that frequently washed over his thoughts.

Sophie's presence lingered in the house like a subtle, ghostly perfume—delicate and an imprint of the stability they had built together. John found comfort in their shared silences and the unspoken understanding between them. However, the quiet also resonated with the whispers of unnamed desires and hidden yearnings.

As the door closed behind him, confining him once again within the well-ordered boundaries of his life, John couldn't shake the feeling that beyond the neatly trimmed hedges and winding driveways, adventure was calling to him like a siren, elusive and intoxicating. For now, however, it remained just out of reach, a whispered secret carried away by the morning breeze.

The morning commute unfolded before him like the opening credits of a movie he had seen too many times. The hum of his car's engine played a familiar tune, blending with the rhythmic clicking of the turn signal as he navigated each well-known corner. Suburban houses passed by his window in a blur of sameness, their manicured lawns and pristine sidewalks a testament to the quiet orderliness of this corner of the world.

John navigated the streets with an absent-minded ease, his hands automatically adjusting the steering wheel while his foot instinctively pressed and released the gas pedal. However, his gaze rarely focused on the road ahead; instead, it was drawn to his reflection in the rear-view mirror. There, a pair of sharp eyes stared back at him, glinting with a spark that belied the monotony of the drive. His mind wandered, not to the meetings that awaited him or the clients he would impress, but to a place where routine tasks and predictable interactions were replaced by the unpredictable thrill of excitement.

Upon arriving at the office, John stepped into the sterile embrace of the corporate world. The air conditioning hit his skin with an artificial chill as he walked through the maze of cubicles. Each cubicle was a carbon copy of the next, lined with grey fabric walls that seemed to absorb light rather than reflect it. John's own cubicle awaited him—a small kingdom of order amidst the chaos of ambition and ladder-climbing.

He settled into his chair, the cushion moulding to the shape it had taken on over years of use. Before him, the computer screen flickered to life, serving as a portal to a digital world filled with emails and spreadsheets. He sifted through the messages with mechanical precision, like a conductor orchestrating a symphony of replies and forwards. Yet, beneath this surface of efficiency, a whisper of discontent stirred. It was subtle, like the brush of a feather or a hint of fragrance carried on the wind, but it was there—a feeling that something vital was missing from his life.

As John shuffled through papers filled with figures and charts, the fluorescent lights overhead cast a pale glow over the scene. It felt as if the vibrant colours of the outside world had been drained away, leaving only shades of grey. He sensed the weight of unseen eyes watching him, while his colleagues engaged in their own silent struggles against monotony, each one reflecting his own restlessness.

Outside, the city buzzed with life—unseen and unheard, yet deeply felt. The sun traced patterns across the high-rise buildings, casting long shadows that crept closer as the day progressed. Somewhere in the distance, behind the glass and concrete, lay the answer to the longing that simmered within John Hawthorne's chest—an answer as elusive as a dream upon waking, and as intangible as the shifting patterns of light and dark that danced on the walls of his cubicle.

John's laughter blended with the noise of voices in the break room, creating a lively atmosphere of midday relaxation. The air was filled with the smell of microwaved meals and coffee, familiar scents that wrapped around him like an old blanket—comforting yet suffocating. He leaned against the counter, sipping his lukewarm coffee, his eyes sparkling with the well-honed wit he shared as he exchanged stories with his colleagues.

Amidst the cheerful clinks of cutlery and the shuffle of shoes on linoleum, John's gaze drifted toward the window. Outside, the world basked under the bold rays of the midday sun. Light filtered through the leaves, casting intricate patterns on the pavement below. It was a canvas of freedom, with each shadow representing a stroke of possibility—a stark contrast to the confined existence within these walls.

For a moment, silence enveloped John as he watched the dance of nature. His heart synced to a rhythm that promised more than just spreadsheets and sales targets. A tightening in his chest signalled an unnamed longing, a silent call that beckoned him toward unknown shores. In that fleeting moment, laughter faded into the background, the break room became distant, and John found himself at the edge of an abyss, gazing into the depths of his own uncharted desires.

The clock's hands lurched forward, breaking the stillness, and with it, the spell was shattered. John returned to the present, the laughter reigniting in his throat as if the moment of introspection had never occurred.

As the day progressed, the warmth of the morning sun was replaced by the cool, harsh glow of fluorescent lights. Shadows grew longer across John's cubicle, with the sterile grey partitions standing as a silent testament to the hours he had spent inside. With careful movements, he packed away the items that represented his work—the pens, the notepad filled with reminders, and the headset hanging limply by the computer screen. Each object was a part of the puzzle that was John Hawthorne: efficient, reliable, and painfully predictable.

He slipped on his jacket, its fabric softly brushing against his skin, a secret promise of the world beyond his mundane routine. The weight of monotony pressed down on him like a physical force, becoming a constant companion that shaped his posture and dulled the brightness in his eyes. As he walked through the emptying corridors, the echo of his footsteps created a solitary rhythm against the silence of departing souls. John felt the sharp edge of solitude nipping at his heels.

As he settled into his car, the seat wrapped around him like the embrace of a partner whose passion had long faded. The engine roared to life, its steady rhythm echoing in the dimming light. He navigated through the evening traffic, the red and white glow of brake lights blending together to create a watercolour of routine and resignation.

Home awaited him, its shape etched into his very being—a sanctuary that both soothed and suffocated. As John drove, he carried with him the ghost of the day—a phantom that whispered of other lives and distant dreams. Its breath was warm against the nape of his neck, stirring the restless spirit that lay dormant within the heart of John Hawthorne.

The key slid into the lock with a sound that echoed through John's spirit, signalling the transition from his public persona to his private self. As he crossed the threshold of his home, he loosened his tie—a silk noose—each pull allowing him to escape more from the day's facade of contentment.

In his bedroom, he removed the corporate armour piece by piece, the fabric falling away like layers of skin and revealing the man beneath—someone who craved excitement and the taste of the unexplored. He put on casual attire, a soft cotton shirt that clung to his torso, hinting at the fitness he maintained not for vanity, but as a vestige of control in a life scripted by others.

Stepping into the open air, John welcomed the embrace of the suburban landscape. He coaxed the dormant lawnmower from the shed, awakening the mechanical beast to tame the unruly yard. As he guided it across the lawn, the scent of freshly cut grass filled the air, an earthy aroma that stirred something primal within him.

He marched back and forth, the rhythmic push and pull of the mower creating a dance of solitude. With each stride, a strip of unruly green surrendered to his efforts, transforming into part of the neat, uniform expanse. It was a meditative ritual; the hum of the engine served as a chant that lulled his racing thoughts into a sense of peace. Yet, restlessness lingered—a current just beneath the surface, threatening to rise and flood his senses with longing.

Once the last blade of grass had been cut by the mower, John stood back with his hands on his hips, surveying his work. The lawn stretched before him, a beautiful expanse of emerald precision, both striking and temporary. A wave of accomplishment washed over him, but it faded as quickly as it came, leaving behind the familiar feeling of dissatisfaction.

"Looks good, John!" called a neighbour from across the street, her voice cutting through the quiet of the early evening.

"Thanks, Diane," he replied, his voice carrying the warmth expected of him, a reflection of the setting sun that painted the houses in hues of gold and amber. They exchanged pleasantries, words tossed back and forth like a well-worn ball—comforting in their predictability, yet confining as the fences that bordered their properties.

As the neighbour retreated into her home, John stood alone once more, and the silence returned like an old friend. He looked at the neat rows of houses; the idyllic scene was a canvas on which his doubts cast long shadows. The serenity of the suburbs both soothed and smothered him—a safe haven that whispered of other lives unlived and passions unkindled in the quiet desperation of everyday life.

With a sigh, he put the mower back in its shed, the door closing with a finality that echoed the end of another day. The veil of twilight descended upon the neighbourhood, a shroud that promised rest while hinting at the darkness lurking beneath the most tranquil of façades.

John sank into the weathered wicker chair on his porch, a cold beer cradled in his hand as he welcomed the gentle evening breeze. It brushed the sweat from his brow, a comforting touch to soothe the day's exertions. Around him, the world unfolded its twilight symphony—the distant laughter of children chasing the last rays of sunlight, and the persistent hum of cicadas marking the slow descent into night. Each sound was a thread in the tapestry of suburban tranquillity, yet each one whispered to John of a life too neatly trimmed, like the lawns that stretched before him.

The amber liquid in his glass caught the fading light, casting a warm glow against the backdrop of encroaching shadows. He brought the beer to his lips; the cool bitterness was a welcome contrast to the warmth lingering in the air, a remnant of the day's heat. As he sipped, his gaze wandered, tracing the familiar outlines of homes that were both a sanctuary and a prison.

A sudden rumble broke the calm, disrupting the quiet of this corner of the world. John leaned forward, looking past the picket fences as a moving truck lumbered into view, its engine growling like a beast that disturbed the evening's tranquillity. It came to a stop next door, an anomaly amidst the stillness, a sign of impending change.

With his interest piqued, John set down his glass and rested his elbows on his knees, watching with a curiosity that felt almost inappropriate. The side of the truck creaked open, revealing a spacious interior filled with secrets and histories belonging to strangers. A sense of anticipation curled within him, a whisper of excitement that slithered through his mind, hinting at the unknown and promising a disruption to the carefully curated monotony of his life.

He squinted, trying to see more than just the silhouette of movement inside the vehicle. Who were these newcomers? What stories did they bring to this orderly neighbourhood, where every tale seemed already told and every ending written?

As each box and piece of furniture transitioned from shadow to the hands of unseen movers, John felt a pull—a seductive tug at the edges of his consciousness. It was the allure of the unknown, the scent of fresh ink on the pages of life—both potent and intoxicating. As the sky shifted to hues of bruise and blossom, creating a canvas ripe for new beginnings, John Hawthorne sat on his porch. The cooling breeze, fading daylight, and rhythmic thrum of the cicadas wove together, creating a blanket of expectancy that settled on his shoulders with deceptive weight.

The dance of dusk enveloped the suburban street in a gentle gloom as John's eyes followed the movements of people weaving through shafts of fading light, their silhouettes outlined against the orange-tinged sky. Boxes and furniture appeared like relics unearthed from a crypt, each silently testifying to lives he had yet to know. The steady shuffle of feet on the concrete was punctuated by the soft thuds of possessions being set down, creating a staccato rhythm that spoke of both endings and new beginnings.

John observed from his porch a solitary figure shrouded in shadows, as potential emerged within the mundane scene before him. The clink of his beer bottle against the railing marked the passage of time in this everyday theatre. As he watched, his mind unravelled a tapestry woven with speculation. Who were these neighbours whose arrival hinted at promises of change? A writer seeking solace in the quiet neighbourhood? A couple caught up in the thrill of new love? His imagination flickered like the candlelight in the windows across the street, casting shifting patterns upon the canvas of his thoughts.

The sun, once a fiery orb, now danced at the horizon, captivating the world with the warmth of twilight. Its descent unveiled a beautiful array of colours, creating a symphony across the clouds. Long shadows stretched across the street, cradling the scene in an embrace that hinted at secrets to be revealed by nightfall.

John finished his beer, the last drop of liquid courage giving him the confidence to face the coming night. He stood up and stretched lazily, his muscles slowly relaxing after a long day. For a moment, he lingered, enjoying the crisp scent of the approaching nightfall. The moving truck, an unwelcome sight in the familiar landscape, served as a stark reminder of the changes that sweep through life, often ignoring the comfort of routine.

With a sigh that reflected his restlessness, John turned away from the unfolding story next door. It was time to retreat indoors, to the solitude of four walls that were all too familiar. Yet, the echo of the moving truck and the scent of fresh beginnings clung to him like a second skin as he crossed the threshold into the quiet predictability of his home.

The kitchen was softly illuminated by the under-cabinet lights as John set a pot of water on the stove. The hiss of the gas flame broke the silence. He moved with the precision of routine, yet the clinks and clatters of dishes echoed like whispers of change within the empty space. As he chopped vegetables for a simple stir-fry, the rhythm of the knife against the cutting board served as a metronome, ticking away the seconds of anticipation that had settled in his mind.

With each slice, John's thoughts cut through the veil of normalcy, drifting back to the moving truck, which had left a lasting impression on the landscape of suburbia. As dinner sizzled in the pan, a symphony of crackles and pops played in contrast to the quiet hum of his longing. The aroma of garlic and spices filled the air, simple yet rich, reflecting the dichotomy of his life—comfortable but yearning for complexity.

John settled down at the dining table, the familiar creak of the chair serving as a gentle reminder of evenings gone by. With a fork in hand, he took a bite, the flavours mingling with a savory sense of curiosity. Each mouthful was accompanied by images of unknown faces and untold stories that might be unfolding next door. A sense of anticipation grew within him, a subtle intoxication swirling through his veins.

Dinner concluded in solitude, with the echo of utensils serving as a stark reminder of the emptiness of the house. The very walls seemed to pulse with a rhythm of possibility, yearning alongside him for the injection of new life into their well-worn grooves. As he cleared the table, the soft scrape of porcelain against wood felt like the closing of one chapter and the tentative opening of another.

As night draped its velvet cloak over the world outside, John ascended the stairs, each step echoing the day's events. He prepared for bed, going through the familiar rituals of brushing his teeth and pulling back the covers, which grounded him in the moment but could not anchor the drift of his thoughts. With the lights extinguished, he lay in the dark, a solitary figure beneath the expanse of a comforter that enveloped him like a promise.

The day replayed behind his closed eyelids—the monotonous click of keyboards, laughter that never quite reached the eyes, and the comforting banality of mowed lawns. Amidst it all was the image of the moving truck. It loomed in his mind, a harbinger of the uncharted, its silhouette etched against the dusk, stirring within John a mix of trepidation and intrigue.

As his breath fell into the steady rhythm of impending sleep, John surrendered to the night. The image of the moving truck lingered, its existence straddling the line between reality and a dreamscape. It stood solid and inscrutable, its contents hidden behind metal walls, symbolizing the unknown that beckoned from just beyond the horizon of John's neatly plotted life.

And as he drifted into slumber, it was not the tranquillity of his ordered existence that cradled him, but the whisper of change—the allure of a new dawn that might finally satisfy the restless spirit smouldering quietly within the man named John Hawthorne.

Chapter 2: Jessica's Arrival

John stepped out onto his porch, feeling the cool wood beneath his bare feet as he leaned against the whitewashed railing. His gaze drifted across the street, where the large moving truck was still parked, its side wide open to reveal the contents of someone's life: stacked cardboard boxes and covered furniture. The air was thick with the anticipation of change, and the morning sun cast long shadows that seemed to reach out toward John, inviting him into the quiet drama of the day.

As he watched, a car—a sleek convertible that gleamed like a drop of mercury under the burgeoning light—pulled up behind the truck. The driver's door opened with a smooth click, and she emerged. She stepped into the world around her as though it were a stage set for her entrance alone. Her long chestnut hair unfurled in a fluid motion, catching stray beams of sunlight that transformed it into a silken banner of warmth.

She moved with an undeniable grace, her confident strides leaving whispers of her presence in the air—hints of jasmine and adventure. The movers, dressed in their plain uniforms, paused in their routine of heavy lifting as her voice broke through the morning's silence. Her instructions were not loud, but they held the weight of authority, each syllable imbued with elegance, and each pause a deliberate touch of command, delivered with an artist's finesse.

John stood frozen in place, captivated by the scene unfolding before him. There was something magical about the way she engaged with her surroundings, as if the very air shifted to accommodate her presence. He found himself an observer on the threshold of his own home, enveloped in the subtle energies of possibility that radiated from this woman who had entered his familiar world, bringing with her the promise of untold stories.

John's gaze lingered as he traced the outlines of her silhouette while she moved effortlessly among the movers. The air seemed charged with her presence, and he felt his breath catch in his chest, the rhythm of his anticipation matching the quickened pace of his heart. She was like a living sonnet, each movement a line of poetry that held him spellbound.

The sun shimmered in her hair, giving her an ethereal crown, while a gentle breeze carried whispers of jasmine that tantalized his senses. John's world, once predictable with its suburban rhythms, now pulsed with an enigmatic vibrancy, all because of this stranger who had unknowingly captured his attention.

Compelled by a force he couldn't define, John descended the steps of his porch, his feet carrying him toward the epicentre of his sudden fascination. His smile was practiced, the embodiment of neighbourly charm, yet beneath the surface, a storm of nerves fluttered like captive birds against his ribcage.

"Good morning, my name is John Hawthorne," he called out, his voice surprisingly steady despite the internal tumult. To any onlooker, he would appear the epitome of calm—a man in control—but the reality was a surging sea of emotions, each wave crashing against the walls he had meticulously built around his orderly life.

The morning light, now a golden cascade, seemed to pause in reverence as she turned, her gaze locking onto John's with a force that robbed him of reason. Her eyes glinted like twin emeralds, alive with a fire that danced and beckoned. The air between them crackled, charged with the electricity of an impending storm.

"John Hawthorne," she said, her voice a melody that resonated within his chest, "I'm Jessica Sterling." The corners of her lips curled upward in a smile that held secrets and promises, each word dipped in an allure that was as intoxicating as it was dangerous.

"Looks like you could use an extra set of hands," John offered, his own voice a traitorous mix of composure and raw edge. He nodded toward a box that seemed to groan under the weight of its contents, its cardboard sides bulging, straining to contain whatever treasures lay inside.

Jessica's laughter, light and infused with warmth, filled the space between them. "That would be wonderful, thank you." She gestured gracefully towards the burden, accepting his proposition with an ease that belied the gravity of the task.

As they approached the box, their steps fell into a silent rhythm, a dance preordained by the subtle forces that pulled the strings of destiny. John bent down, his fingers grazing the rough surface of the container, while Jessica mirrored his movements on the opposite side. Together, they heaved the box upwards, the strain in their muscles a testament to the weight of both the object and the moment.

The box lifted, and with it, an unspoken understanding rose—a recognition of the energy that flowed between them, binding them in a shared purpose, yet hinting at depths yet to be explored. They moved together, a synchrony that felt as ancient as time itself, carrying their load with a coordination that suggested they were two halves of a whole, only just now made complete.

Their conversation hung suspended, a delicate thread weaving through the tapestry of their encounter, binding them in a narrative that was only beginning to unfold. As they journeyed in tandem, the box between them became a vessel for their burgeoning connection, a silent witness to the nascent spark that had ignited without warning beneath the suburban sun.

Their hands met inadvertently, a fleeting touch over the cardboard edge that crackled with a charge neither had anticipated. John's fingers brushed against Jessica's, and for a moment, electricity surged through him—a silent strike that left his nerves alight and his heart throbbing in a bewildering cadence. The texture of her skin was a whisper against his, sending ripples through the still air of the afternoon. He withdrew slightly, startled by the intensity of the contact, yet craving its return.

"Careful," he murmured, more to himself than to her, as they secured their hold on the box.

"Always am," Jessica replied, her voice a melody that seemed to dance around him, wrapping him in layers of allure. She shifted her grip, and the distance between their hands grew, leaving John oddly bereft.

As they moved, the weight of the box forced them into a slow march, their steps measured and deliberate. The sunlight filtered through the swaying branches above, casting dappled shadows across Jessica's face, turning her emerald eyes into shifting pools of light and dark.

"So, what brings you to our little corner of the world?" John asked, breaking the silence that had enveloped them. His voice was steady, betraying none of the turmoil that her presence stirred within him.

Jessica glanced sideways at him, her gaze sharpening with a hint of curiosity. "A fresh start," she said simply, her words floating out like a secret carried on the breeze. There was a weight behind them, though, a gravity that hinted at more than just a change of scenery.

"Fresh starts can be good," John ventured, intrigued by the mystery that clung to her like a second skin. "Sometimes, it's all we need."

"Indeed," she agreed, the corner of her mouth tilting up into a smile that didn't quite reach her eyes. It was a smile that spoke of knowledge and experiences far beyond what her youthful countenance suggested.

They navigated the path to her new abode, the box a shared burden that somehow felt lighter with each step. The conversation ebbed and flowed, but questions lingered, hanging like ripe fruit in the thickening air. John wanted to pluck them one by one, to taste the truth of what lay hidden beneath Jessica's composed exterior. Yet he held back, wary of trespassing too quickly into the garden of secrets she cultivated with such care.

The scent of freshly cut grass mingled with the subtle perfume that wafted from Jessica—the fragrance delicate yet intoxicating. It wrapped around him, drawing him closer to the enigma that was Jessica Sterling. As they set the box down upon the threshold of her new beginning, John couldn't help but feel that he, too, was on the precipice of something entirely unfamiliar and undeniably compelling.

They continued in step, the box a silent mediator in their impromptu partnership. John's wit found its mark, a quip about the eccentricities of local fauna slipping from his lips with the ease of old friends sharing inside jokes. "You'll find the squirrels here have quite the aristocratic air about them," he said, a playful glint in his eye.

Jessica's laugh broke free, a rich, melodic sound that seemed to dance on the sunlight filtering through the oak leaves above. It was a genuine expression of delight, one that etched itself into John's memory, warming the secret places of his heart that yearned for such unrestrained joy.

"Is that so?" she replied, her eyes sparkling with amusement. "I suppose I'll have to prepare my best curtsy then."

The camaraderie between them was as natural as the breeze whispering secrets to the swaying grass. A bond, tenuous yet undeniable, spun its delicate web, drawing them closer with each shared smile and knowing glance.

As they approached the final resting place for the cumbersome box, they lowered it gently to the ground, their movements synchronized in an intimate ballet of cooperation. The box settled with a soft thud, but neither stepped away immediately, caught in the gravity of the moment.

Their eyes met, locking in a silent conversation that words would only diminish. In Jessica's gaze, John discovered an ocean of hidden depths, and he found himself drawn to the brink, tempted by the siren call of her emerald eyes. There was an invitation there, subtle as the shifting shadows, yet as potent as the electric touch they had shared just moments before.

The air around them seemed charged, heavy with anticipation, as if the universe itself held its breath, waiting for the inevitable collision of their separate worlds. John felt the pull, an irresistible force tethered not to the mundane, but to the extraordinary promise that Jessica embodied.

It was a look that spoke of possibilities—the kind that whispered of moonlit confessions and the thrill of shared secrets. And though the space between them remained unbreeched, the connection that sparked to life was as tangible as the warm earth beneath their feet.

The silence that fell between them was thick with unspoken thoughts, a delicate veil that neither was quite ready to lift. John stood motionless, caught in the stillness of time as his gaze traced the contours of Jessica's form. The sundress she wore clung to her like a second skin, its fabric dancing gently in the summer breeze, outlining the curves that spoke of a femininity both bold and unapologetic. There was an artistry in the way it moved with her, a silent testament to the life force she carried within.

Sunlight played across her hair, turning it into ribbons of burnished copper, and for a moment, John imagined the softness of those tresses between his fingers. The air was laced with the subtle scent of her perfume, a fragrance that seemed to weave itself into the very fabric of the day, intoxicating in its understated complexity. It was a scent that promised hidden layers, much like the woman who wore it, and

John found himself leaning subtly into the breeze, wanting—no, needing—to capture more of it.

"Thank you, John," Jessica's voice sliced through the quietude, rich and melodic, pulling him back from his reverie. "Really, I can't tell you how much I appreciate the help." Her smile was genuine, touching the corners of her eyes in a way that made them sparkle with sincerity and something else—something deeper.

Her excitement about the move was palpable, vibrating in the space around her with the intensity of a plucked string. Yet beneath it, there lay a shadow, a nuance of emotion that hinted at stories untold, stories that lingered on the edge of revelation, shrouded in mystery. The sunlight seemed to cast more than just shadows; it threw into relief the intricate tapestry of her past, each thread a story waiting to be unravelled.

John nodded, his own smile a mirror of mixed emotions. "It's no trouble at all," he replied, though the words felt inadequate against the backdrop of his racing heart. In that simple exchange, there was a transaction of more than just gratitude; there was the weaving of a connection, the kind that could not be easily broken or forgotten.

John stood motionless, watching as Jessica turned away from him and walked back towards the flurry of movers. Each step she took seemed to echo in his pulse, sending ripples through the stillness that blanketed his thoughts. The afternoon sun dipped lower, casting a golden hue over the scene, making the ordinary act of moving house appear like a dance of light and shadow. There was an air of finality in her stride, a sense of closing one chapter and stepping into another.

The subtle sway of her dress against her legs, the purposeful yet graceful way she communicated with the movers—everything about Jessica exuded a quiet command that fascinated John. As he observed her blend into the orchestrated chaos, his mind swirled with conjecture and curiosity. Who was this enigmatic woman who had suddenly appeared in his orbit, disrupting the gravitational pull of his neatly ordered life?

He felt it then—a burgeoning anticipation, a prelude to a symphony not yet played. This encounter, he sensed, was merely the overture to something far more profound. There was a story unfolding before him, one that promised to be as complex as the intricate patterns of a spider's web glistening with morning dew.

Turning on his heel, John made his way back to his porch, but with each step, a restlessness stirred within him. It was as if Jessica's presence had awakened dormant desires, teased out longings he had pressed into the silent corners of his heart. He couldn't quite put a name to the sensation—it was like the whisper of velvet against skin, enticing and unsettling all at once.

His hands, previously steady and sure, now trembled slightly as he pushed them into the pockets of his jeans. The comfortable predictability of his existence suddenly felt like a well-worn garment that no longer fit. There was a shift in the air, a current that tugged at him, suggesting that the path he had so carefully trodden was about to diverge in ways unimaginable.

A faint breeze caressed his face, carrying with it the lingering scent of Jessica's perfume—a haunting melody that played upon his senses, refusing to be ignored. He paused at the steps to his porch, caught in the liminal space between his known world and the mysterious allure of the unknown.

With a deep breath, John stepped onto the porch, his gaze inadvertently searching for hers once more. Though she was focused on the task at hand, there was a magnetism that drew him, an unspoken invitation embedded in the very air that separated them.

John was leaning against the wooden railing of his porch, his eyes tracing the contours of Jessica's form as she moved with assured grace among the boxes and furniture. A mix of intrigue and yearning settled into his bones, a silent promise that whispered of more to come.

John's hand grazed the worn grain of the porch railing, its splintered edges a stark reminder of the tangible world as he struggled against the pull of an intangible force. Against the backdrop of his quaint and quiet life, Jessica was a vibrant stroke of colour, her presence igniting an undercurrent of longing that rippled beneath the surface of his calm exterior.

The scent of freshly cut grass mingled with the distant hum of the moving van, grounding him in the here and now while the taste of possibility lingered on his tongue, sweet and intoxicating.

With each step he took away from the edge of his porch, John felt the subtle shift within him deepen—a visceral tug that moulded his restlessness into a yearning for the unexplored depths that Jessica's emerald gaze promised. There was an electric charge in the space she occupied, a silent siren call that resonated with the hidden chambers of his heart.

As he reached the threshold of his front door, a pause arrested his movements. Compelled by a force beyond his understanding, John cast a final glance over his shoulder.

There she was, directing the movers with a dancer's poise. Her chestnut hair caught the rays of the sun, igniting with a fiery glow that outlined her figure in a halo of warmth. Even at a distance, the aura of her confidence was palpable, stirring the air into whispers of silk against skin.

For a moment, their eyes connected across the expanse—the briefest of exchanges, yet laden with the weight of unspoken promises. It was a look that spoke of new beginnings and veiled secrets, a look that hinted at shared laughter and uncharted territories of desire.

John turned, stepping through his doorway and into the cool of his home, the image of Jessica imprinted behind his eyelids. As the door closed softly behind him, sealing off the outside world. The promise of more hung in the air, as tangible as the lingering touch of sunlight on his skin.

Chapter 3: The Pool Encounter

John stepped onto the scorching pavement surrounding the community pool, a mirage of heat waves shimmering above the concrete. The afternoon sun was oppressive, its fiery touch clinging to his skin with a relentless fervour. He squinted against the blinding glare, casting his gaze over the exuberant tableau before him—children playing a cacophony of splashes and laughter, parents lounging under the intermittent shade of broad umbrellas.

The air buzzed with the sound of summer in full swing, yet it was as if John moved through a silent film, the noise around him fading into a distant hum. His presence was an unnoticed ripple in the vibrant oasis, his mind adrift on the currents of his own restlessness.

Then, amidst the chaos, his attention snagged on a solitary figure reclining languidly by the water's edge. Jessica Sterling. Her green bikini was a verdant promise against her sun-kissed skin, a stark contrast that drew the eye like a beacon. She lay stretched out on a lounger, the embodiment of leisure, her chestnut hair splayed behind her in a dark fan against the white cushion.

As if compelled by some magnetic force, their gazes locked across the crowded space. It was a moment suspended in time, a silent communication that thrummed with unspoken understanding. The world seemed to tilt, the sounds of merriment dimming further, replaced by the resonant beat of John's heart in his ears.

In the limpid pools of Jessica's emerald eyes, he found an echo of his own hidden desires—a longing for a connection that transcended the ordinary, a yearning for something that promised to unsettle the carefully structured life he'd built. A shiver of anticipation traced his spine, as though the sultry air had suddenly become charged with electricity.

They held each other's gaze for a breath, a beat, a pulse of time that spoke volumes. There was recognition, a mutual awareness of the precipice upon which they both teetered. And then, just as quickly as it had materialised, the moment evaporated, leaving behind a lingering sense of what could be, an uncharted territory ripe with possibility.

John felt the heat of the day wrap around him again, a stifling blanket that now seemed infused with the intoxicating scent of chlorine and sunscreen. With each step closer to where Jessica lay, the everyday scene regained its volume, but it couldn't drown out the silent symphony that played between them—a prelude to the slow-burn dance that awaited.

John's stride carried a casual confidence, the kind that came from years of navigating suburban pleasantries and manicured lawns. As he approached Jessica, the vibrant cacophony of the community pool seemed to recede into a hazy backdrop, leaving only the sound of his own heartbeat echoing in his ears. The sun bore down on them, relentless and scorching, but it was the heat emanating from her presence that truly made his skin tingle with anticipation.

"Quite the scorcher today, isn't it?" John quipped, breaking the silence with an ease that belied the quickening pulse within him. His shadow fell over her like a cool reprieve from the sun's glare, casting them both in a shared, intimate dimness.

Jessica's lips curled into a knowing smile, her eyes gleaming with mischief. "I've always thought the best way to beat the heat is to surrender to it," she replied, her voice a melody that seemed to stir the air around them.

Their banter flowed as easily as the water in the pool, light-hearted yet charged with an undercurrent of something deeper, something neither of them could—or perhaps wanted to—name just yet.

"Care to put that theory to the test?" John extended a hand, an invitation hanging between them like the subtle fragrance of her sun-kissed skin.

"Lead the way," Jessica said, accepting his offer with a grace that seemed to defy the oppressive atmosphere.

Together, they stepped towards the pool, their movements synchronised in silent concordance. The moment their bodies met the embrace of the water, the world shifted into refreshing clarity. The liquid coolness enveloped them, soothing the fire of the afternoon sun, offering a respite that sank deep into their cores.

John felt the contrast keenly—the blistering heat of the day against the serene chill of the pool. It was a duality that mirrored the opposition within him: the stable, structured life he knew so well, up against the thrilling lure of the unknown that Jessica represented. She swam with an effortless elegance beside him, her body cutting through the water with fluid strokes, leaving ripples of promise in her wake.

As the two of them moved in the tranquil refuge of the water, there was a palpable sense of crossing into uncharted territory. The mundane faded away, leaving behind only the heady mix of chlorine and the subtle dance of sunlight filtering through the ripples above.

John's laughter mingled with the sound of splashing as he feigned a clumsy stroke, his hand brushing against Jessica's arm under the guise of an accidental encounter. The fleeting touch sent a jolt like electricity through him, and he could tell by the quick upward quirk of her lips that she felt it too. A dance of ripples encircled them, distorting their reflections below—a fitting metaphor for the blurring lines between playful jest and earnest desire.

"Careful there, John," she teased, her voice a siren song amid the cacophony of poolside revelry. "Wouldn't want you to drown in your own charm."

"Ah, but what a way to go," he shot back, grinning as he executed a deliberate splash in her direction, sending droplets cascading down her sun-kissed shoulders.

Jessica retaliated, a cascade of water arcing gracefully from her fingertips, glittering in the sunlight before they showered over him. Their eyes locked, the world around them fading into obscurity, leaving only the sensation of cool water and warmer intentions swirling between them.

Eventually, the laughter subsided, replaced by a charged silence as they treaded water at arm's length. Every shared glance was laden with unspoken words, each teasing remark loaded with possibility. The tension was a living thing that moved with them, wrapping around their limbs like the gentle lapping waves.

With an unspoken agreement, they swam to the edge and hoisted themselves out of the pool. Water trailed in rivulets down their bodies, gravity pulling each drop toward the sunbaked concrete. They claimed a pair of loungers side by side, the heat radiating off the surface a stark contrast to the cool embrace they had just left behind.

John reclined, feeling the warmth penetrate his skin, seeping into his muscles and bones. He listened to the rhythmic dripping of water from their bodies, a natural metronome marking the passing moments of silent contemplation. His breath came easier now, yet it was peppered with anticipation of what lay beyond this interlude of sun and calm.

Beside him, Jessica stretched out, her silhouette a vision of languid grace. She reached for a towel, dabbing at her face with delicate pats before spreading it beneath her. The sun illuminated her features, casting a glow that seemed to capture the very essence of summer's allure.

As the heat worked its magic, drying their dampened attire, John caught himself stealing glances. He watched the rise and fall of Jessica's chest with each breath, the way droplets clung stubbornly to her skin, defying evaporation. It was a moment suspended in time, every detail etched into his memory with vivid clarity—the beginning of something he couldn't yet define but knew he would chase to whatever end awaited.

The sun, a golden orb descending towards the horizon, drenched the poolside in its warm, amber glow. John shifted in his lounger, turning to face Jessica, whose presence was as intoxicating as the fragrant bloom of night-blooming jasmine carried on the evening breeze.

"Have you ever been scuba diving?" he asked, finding an opening into the depths of their conversation. His voice was casual, but his heart thrummed with a rhythm that betrayed his calm exterior.

"Only once," she replied, her eyes sparkling with the reflection of the water's surface. "In the Caribbean. The underwater world is so surreal, like stepping into a dream." Her words painted a picture, vibrant and alive, inviting him into her past adventures.

"Sounds mesmerising," he murmured, picturing her enveloped in the embrace of the ocean's depths. They exchanged tales of travel and escape, each anecdote peeling back another layer, revealing kindred spirits caught in the web of mundane existence, both yearning for more.

As they spoke, John found himself ensnared by the ease of their interaction, the way her laughter seemed to resonate within his chest. It was as though they were old friends, reuniting after years apart, comfortable and familiar despite the brevity of their acquaintance.

The conversation flowed, meandering through topics as if they were strolling down a garden path. She shared stories of moonlit walks on foreign shores, while he recounted the thrill of navigating the chaotic streets of distant cities. Their words danced together, creating a tapestry of experiences shared and separate, yet somehow intertwined.

A silence fell between them—a silent reprieve heavy with unspoken thoughts. John lay back, letting the last rays of sunlight caress his face, stirring the shadows around them into a soft, velvety darkness. He closed his eyes, inhaling deeply, allowing the scent of chlorine and sunscreen to anchor him to the moment.

In the quietude, John's mind wandered, drawn irresistibly towards the enigma lying beside him. Jessica, with her enigmatic past and intriguing confidence, had slipped under his skin without warning. The pull towards her was undeniable, magnetic, as if she were the north to his compass needle.

He wrestled internally, caught in a tempest of desire and duty. A part of him craved the adventure she embodied, the promise of unknown pleasures and secret whispers in the dark. Yet, there was the life he had built, the commitments he had made, anchors of responsibility that tethered him to a reality he could not simply abandon.

John opened his eyes, staring up at the sky now streaked with hues of pink and orange. The day's heat lingered, a ghostly touch upon his flesh, mirroring the smouldering conflict within his soul. He turned his head, meeting Jessica's gaze, her eyes alight with a fire that mirrored the sunset. There was danger in those depths, a siren call that whispered of tempests yet to come. And for a moment, he allowed himself to drift closer to her flame, even as the voice of caution murmured its insistent warning in his ear.

A gentle prod at his shoulder jolted John from his reverie, the touch electric, snapping the taut wire of his thoughts. Jessica's fingertip was light against his sun-warmed skin, yet it carried the weight of unspoken words and uncharted possibilities between them.

"Lost in thought?" Her voice was a velvet tease, pulling him back to the present with effortless ease. The corners of her lips curved upwards in knowing amusement, as if she held the secrets of his inner turmoil cupped delicately in her hands.

"Something like that," John admitted, the edges of his own smile betraying the intensity of his internal struggle. Their laughter mingled in the thick air, a shared note in the symphony of splashing water and joyful cries that surrounded them. The energy between them crackled, an invisible current charging the space with anticipation.

He studied her face, lit by the soft glow of the sinking sun, noting how the fading light played across her features, casting shadows that hinted at the depth of her mysterious allure. In the golden hour, she seemed both part of this world and yet apart from it—untouchable but undeniably present.

"Would you—" he began, the words catching slightly in his throat, "care for a drink? At my place, I mean." His heart thrummed a reckless rhythm, emboldened by the connection they had woven with each word and glance.

Jessica's eyes locked onto his, a spark igniting within their emerald depths. A slow, deliberate smile graced her lips, her interest blooming like a night flower coaxed open by moonlight. She tilted her head ever so slightly, as if weighing the gravity of his invitation against the tapestry of her own enigmatic desires.

"That sounds... intriguing," she replied, the word hanging between them, ripe with latent promise. Her voice was a siren song, luring him further into waters whose currents he could not predict, yet longed to navigate.

In that moment, the world around them seemed to recede—the clamour of the poolside fading into a distant murmur. All that remained was the heat of the day clinging to their skin and the simmering tension that now defined the space where their lives intersected.

"Later then," she said, her tone threaded with flirtation and an allure that defied easy understanding. The promise of the evening lay ahead, shrouded in the sultry haze of the approaching night.

Jessica's eyelashes fluttered with a coyness that belied the sharp glint of curiosity in her gaze. "I suppose I could be persuaded," she murmured, the corners of her mouth curling into a knowing smile. Her response was laced with an invitation that went beyond mere words, a silent dance of possibilities that stretched out into the night awaiting them.

"Later it is," John agreed, his voice a low rumble of anticipation. There was an unspoken understanding that coursed through the air, a shared excitement for the clandestine hours they would steal away from the rest of the world. The prospect of the evening unfurled before him like a secret garden, its paths untrodden and scents undiscovered.

With a final glance that smouldered with unvoiced promises, John tore himself away from the magnetic field of Jessica's presence. He stepped back onto the pavement, the sun's dying embers painting long shadows on the ground as the day began to fold into twilight.

The walk to the exit was a study in restraint, each step pulsating with the rhythm of what lay ahead. The heat lingered stubbornly around him, clinging to his skin like a lover reluctant to part. It served as a physical echo of the tension that now thrummed between him and Jessica—a tension both delicious and dangerous.

John's mind raced with the countless scenarios the evening could unfold, each more tantalizing than the last. The mundane reality of his life receded, replaced by the vivid colours of risk and desire. As he pushed open the gate and stepped through, it felt like crossing an invisible threshold into a realm where the ordinary rules no longer applied.

The heat of the day may have been oppressive, but it was nothing compared to the scorching path of his thoughts, setting ablaze every rational objection. This was more than a casual drink; it was a tacit challenge to the life he knew—one that he found himself unable to resist.

The world beyond the iron-wrought gates of the community pool seemed to dim, as though night itself were an accomplice to the impending rendezvous. John's footsteps echoed softly against the pavement, a staccato beat in the otherwise hushed suburban symphony. With each stride, he felt the weight of his decision anchoring him deeper into a future rife with uncertainty and brimming with clandestine promise.

Amber streetlights flickered to life, casting a warm glow that danced upon his path, illuminating the contours of his face—each line etched by the years of a life lived within the confines of expectation. The evening breeze whispered through the trees, carrying with it the scent of jasmine, a fragrance that tangled with the remnant chlorine on his skin, crafting an intoxicating blend that lulled his senses further into the labyrinth of what-if.

He paused for a moment, allowing himself to be wrapped in the velvet cloak of twilight. The crickets' chorus rose in crescendo around him, nature's own ode to the thrill of the chase, the perilous beauty of potential. There was a depth to the darkness that settled over the world, a profound echo that resonated within him, harmonizing with his own unvoiced desires.

In the quiet, John confronted the duality of his existence—the steadfast husband, rooted in familiarity, and the restless soul, yearning for the rapture of connection that transcended mere flesh. He had walked the straight line so long; now, the allure of the unknown beckoned, whispering sweet sedition into his ear.

As the first stars pierced the navy canvas above, a surge of adrenaline coursed through him, quickening his pulse with its fervent rhythm. It was a sensation unfamiliar yet addictive, like the first drop of wine on a parched tongue, promising a richness that could either sate or ruin. In this fleeting interlude between day and night, John stood on the precipice of two lives, the air charged with the electricity of decisions yet made.

"Life," he mused silently, "is but a series of choices." His voice was a ghost in the stillness, a spectre of the man who once believed he had no choices left to make.

With a deep breath drawing in the cool air of encroaching night, John stepped forward, surrendering to the inexorable pull of what awaited. The risk was palpable, a living entity that coalesced in the space between heartbeats, yet so was the thrill—the ineffable dance of what lay just beyond reach.

And as he walked, the shadows lengthened, stretching out before him like the opening act of a play whose script remained unwritten. A play wherein the lead actor teetered on the knife-edge of temptation, driven not by the lines delivered but by the ones left unsaid, pregnant with meaning.

Tonight, he realised, might just be the prologue to a story untold, a chapter in the book of his life marked by the reckless abandon of passion, the sublime terror of true intimacy. John Hawthorne, a polite and friendly suburbanite and friend to many but known by few, took his first steps into the unfolding drama of their entangled lives, his heart whispering silent promises of things to come.

Chapter 4: Wine and Whispers

The evening's fading light cast a golden hue over John Hawthorne's meticulously kept patio, the setting sun painting long shadows across the flagstones. He was poised in his favourite chair, a vessel of tranquillity amid the whispering symphony of suburban life that swirled just beyond the confines of his orderly garden. His eyes, reflecting a restive spirit, lifted at the sound of the gate unlatching, anticipation tightening in his chest.

Jessica appeared at the threshold, her presence an immediate contrast to the day's quiet decline. She carried with her not just a bottle of wine but an air of enigma that seemed to swirl around her like the summer breeze. With each step onto John's domain, her sundress—hued in the vibrant shades of a blooming sunset—swayed around her legs, its fabric dancing to the silent music of her movements. Her stride was confident, the embodiment of a woman who understood her effect on the world—and particularly on the man waiting for her.

John rose, as if drawn up by the strings of Jessica's invisible allure. A warm smile played upon his lips, softening the angularity of his jaw, a subtle testament to the comfort he found in her company. "Château Montelena," he remarked, his voice carrying both admiration and a touch of surprise as his gaze fell upon the label of the wine she presented. "An excellent choice." The words were casual, yet they carried the weight of their burgeoning connection—a rapport laced with humour and the unsaid.

"Only the best for this evening," Jessica replied, her voice smooth, touched with the hint of flirtation that seemed as natural to her as breathing. Her emerald eyes locked with his, a challenge and an invitation all at once.

The familiarity between them was palpable, an ease that spoke of shared secrets and laughter, of moments spent in one another's orbit that had slowly chipped away at the facade of mere neighbourly affection. Yet beneath that camaraderie, a current of tension hummed, electric and unacknowledged, as they both lingered in the space between propriety and the yearning for something more.

The evening breeze, a whispering accomplice to the night's endeavour, danced through the leaves, carrying with it the soft creak of aged wood as John and Jessica settled onto the patio swing. It moved with a gentle rhythm, like the pulse of the earth itself, each sway an echo of heartbeats syncing in quiet anticipation. The swing's motion was both a cradle and a catalyst, rocking them into a world that felt removed from the mundane, where every rustle of foliage seemed to conspire in their intimate seclusion.

Their shared humour was a language unto itself, a bridge spanning the gap between friendship and the precipice of something far more enthralling. As the swing continued its soothing arc, the laughter subsided into comfortable silence, leaving only the symphony of nature and the unspoken dialogue of glances and half-smiles.

The lull in their laughter tapered into a stillness that seemed to wait anxiously. John watched as Jessica reached for her glass, the moonlight casting prismatic colours onto the surface of the wine within. He found himself captivated, not just by the play of light, but by the elegant curve of her wrist, the way her fingers curled around the stem.

"Have you heard the latest album from The Velvet Labyrinths?" she asked, her voice low and smooth, like the hum of a cello in a quiet room. It was a deep dive into their shared love for music that lived in the shadows, far from the blaring mainstream.

John's eyes lit up, a spark kindling behind his casual facade. "Yes," he exhaled, a rush of excitement betraying his composed exterior. "It's like they've distilled the essence of midnight into sound."

Jessica's laugh was soft and knowing, a secret shared between thieves. She leaned in closer, her body language an open book with pages fluttering in the breeze. Her sundress brushed against his jeans in a whisper of fabric, a touch as light as air yet heavy with intent.

He could feel his pulse quicken, a silent percussion in the symphony of the night. His gaze lingered on her, tracing the silhouette of her face, the gentle slope of her neck, and the cascade of chestnut hair that framed her like a masterpiece. She was a siren song made flesh, and he was all too willing to be drawn into her depths.

"Midnight," she mused, her lips curving into a smile that held promises untold. "A time when secrets unveil themselves, don't you think?"

"Indeed," he whispered, his voice a thread in the tapestry of shadows and moonlight. In those words, a confession of his own longing for the mysteries she embodied, for the adventure she promised in every glance, every lean of her supple frame closer to his own.

Their knees brushed beneath the swing, a fleeting touch that sent ripples through the calm waters of John's self-restraint. He was caught in the gravitational pull of her presence, each subtle shift in her body language charting a course through the uncharted territories of his heart.

The night had fallen into a comfortable stillness, disturbed only by the occasional creak of the patio swing and the symphony of crickets hidden in the dark tapestry of the garden. They paused, glasses cradled in their hands, wine reflecting the scant light like liquid rubies. The moment stretched between them, taut as a string quivering with notes unsung.

Jessica's gaze was lost in the depths of her glass, the silence wrapping around them like a velvet shroud. John watched her, the contours of her face softened by shadows, his own breath barely a whisper against the thickening air. The wine touched his lips, a brief respite from the tension that seemed to curl around his thoughts, an unspoken attraction simmering beneath the veneer of calm.

A soft sigh escaped her, dispelling the hush as she set her glass aside with a gentle clink. "Imagine," Jessica began, her voice a brushstroke of colour on the canvas of silence, "if we could escape to anywhere in this very moment. No plans, no maps—just the stars as our guide."

John's imagination flickered to life, kindled by the playful lilt of her words. "And where would you find yourself in this boundless dream?" he asked, his intrigue piqued, a smile tugging at the corner of his mouth.

"Everywhere," she replied, her eyes gleaming with wanderlust. "I'd chase the aurora borealis in the wilds of Iceland, dance under the lantern-lit skies of Morocco, and lose myself in the labyrinthine streets of Prague."

Her descriptions unfurled with a fervour that was both vivid and intoxicating, painting images of exotic locales and thrilling escapades. Each word was a promise of mysteries to explore, worlds to unravel—a siren call to the unknown that vibrated through the charged air.

"And you, John?" she prompted, leaning slightly forward, her interest genuine, her presence enveloping him in warmth.

"Perhaps the forgotten corners of the earth," he mused, drawn into the allure of their shared daydream. "Ancient temples shrouded by jungle canopies, cities abandoned to time, places where history whispers its secrets to those who dare listen."

Their exchange wove a tapestry of adventure, each thread a connection binding them closer, their dreams interlacing like vines in an overgrown garden of possibility. The more they conversed, the more the world beyond the patio seemed to fade into obscurity, leaving only the two of them suspended in a realm of what-ifs and maybes.

The moon, a voyeur in the heavens, seemed to conspire with destiny as its silver light caressed Jessica's chestnut hair, imbuing her with an ethereal luminescence. Each strand shimmered like the delicate threads of a spider's web jewelled with dew, weaving a halo around her that was not of this mundane world. John found himself entranced, his eyes captured by the celestial artwork that danced upon her head.

A breeze, playful and conspiratorial, whispered through the patio leaves, carrying with it the secret scents of a night in bloom. It nudged against the wooden swing where they sat, eliciting a gentle creak that punctuated the quietude of their shared space. Their knees, in moments of unspoken accord, brushed together beneath the flowing fabric of her sundress—a touch so fleeting, yet laden with an electric promise that lingered far longer than the contact itself.

As the swing swayed, their shoulders gravitated toward one another, almost touching, the gap between them charged with the energy of unarticulated yearnings. The subtle shifts in their posture spoke a language of desire and restraint, each lean and recoil a verse in the silent poem of their proximity. For every inch closer that Jessica shifted, a corresponding pulse raced through John, each beat spelling out the contours of temptation.

Their conversation meandered through the labyrinths of intimate discourse, yet it was in these small gestures—the accidental touches and the gravitational pull of bodies—that the true dialogue unfolded. There, amidst the symphony of crickets and the rustling of leaves, the air between them thickened with the sweet tension of possibility, a narrative written not in words but in the very space that both separated and connected them.

Amidst the symphony of the nocturnal chorus and the soft whisper of leaves, John's heart had become a turbulent sea, waves of desire crashing against the shore of restraint. The moonlight bathed Jessica in an ethereal radiance, her emerald eyes reflecting the stars above—a celestial map charting the course to his undoing.

Every laugh they shared was like a siren song, calling him closer to the jagged rocks of forbidden longing. The gentle sway of the swing seemed to rock John between two worlds, one where he was a man bound by vows and verdant lawns, the other a wilder domain, ungoverned by the hands of the clock or the expectations of neatly trimmed hedges. In this twilight realm, it was Jessica's presence that seemed as necessary as air, her every gesture and smile stirring the embers of a dormant blaze within him.

The wine swirled in his glass, a crimson tempest mirroring the turmoil in his veins—each sip an attempt to quell the fire she kindled. He wanted to reach across the chasm of propriety, to explore the contours of her laughter, the texture of her thoughts, the warmth of her skin. But the spectre of consequence loomed over him like a ghost, its cold fingers tightening around his conflicted soul.

"Jessica," he would think, "Jessica," the name rolling silently through his mind, a mantra of both yearning and warning. His gaze traced the line of her neck, the curve of her shoulder, the cascade of chestnut hair. And within that gaze lay the battle he fought—a skirmish between longing and loyalty, each glance an admission of what he dared not speak.

When Jessica leaned towards him, the world seemed to hold its breath. Her lips, a mere whisper from his ear, grazed his skin with the faintest touch, sending shivers cascading down his spine. An electric jolt shot through him, igniting every nerve ending with the intensity of lightning striking barren ground.

"Imagine us, under the Northern Lights," she breathed, her voice a velvet caress that wrapped around his senses. "The sky ablaze with colour, no one else around for miles... just us."

The very air crackled with the energy of her words, each syllable painting visions of far-flung escapades, of freedom unbound and passion unleashed. John's pulse quickened, his body acutely aware of her proximity—an exquisite torture, a delicious agony that held him captive in the space between breaths.

In the shadows of the patio, tangled in the sweet vine of longing, John Hawthorne found himself at the precipice of the unknown. Desire beckoned with its seductive finger, fear whispered of the abyss, and in that moment, he danced on the edge of both.

The silence that settled in the wake of Jessica's whispered invitation was thick, charged with a current that pulsed through the humid air. John's heart hammered against his ribcage, a relentless drumbeat echoing the tumultuous storm of his emotions. The taste of the wine lingered on his tongue, bittersweet and complex, much like the situation he found himself ensnared within.

The moon hung low, a silver orb casting an ethereal glow over the patio, bathing everything—the swing they shared, the half-empty glasses, the intimate proximity of their bodies—in its haunting light. It was as though they were enveloped in a world apart, a realm where time slowed and the rules of reality blurred at the edges.

John's gaze drifted to the glass in his hand, watching the way the moonlight danced across the surface of the wine, creating a kaleidoscope of crimson and violet. But the beauty of it couldn't distract from the chaos within. His mind raced with the possibilities of what could be, each thought more perilous than the last. Daring him. Taunting him.

He felt the warmth of Jessica's thigh pressed against his own through the thin fabric of her sundress, the innocuous contact sending a surge of awareness through his veins. Her scent lingered in the air, a heady mix of jasmine and something uniquely hers, wrapping around him, an invisible tether pulling him closer.

In the quiet that surrounded them, every breath she took seemed amplified, a siren's call to the part of him that yearned to close the distance, to claim the moment for what it could become. But another voice, a whisper of caution and conscience, held him back, reminding him of the life he had built, the promises made.

The soft rustling of leaves in the breeze played a delicate symphony, a backdrop to the internal noise that threatened to overwhelm him. He wanted to speak, to break the spell, yet words failed him, lost in the labyrinth of his longing and the spectre of consequence.

Jessica's eyes sought his, pools of midnight reflecting questions he wasn't sure he dared answer. In their depths, he saw the reflection of his own soul, wrestling with desires too powerful to ignore, yet too dangerous to indulge.

A firefly flitted by, a lone beacon in the darkness, its light winking in and out like the flicker of opportunity that hovered just beyond his grasp. The night held its breath, waiting for a decision he couldn't make, a step he couldn't take.

So there he sat, suspended in the space between action and restraint, desire and duty—a man caught in the web of his own making, a heart racing with the thrill of the forbidden, and a mind haunted by the shadows of 'what if.' The tension palpable and unrelieved, a slow-burn fire smouldering in the quiet of the night.

Chapter 5: The Almost Kiss

John shifted in the chair subtly, the movement small and deliberate as he angled himself towards Jessica. John's knees almost brushed against Jessica's, a whisper away from contact. He could feel the heat radiating from her skin, the space between them charged with an electric tension that defied the calm suburban setting.

"Here's to... whatever may come," John said, his voice steady but laced with a current of anticipation.

"Whatever may come," echoed Jessica, her gaze never leaving his as they raised their glasses in a toast that felt like a sacred pact.

Their glasses met in a soft clink, the sound delicate but pronounced against the backdrop of the evening's symphony – the distant hum of cicadas serenading the darkness. The wine's aroma rose in the air, rich and potent, weaving through the scent of freshly cut grass and the underlying earthiness that heralded the end of day. It mingled with Jessica's own perfume, something floral with a hint of spice, creating a heady blend that hung around them, thickening the atmosphere with its intoxicating bouquet.

The night played a coy dance around the edges of the patio, casting long shadows that seemed to reach for the pair as if to drag them into the night's embrace. The world beyond their cocoon receded into insignificance, leaving nothing but the subtle glow of the outdoor lanterns to illuminate the contours of Jessica's face. Her eyes, those

41

emerald pools shimmering with secrets and silent promises, held him captive.

John's heart thrummed a rhythm that resonated with the nocturnal chorus, each beat an echo of the raw desire he fought to keep sheathed. In this moment, suspended between the safety of what he knew and the abyss of what could be, he tasted the thrill of the forbidden, a flavour more intoxicating than any vintage they could possibly drink.

John's chuckle resonated beneath the veil of dark, a warm sound that fluttered through the thickening air like a moth drawn to the lantern's glow. Across from him, Jessica's laughter joined his, a musical counterpoint that spoke of shared amusement and clandestine delight. The banter between them was light, a playful volley of words that danced on the precipice of flirtation.

"Clearly, you've never experienced a true adventure until you've tried midnight kayaking," Jessica teased, her eyes alight with mischief. "The stars above, the water below—it's like being suspended in space."

"Ah, but you forget," John parried back with feigned solemnity, "I'm a man of terra firma. My idea of an adventure is successfully navigating the wilds of the Sunday farmers' market."

Their laughter mingled once again, easy and genuine, a testament to the growing comfort weaving its way into their interactions. Each quip and clever retort edged them closer, as if their words were stepping stones leading to the brink of something more profound than either dared to admit.

As the conversation rose and fell, the space between them seemed to shrink, an invisible thread pulling tighter with each passing second. A lull settled over them, a pause heavy with unspoken thoughts, and Jessica leaned in, her gaze fixed upon John with an intensity that pierced through the casual facade.

John felt a shiver cascade down his spine, an electric charge that jolted him from within. Her emerald eyes held a depth that beckoned him, promising the unravelling of mysteries he wasn't certain he had the courage to explore. And yet, the yearning to dive into those depths was overwhelming, drowning out the rational voice that whispered warnings of caution and restraint.

For a fleeting instant, the world around them evaporated, reduced to nothing more than background noise to the silent dialogue that passed between their eyes. The only reality was the two of them, caught in a moment as delicate and dangerous as a spider's web glistening with morning dew.

A subtle breeze stirred, whispering secrets through the jasmine-laden air as it wound its way around John and Jessica. It was a cool caress against their skin, a conspirator in the night's seductive dance, carrying with it the intoxicating perfume of flowers that seemed to bloom only for them. The scent enveloped them, a fragrant shroud that hinted at promises yet unvoiced, each petal's aroma weaving into their cocoon of intimacy like a silent incantation.

John's gaze lingered on Jessica, tracing the contours of her face illuminated by the soft glow of patio lights. Her laughter still echoed in his ears, a melody that played upon his senses, stirring within him a symphony of desire and hesitation. The breeze rustled through the leaves, a sound that mirrored the restless stirring of his soul. He was acutely aware of the scant inches separating their knees, the magnetic pull that beckoned him closer with each gentle gust.

In the quietude of his thoughts, John grappled with an inner tumult that threatened to spill over. He longed to bridge the gap between them, to dissolve the barriers with a single touch—a touch he knew could unravel the very fabric of the world they knew. His heart raced, pounding out a rhythm of perilous temptation, each beat a drum call to abandon caution and surrender to the fervour that smouldered beneath the surface.

It was a risk, a forbidden fruit dangling just within reach, and the thrill of it sharpened his senses, honing his awareness of every breath, every shift in Jessica's posture. The wine in his glass, rich and dark, seemed a mere shadow compared to the heady rush of adrenaline that coursed through him. He revelled in the uncertainty, the dangerous allure of a path veiled in shadows, where every step could either lead to ecstasy or precipice.

The night air hummed with the energy of unseen forces, the rise and fall of a tide that pulled at the corners of his resolve. In the depths of his mind, John danced with the spectres of consequence and passion, each vying for dominance, each whispering sweet nothings to sway his decision. And amidst the silent battle, the jasmine continued to bloom, a testament to nature's own recklessness, urging him toward the edge of reason with its silent, scented promise.

The night seemed to hold its breath as John and Jessica drew imperceptibly closer, the space between them charged with the silent whispers of longing. The jasmine-scented breeze had woven around them a cocoon of intimacy, and under the cloak of darkness, their knees almost touched, a testament to the magnetic pull neither could deny.

In the fraught silence, the sound was sudden and stark—a ringtone cleaving through the fabric of the night like a knife through velvet. The spell shattered, splintering the moment into fragments of what might have been. The obtrusive melody belonged to Sophie's phone, its electronic trill jarring against the organic chorus of cicadas that hummed in the distance.

Jessica's eyes, those pools of emerald that had glowed with invitation, now flickered with a change so swift it was almost missed. Anticipation melted away, replaced by a mask of composure as elegant as the curve of her wine glass. She leaned back, the movement fluid and graceful, an artful retreat from the precipice upon which they had teetered.

"Looks like reality is calling," she said, her voice still threaded with the remnants of their shared laughter, yet laced now with a note of finality.

With a smooth motion, she rose from the chair, the silhouette of her form-fitting dress cutting a sharp line against the backdrop of the patio's ambient lighting. There was an elegance to her exit, unhurried but deliberate, leaving behind a palpable sense of unfinished business that clung to the night air like the fragrance of the unseen flowers.

As the echo of her footsteps faded into the evening, the oppressive silence settled back over the patio, underscored by the persistent ring of Sophie's call—a reminder of boundaries and the razor's edge on which desire balanced.

John's fingers, betraying the calm facade he projected, trembled ever so slightly as they reached for the vibrating phone. The device felt foreign and unwelcome in his hand—a harbinger of reality cutting through the thick veil of yearning that had moments before enveloped him. "Hello?" His voice, remarkably steady, belied the maelstrom that churned within—a tempest of relief at the interruption and a poignant sting of disappointment.

"John, are you still up?" Sophie's familiar tone, tinged with the sleepiness of interrupted dreams, seeped through the speaker. The mundane concern laced within her words was a world away from the electric tension that had charged every glance exchanged with Jessica on this very patio.

"Of course," John replied, ensuring his response carried none of the weight of his internal conflict. "Everything okay?"

"I'll be home in two days," she said, a yawn punctuating her speech. The banality of the conversation acted as an anchor, pulling him back to a harbour he knew too well.

"Get some rest; we'll talk tomorrow," he assured her, and with a click, the connection was severed. The silence that followed was profound, heavy with the words that had almost found life between him and Jessica. The night, now devoid of her laughter, seemed to have expanded, creating a vacuum that filled the space around him.

He remained seated, his form a solitary shadow amidst the ambient glow of the patio lights. The air, previously charged with the scent of jasmine and anticipation, now carried a coolness that whispered across his skin—a gentle caress to soothe the smouldering thoughts that flickered like wayward sparks in his mind. John closed his eyes, taking in the night's symphony—the distant hum of cicadas providing a rhythmic backdrop to his tumultuous heartbeats.

The patio, once a stage for their flirtatious dance, held onto the remnants of their proximity. It was as if the stones beneath his feet retained the warmth of their near touch, the soft glow of the table candle casting long shadows that reached out like fingers, grasping for what might have been.

John breathed deep, letting the fragrance of the earth after dusk fill his lungs, mingling with the fading aroma of the wine they had shared. It was a heady mixture, one that fuelled his imagination and stoked the fires of 'what if.' Yet, as the cool breeze swept over him once more, it seemed to carry away the edges of his longing, leaving behind a resolve tempered by the night's revelations.

There, under the cloak of darkness, John Hawthorne sat, a man caught between two worlds. One foot rooted in the safety of the known, the other dangling over the abyss of desire's sweet chasm. And as the stars above blinked indifferently at his plight, he couldn't help but wonder which path tomorrow would illuminate.

The darkness of the bedroom loomed around John like a tangible entity. He lay motionless on his back, the cotton sheets beneath him crisp and cool against his skin. Above, the ceiling stretched into an expanse of shadow, becoming a canvas for the flickering dance of his thoughts.

Memories of Sophie, vibrant and vivid, cascaded through his mind—the first time they met, when her laughter had seemed like the only sound in a room full of chatter; their wedding day, suffused with promises and hopeful gazes under a canopy of white. He remembered how her blonde hair had captured the sunlight, framing her face with halos of gold, her blue eyes reflecting a future filled with shared dreams.

Yet now, amidst the weight of his choices, those hues of happiness were tinged with the grayscale of doubt. The scent of jasmine from the patio lingered on his senses, interwoven with a guilt that clung to him more stubbornly than any perfume. It was as though he could still feel Jessica's nearness, her emerald gaze burning through the veil of night, igniting a flame within him that he feared could not be quenched.

John turned restlessly, the sheets whispering against his body like secrets being exchanged in hushed tones. He closed his eyes tight, trying to shut out the allure of what lay just beyond reach, but it was no use. Desire was a siren call, the melody sweet yet fraught with peril, each note a step closer towards something forbidden.

His heart wrestled with itself in the quietude, duty and longing entwined in a tumultuous embrace. He thought of Sophie's steady voice, the way she spoke with such clarity and purpose—her words always a guiding light in his life. But now, that light flickered uncertainly as the shadows of temptation crept closer, threatening to extinguish its comforting glow.

In this chamber of solitude, John grappled with the duality of love's nature—a fortress of safety and a battlefield of the soul. As the hours trickled by, the soft rhythm of his breathing was the only sound that punctuated the silence. And in that stillness, John Hawthorne, the man who wore his ease like a well-fitted garment, found himself unravelling, thread by delicate thread, under the scrutiny of the night's watchful eyes.

John shifted beneath the cocoon of his blankets, a restless spectre in the dark. The moon outside cast a sliver of light across his form, painting him silver and shadow. His skin prickled with the remnants of a day that had seared itself onto his consciousness, the warmth of Jessica's nearness still lingering like a phantom touch against his flesh.

He lay there, wrestling with the call of what could be, his mind a tumultuous sea of memories and maybes. The scent of jasmine from the patio seemed to have followed him, infusing the air with its intoxicating promise. The stillness of the room was a stark canvas against which his thoughts ran wild, vibrant hues of longing splashed against the muted tones of loyalty.

Sophie's laughter echoed distantly in the recesses of his mind, a haunting melody that once danced through their shared life, now competing with the new rhythm that pulsed with each beat of his heart. He could feel the familiar weight of their history, the comfort of the life they had built, yet it felt as though he stood on the precipice of an abyss, peering into depths unknown.

The battle within him raged, duty clashing with desire, each claiming him as their own. John's breaths grew deeper, more deliberate. In the quiet hours before dawn, he found a semblance of peace, a fragile truce between the parts of himself at war.

A resolve began to take shape, hardening like steel tempered by fire. There was no road map for the journey ahead, each step shrouded in mist and mystery, but he knew he must tread forward. The future beckoned, a tapestry of shadows and light yet to be woven, and he would not shy away from its call.

John pledged to meet the days ahead with eyes wide open, embracing the uncertainty that cloaked them. The future was a tantalizing enigma, a riddle wrapped in the folds of fate, and he—its willing seeker, ready to unravel its secrets.

Chapter 6: Maggie's Warning

The quaint chime of the bell above the cafe door heralded John's arrival, a soft counterpoint to the murmur of conversation and the hiss of steam from the espresso machine. The air was a tapestry of roasted coffee beans and freshly baked pastries, inviting and familiar. He paused on the threshold, taking in the homey ambiance, a warm haven against the cool indifference of the outside world.

His gaze wandered through the thrumming space, slices of life unfolding at each table, until it landed on Maggie Wilson. There she sat, an island of vibrancy amidst the gentle chaos, her curly red hair a vivid flame in the dimly lit corner. She had ensconced herself in the nook, yet her laughter seemed to reach out, weaving through the air like music.

As John threaded his way between the tables, the rhythm of the cafe seemed to change, almost as if its patrons sensed the shift in the narrative with his entrance. With every step he took, the noise around him faded into a hush, anticipation thickening in his chest.

Maggie's eyes lifted from her cup, locking onto his with a smile that bloomed like a revelation, as if she had been waiting for this moment all along. Her gesture was simple—a tilt of the head, a beckoning hand—and yet it was charged with an unspoken understanding that spoke volumes of their shared history.

"John," she greeted, her voice a warm caress against the backdrop of clinking cups. "You're right on time."

"Wouldn't dream of being late," he replied, sliding into the seat across from her with practiced ease. The chair felt like an old friend, the grain of the wood familiar beneath his fingers.

They exchanged pleasantries, the kind of light-hearted banter that danced around the edges of something deeper. His jokes were a deft mask, a way to test the waters before diving into the truth that lay beneath the surface of their smiles.

"Still running circles around the neighbourhood joggers?" Maggie teased, but her eyes brimmed with an awareness that saw past his casual demeanour.

"Only the slow ones," John shot back, a wry twist to his lips. He leaned back, arms folding as he surveyed her, a silent challenge in the arch of his brow.

Their laughter mingled, a duet that filled the space between them with a resonance that hinted at the intricate dance they were about to begin. It was a prelude, the light brush of a bow against strings before the symphony surged forth, and in that moment, the cafe seemed to hold its breath, waiting for the crescendo that would inevitably come.

John's hand swept through the air, tracing the arc of an invisible comet as he recounted his latest encounter with Jessica. "You should have seen her, Maggie," he enthused, the corner of his mouth lifting in a lopsided grin that failed to mask a flicker of something unspoken. "There's just something about her—like gravity, I can't help but be pulled in."

The cafe's ambient glow cast dancing shadows over John's face, accentuating the restless spark in his eyes—a spark that leapt with each vivid description of Jessica's laughter, the way she tossed her hair, the electricity that seemed to charge the space between them.

Maggie leaned forward, her hands cradling the warmth of her coffee mug as she absorbed his words. The amusement in her gaze was tinged with a silent query, the soft crease between her brows betraying concern. "Gravity can be dangerous, you know," she chimed lightly, her voice a velvet ribbon weaving through the hum of conversation around them. "It might draw you in, but it doesn't always let you go."

A chuckle tumbled from John's lips, a sound more rehearsed than spontaneous. "I'm just orbiting, not planning on landing," he quipped, yet the quick tap of his fingers against the table betrayed a nervous energy, a symphony of doubt at odds with his cavalier words.

"Orbiting too close to a star can still get you burned," Maggie replied, her smile soft but her eyes piercing, seeking the truth behind his jest. The scent of roasted coffee beans mingled with the subtle cinnamon wafting from the kitchen, a sensory echo of the complexities entwining their conversation.

John nodded, a concession veiled by a sip of his own drink, the steam momentarily clouding his vision. He could feel the weight of Maggie's gaze, the gentle tug of her concern pulling at the edges of his resolve. There was a comfort in the familiarity of the cafe, but also a tension, as if the very walls whispered secrets of hidden desires and warnings left unheeded.

Maggie leaned forward, her elbows resting on the scarred wooden table, and her vibrant curls formed a fiery halo around her earnest face. The cafe's ambient chatter softened to a distant murmur as she began, her voice a hushed confessional whisper that drew John into the private world of her reminiscences.

"Once, I found myself tangled in a web not unlike yours," she murmured, her fingers tracing the rim of her coffee cup, a delicate dance of memory. "It started innocently enough, laughter shared over late-night texts, secrets exchanged like sacred vows. But lines blur in the dim light of ambiguity, and soon, every touch was laced with silent promises we never intended to keep."

John's eyes clung to Maggie's, absorbing the shadows of regret that flitted across her features. In the vulnerability of her admission, he glimpsed the depth of her understanding—her empathy rooted in the pain of experience. She spoke of betrayal not as a distant concept, but as an intimate spectre, one that had whispered sweet nothings in her ear before leaving her stranded in the stark daylight of reality.

"John," she said, reaching across the table to still the nervous drumming of his fingers, "the heart is a curious creature, hungry for connection, even when the mind protests its innocence."

The contact sent a jolt through him, and he withdrew his hand as if scorched by the intimacy of her touch. His laugh came out dry, a brittle leaf skittering across the pavement of their discussion. "Maggie, you worry too much," he attempted to deflect, the forced joviality in his tone at odds with the sudden tightness around his eyes. "Jessica and I, we're just friends—comrades in the mundane battle against suburban boredom."

Her gaze didn't waver, a mirror reflecting the storm brewing within him, not fooled by the veneer of his joy. "Even platonic orbits can decay, John," she warned, gentle yet firm, like the first drops of rain presaging a tempest. "Be careful you don't get pulled in by a gravity you underestimate."

He felt the tension coiling in his chest, a serpent ready to strike at the truth he wasn't prepared to confront. Maggie's words lingered between them, heavy as the scent of rain on the horizon, threatening to wash away the illusion he clung to with such desperate tenacity.

Maggie's hand retreated, leaving a space charged with unspoken understanding. She leaned back in her chair, the crimson swirl of her dress mimicking the dance of flames, and watched John with eyes that missed little. The cafe around them hummed with the muted symphony of clinking cups and whispered confidences, but at their secluded table, a different sort of communion unfolded.

"John," she began, her voice a soothing balm, "no matter where this path leads you, remember I'm here—for laughter or for secrets spilled over coffee. You're not alone."

Her words wrapped around him like a warm shawl on a cool autumn evening. He nodded, a silent acknowledgment of her loyalty that felt as intrinsic to his life as the steady beat of his heart. But within the sanctuary of Maggie's assurance lay an unsettling invitation to face the tangle of emotions he'd rather leave in shadow.

"Thank you, Mags," he murmured, grateful yet adrift in the sea of her concern. "I know you've got my back."

"Always," she affirmed with a nod, her curls bouncing like vibrant springs of empathy. Yet her smile held a trace of something more—perhaps a hint of sadness for the struggles she knew too well.

"Let's peel back the layers, John," she urged gently, her fingers tracing patterns on the wooden table as if to draw out the truth. "What's driving you toward Jessica? Is it just companionship, or is there something missing that you're trying to find?"

He hesitated, the question a soft hook baited with sincerity. To evade was simple; to delve into the murky waters of self-reflection was to navigate a labyrinth without a thread. Still, Maggie's presence, both comforting and unyielding, beckoned him closer to honesty's edge.

"Maybe it's... curiosity?" John ventured, the word feeling foreign yet strangely fitting on his tongue. "Or the thrill of something new, a spark I haven't felt in..."

His voice trailed off, the confession dangled between them, stark against the backdrop of the cafe's cozy tranquillity. Maggie's gaze held steady, offering a safe harbor for the tempest of his doubts.

"Curiosity is human," she acknowledged, her tone devoid of judgment, rich with the wisdom of storms weathered and survived. "But it can lead to places with shadows deeper than we expect. Think about what you truly want, John. What are you willing to risk?"

The air seemed to thicken with her words, laden with implications as intoxicating as the dark roast aroma permeating the space. A sigh escaped him, a quiet surrender to the complexity of his desires—a tapestry woven with threads of longing and remorse.

"I don't know," he admitted, and in that moment, with Maggie's unwavering gaze upon him, the admission tasted both bitter and sweet.

John fidgeted with the ceramic mug, his fingers tracing the heat that seeped through its walls. Maggie's words hung in the air like the delicate steam from their coffees, a mist of truth he couldn't quite clear away. His gaze shifted from her eyes to the window, where raindrops raced down the glass—a mirror to the turmoil within him.

"Have you ever felt trapped, Maggie?" he asked, his voice uncharacteristically hushed, as if afraid of the confessions it might unlock. "Like you're following a script written for you by someone else?"

The question lingered, and in the silence that followed, John could feel the weight of denial lifting, even as the gravity of introspection threatened to pull him under. His usual joviality was absent, replaced by an earnest vulnerability that seemed foreign on his lips.

"More than once," Maggie replied, her hand reaching across the table, fingers brushing against his with an almost imperceptible touch. "But sometimes the script is just a comfort zone we cling to, afraid of what might happen if we start improvising."

John withdrew his hand, not out of rejection, but from an instinct to protect himself from the raw honesty of her words. He leaned back in his chair, the wood creaking softly, mirroring the unrest that danced behind his composed exterior. A shadow of doubt crossed his face, a silent acknowledgment of the crossroads ahead.

"Improvisation can be... messy," he said, the edges of his mouth twitching into a half-smile that failed to reach his eyes.

"Life is messy, John," Maggie countered, her voice a low melody that seemed to resonate with the ambient jazz playing in the background. "And sometimes, in that mess, we find the parts of ourselves we've been missing."

The conversation waned as they both took a moment to reflect, the cafe's atmosphere thickening with the scent of spices and the warmth of shared confidences. The intimacy between them was palpable, a connection that transcended the boundaries of mere friendship.

As the lunch hour faded, Maggie offered one last nugget of wisdom, leaning in so only he could hear. "Just remember, desires untangled from the heart can lead us astray. Make sure it's your heart guiding you, not just the thrill of the chase."

John rose slowly, his movements laden with hesitation. Maggie's advice clung to him like the fragrance of the cafe's dark roast—a comforting yet sharp reminder of the depth of their exchange. He reached for his coat, his hands momentarily stilling as if to steady himself against the surge of emotions her words had unleashed.

"Thanks, Maggie," he said, his voice betraying the tremor of a man whose certainties had been unravelled. "You always know how to stir the pot."

With a rueful smile, he turned towards the door, leaving the sanctuary of the cafe behind. Maggie's advice echoed in his mind with each step, a haunting refrain to the symphony of his doubts.

John stepped out of the cafe, the bell's farewell chime dissolving into the cacophony of city life. The air outside was crisp, a stark contrast to the steamy warmth he had left behind. It nipped at his cheeks with an almost taunting freshness, as if challenging the feverish stirrings of his mind. With every breath, tendrils of coolness seeped into his lungs, offering a momentary clarity that was swiftly muddled by the distant hum of traffic—a relentless reminder of the world's persistent march.

His stride carried a purposeful cadence, the soles of his shoes clicking against the pavement in a rhythmic assertion of determination. Yet within each step lurked a tremor of uncertainty, a subtle falter borne from the weight of Maggie's parting words. They were like shadows clinging to the edges of his consciousness, insistent and unyielding.

The city around him was alive with its own secrets, its streets a labyrinth of possibilities veiled in smog. Buildings rose like sentinels, their windows reflecting the afternoon glow and the opaque musings of the many souls within. The faint scent of exhaust mixed with the more earthy whispers of summer, creating a heady perfume that seemed to mirror the complexity stirring inside him.

John paused at the edge of the sidewalk, his gaze drifting towards the horizon where the sky kissed the tops of skyscrapers in a tender bruise of purples and oranges. Maggie's voice lingered in his ears, a siren song of wisdom and warning, both alluring and foreboding. What was it about her words that clawed so deeply at the facade he had meticulously built? Was it the sincerity in her tone or the unwavering belief she held in the truths she spoke?

A gust of wind swept through the street, tugging at his coat and ruffling the neat lines of his hair. It whispered of change, of the tumultuous dance between desire and duty, passion and placation. John stood at the crossroads of his own making, the future an enigma shrouded in the allure of what ifs and maybes.

As the sun began its slow descent, casting elongated shadows across the pavement, a sense of ambiguity settled over him. Maggie's advice, a beacon in the tempest of his thoughts, offered no easy answers but promised the dawn of introspection. He could feel the precipice beneath his feet, the beckoning edge of transformation that could either elevate or undo him.

With a last look at the waning day, John turned from the horizon, his silhouette etched against the dimming light. His departure carried the silent echo of Maggie's counsel. The choices that lay ahead were his alone to make, each path fraught with the peril and promise of the unknown.

Chapter 7: Sophie's Return

John stood motionless amid the bustle of the airport terminal, his gaze piercing through the swarm of bodies as if searching for a lighthouse in a tempestuous sea. Each passing second throbbed in his chest—a drumbeat of anticipation mingled with a sharp sting of guilt—while he practiced the curvature of a smile that felt more like a mask than a greeting.

The air was thick with the scent of coffee and the cacophony of rolling suitcases and muffled announcements, yet John remained insulated in his private chamber of contemplation. His fingers twitched at his side, betraying a restlessness that contrasted sharply with the orderly neatness of his casual attire. The short brown hair that usually framed his face with such precision seemed to fall a touch too carelessly today, hinting at the turmoil hidden beneath his calm facade.

Suddenly, from the shifting sea of strangers, a beacon emerged. Sophie's form cut through the throng with the quiet determination that he'd always admired. Her short blonde hair caught the sparse sunlight filtering through the terminal windows, crowning her with an ethereal glow. As her blue eyes locked onto John's, they lit up with a warm recognition that sent a jolt through his heart.

She waved, her gesture cutting through the distance between them, cradling a smile that spoke of homecomings and long-awaited embraces. The sight of her, so full of life and expectation, drew him forward as if by a magnetic pull.

"John," she called out, her voice a familiar melody that reverberated against his skin.

In two strides, John closed the gap, reaching out to enfold Sophie in an embrace designed to shield, to comfort—to conceal. His arms wrapped around her, strong yet trembling, seeking solace in the press of her body against his. Her presence was a balm, soothing the rough edges of his conscience, yet the hug carried a weight far heavier than their intertwined forms. It was laden with unspoken truths, with silent confessions that lingered just on the precipice of revelation.

"Welcome back," he murmured into her hair, each word infused with a subtle tremor that belied the steady tone he fought to maintain.

Sophie's reply was a contented sigh, her arms tightening around him as if to anchor herself in the reality of their reunion. In that prolonged moment, the world outside their cocoon ceased to exist—their shared breaths, the only currency of exchange.

And for John, amidst the sensory tapestry of Sophie's soft perfume and the hushed rustle of her jacket, lay an undercurrent of danger, a seductive undertone of secrets held too close. The slow burn of tension simmered within him, even as he mustered the strength to step back, to look into the eyes of the woman he loved, all while grappling with the shadow of another etched upon the canvas of his heart.

John released Sophie from their embrace, stepping back to observe her as she brushed a loose strand of blonde hair behind her ear, her blue eyes reflecting the fluorescent lights overhead. They began the familiar dance of small talk, Sophie's voice a melodic stream recounting the cobblestone streets of Prague, the taste of fresh pastries in Paris, the symphony of bustling markets in Marrakech. Each word painted vivid pictures, yet John's mind wandered, caught in a web of memories tinted with the emerald hue of Jessica's gaze.

"Sounds like you had an amazing time," John said, his voice steady despite the dissonance inside him. His smile was measured, a mask sculpted from years of suburban pleasantries, but it did little to still the storm that raged quietly within—a tempest born of guilt and longing.

"Absolutely," Sophie replied, her enthusiasm genuine as she delved into anecdotes about street artists and ancient architecture. "It was like walking through history."

As they walked towards the car, John's hand found the small of Sophie's back, a gesture as automatic as breathing, yet tainted with the phantom touch of another. He steered them through the parked cars, each step an attempt to close the chasm that had formed since Jessica moved into the neighbourhood, bringing with her the scent of forbidden fruit.

"I thought maybe we could have dinner tonight at L'Amore," John suggested once they were enclosed in the leather-scented confines of the vehicle. The engine hummed to life, a low purr that seemed to resonate with the undercurrent of his own restlessness.

Sophie's face brightened, her smile reaching her eyes, dispelling the exhaustion etched by long flights and layovers. "That would be lovely, John. A perfect way to come home."

The words should have comforted him, but they felt like stones in his stomach, heavy with the knowledge of the emotional gulf he was attempting to bridge. He drove the car onto the road, the cityscape blurring past them, a juxtaposition to the clarity of his transgression.

John glanced at Sophie, her profile bathed in the soft glow of the setting sun streaming through the window, casting golden highlights in her hair. She was everything stable, everything real, and yet he couldn't shake the allure of the unknown that Jessica represented—the siren song of a life less ordinary, whispering promises of excitement that echoed the restless beat of his heart.

"Can't wait," he lied, the words a silken thread woven into the fabric of their conversation, laced with the hope that perhaps the evening could rekindle a flame that had dimmed in the shadow of temptation.

John moved his way through the maze of candlelit tables, leading Sophie to a secluded corner of the restaurant. The ambiance was intimate, with dim lighting casting dancing shadows on the walls and soft music that seemed to weave through the air, wrapping around them like silk. He pulled out her chair, the smooth motion a practiced gesture of chivalry, but as he did so, his mind betrayed him, drifting back to another night, in a setting not unlike this one—where laughter had been shared under similar velvet tones, but the eyes he'd sought then were not Sophie's clear blue but Jessica's deep emerald green.

Sophie settled into the chair with an appreciative smile, her gaze lingering on John, unaware of the silent battle waging within him. He took his seat across from her, the flicker of the candle flame reflected in the pristine white tablecloth, creating a barrier of light between them—a divide that felt insurmountable despite the few feet of distance.

They perused the menu, the words blurring before John's eyes as he struggled to maintain the facade of normalcy. Sophie, ever observant, reached across the table, her fingers brushing against his hand in a tender, familiar gesture. The contact sent a jolt through him, and he flinched slightly, the touch a stark reminder of the physical connection he craved yet feared.

"Is everything alright, John?" Sophie's voice was laced with concern, the timbre resonating within the hollow space of his chest.

"Of course," he replied, squeezing her hand in reassurance, the pressure of his grip seeking to ground him in the reality of her presence. His heartbeat hammered against his ribs, an erratic drumbeat that echoed the turmoil he fought to conceal.

The warmth of Sophie's hand seeped into his skin, a beacon amid the fog of his desires. He drew in a breath, the subtle scent of her perfume mingling with the rich aromas wafting from the kitchen, and for a moment, he allowed himself to sink into the comfort she offered—a lifeline amidst the tempestuous sea of his own making.

Yet even as he clung to the sensation of her touch, part of him remained adrift, caught in the undercurrent of memories that whispered of forbidden pleasures and the intoxicating danger that lay just beyond the precipice of choice.

Sophie's laughter twirled through the air, a lilting melody that John wished he could lose himself in. Her stories spilled forth effortlessly, tales of distant lands and close encounters that should have captivated him. He offered chuckles at just the right beats, his timing impeccable as ever. Yet, beneath the practiced ease, an undercurrent of distraction pulled at the edges of his attention.

"...and then the monkey simply snatched the sunglasses off my head," Sophie recounted, her blue eyes sparkling with mirth.

"Quite the cunning little thief," John replied, his laugh hollow to his own ears. But his mind was not there at the table adorned with white linen and flickering candles. It wandered, unbidden, to Jessica's emerald gaze—the way it had pierced through his defences, promising secrets and depths unexplored.

The clatter of dishes announced the arrival of their dinner, a welcome interruption. The server set down plates of exquisitely arranged cuisine before them, the scents of garlic and herbs wafting up to meet John's senses. He took a deep breath, allowing the earthy fragrance of truffle oil to anchor him back to the here and now.

"Ah, the Chateauneuf-du-Pape. Excellent choice, Sophie." He lifted his glass, swirling the ruby liquid before taking a sip. The velvety wine coated his tongue, a complexity of flavours vying for his attention, yet not quite reaching his numbed palate.

"Thank you. I thought it'd pair well with the lamb," she said, cutting into her meal with a grace that matched her composed demeanour.

"Indeed, it does." John forced the words out, draping them in appreciation he hoped sounded genuine. His taste buds recognized the harmony of the dish, the tender meat melded with the boldness of the wine, but his heart remained untouched, stubbornly resistant to the sensory indulgence.

As Sophie savoured her meal, John studied her profile, the soft light casting shadows that played upon her features. There was beauty there—familiar and comforting—but it was eclipsed by the haunting image of Jessica's laughter, the way her head had tilted back, hair tumbling like a cascade of autumn leaves.

He reached for another bite, the clink of cutlery against porcelain punctuating the moment. Each sound, each scent, was a lifeline thrown into the swirling thoughts that threatened to pull him under. With every chew, he willed the present to become more potent than the past, for the taste of the meal to erase the lingering phantom of Jessica's kiss that seemed to burn against his lips still.

But the ghost of another life, a life of thrilling whispers and intoxicating glances, refused to be exorcised by mere food and wine. It hovered at the periphery of his consciousness, an ever-present siren call that no amount of culinary distraction could silence.

The flicker of candles danced across the table, casting an amber glow on Sophie's earnest face as she leaned forward. The wine in her glass swirled with the motion, releasing a bouquet that mingled with the scent of fading lilies centrepiece. "How about a weekend getaway? Just you and me," Sophie suggested, her voice weaving through the soft murmurs of the restaurant, a melody John had always adored.

John offered a nod, the movement mechanical, his practiced smile concealing the tempest within. The gentle pressure of her fingers against his own was meant to be reassuring, yet it sent his thoughts spiralling once more to Jessica—her daring laugh, the electric touch of her skin against his in fleeting moments stolen from reality.

"Sounds perfect," he replied, the words hollow to his own ears as they bridged the chasm between longing and duty. He watched the reflection of candlelight in Sophie's eyes and tried to anchor himself to their blue depths, only to be drawn again to the verdant allure of a memory that refused to be dimmed.

The ride home was a silent passage through shadowed streets, the city lights streaking by like the tail of a comet—a celestial body untethered from the earth, much like John's wandering heart. Once inside the comforting walls of their home, Sophie's suggestion of a movie seemed to offer an escape, a way for John to slip beneath the surface of his own disquiet.

"Sure, let's find something light," he agreed, his voice betraying none of the weariness that settled upon him like a shroud. As she busied herself with the task, John sank into the couch, the fibres embracing him in familiar softness. Yet, even as the screen came to life with colours and sounds designed to captivate, John felt the grip of his secret tighten around him.

The weight of unspoken confessions pressed down, heavier than the darkness that filled the corners of the room. The characters on the screen played out their scripted lives, but John was lost in an unscripted turmoil, caught between the woman who lay beside him, her head resting trustingly on his shoulder, and the siren call of what could never be his without toppling the world he knew.

The glow from the television cast flickering shadows across the room, dancing over Sophie's features as she nestled closer to John. Her head found its familiar nook on his chest, her breaths syncing in rhythm with the rise and fall of his own. He should have been comforted by her warmth, by the soft press of her body against his side, yet a restless energy coursed through him, an undercurrent that whispered of forbidden thoughts.

As the protagonists on screen shared a triumphant kiss, a pivotal moment meant to stir hearts, John's gaze was unfocused, the scene before him blurring into irrelevance. Instead, he saw Jessica's laughter—the way it would throw her head back, revealing the elegant line of her throat—and felt the ghost of her touch, a phantom sensation that trailed fire along his skin. His heart raced, not from the movie's crescendo of music, but from a dangerous longing that threatened to consume him whole.

Sophie shifted, pulling back slightly to look at him as the credits rolled, her blue eyes seeking his. They were deep pools of trust and expectation, searching for the man she knew, the man who had vowed to be hers alone. But in that prolonged gaze, John felt exposed, as if she could see straight through to the chaotic tangle of emotions he fought so desperately to hide.

"Did you enjoy the film?" Sophie's voice cut through the silence, her words anchored in the ordinary, yet laced with an unwitting edge that made him flinch inwardly.

"Of course," he lied smoothly, mustering a smile that felt like a betrayal. He leaned forward, the space between them charged with an invisible tension. As their lips met in a kiss that should have been familiar and comforting, John tasted the ghost of another—a taste sweeter and more intoxicating than any wine they had shared at dinner. It was Jessica's essence that lingered on his tongue, a vivid reminder of a passion that had ignited without warning and now refused to be extinguished.

He pulled away, the aftertaste of deceit heavy in his mouth. The air around them seemed to close in, filled with unspoken questions and the weight of a secret that lay between them like a chasm. John looked away, pretending to be absorbed by the meaningless scroll of text on the screen, all the while feeling Sophie's gaze upon him, heavy with the love he no longer trusted himself to return.

The journey to the bedroom was a silent procession, each step heavy with the weight of unspoken words. The soft patter of their footsteps on the plush carpet was a stark contrast to the tumultuous storm raging in John's conscience. He felt Sophie's arms encircle him, her embrace both a sanctuary and a prison. In the darkness of their shared space, he closed his eyes, allowing himself to be momentarily lost in the warmth of her touch.

Yet, even as he surrendered to the familiarity of her presence, the guilt inside him twisted like a knife. Desire for another had infiltrated his heart, casting long shadows over the love he had vowed to cherish. It was a battle between loyalty and longing, fought in the quiet spaces where only he could see.

The room around them was suffused with the gentle glow of the nightstand lamp, painting their surroundings in soft amber hues. Shadows danced upon the walls, as if reflecting the flickering uncertainty within John's soul. Sophie's voice broke through the stillness, a whisper that seemed to resonate directly with his heartstrings. "I've missed you," she breathed, words drenched in affection.

John's response was automatic, yet laced with an undercurrent of sorrow. "I've missed you, too," he murmured, the words scraping against the raw edges of his deceit. Her love was like a warm light in the cold void of his duplicity, but it only served to deepen the shades of his inner conflict.

As he held her close, the contours of her body pressed against his, a stark reminder of their shared history and the intimacy that had once been untainted. Her scent enveloped him, a mixture of lavender and something uniquely Sophie—an olfactory echo of countless nights entwined in each other's arms. Yet now, that familiarity was tinged with the bitter sting of betrayal.

Sophie's love washed over him, as soothing and profound as it had always been. But where it once ignited flames of passion, it now kindled embers of remorse, each tender word fanning the coals of a secret he harboured in the dark recesses of his heart. His whispered affirmations were a hollow mimicry of the fervour they used to embody, each syllable a testament to the chasm that had opened within him.

In the dim comfort of their bedroom, enveloped by the velvet night, John Hawthorne was a man adrift, caught between the anchoring pull of a wife's undying affection and the tempestuous call of a desire he had never sought but found all-consuming. The night whispered on, cloaking their forms in its enigmatic shroud, holding them in a moment suspended between truth and illusion.

The room lay shrouded in shadows as the moon cast its pale glow through the sliver of curtains left ajar. John watched the silver light dance across the ceiling, painting ethereal patterns that seemed to mock the stillness of his predicament. Sophie's breathing settled into the steady rhythm of sleep beside him, her chest rising and falling with a tranquil assurance that belied the turmoil churning within him.

He lay motionless, the soft sheets a cool contrast to the heat radiating from his skin—a skin still tingling from Sophie's touch, yet craving another's. The faint scent of their earlier love-making lingered in the air, commingled with the subtle perfume of guilt that clung to him like a second skin.

John's mind was adrift on a sea of memories, each wave crashing against the brittle shore of his resolve. He could almost feel Jessica's phantom caress trailing fire down his spine, her laughter echoing through the recesses of his thoughts. It was a siren song that threatened to pull him under, to drown him in the depths of desire he had never meant to explore.

In the oppressive silence of the room, it was the echo of his own heartbeat that sounded loudest—a drumbeat out of sync with the tranquillity that surrounded him. Each throb was a reminder of the duality of his existence; the man who lay with his wife was not the man who walked in the daylight, smiling at passersby with a charade of contentment.

A car passed outside, its headlights flitting across the walls like the fleeting nature of his fidelity. He pondered the path before him, the unseen crossroads where each choice led further into the labyrinth of deceit or back toward the light of honesty. Yet even as clarity sought to emerge from the fog of his desires, the allure of the forbidden whispered seductively in his ear, promising the taste of a life less ordinary.

As the night pressed closer, suffocating in its silence, John felt the weight of the unspoken truths between Sophie and himself—a distance measured not in inches but in secrets. He knew that with the dawn would come the inevitable reflection in the mirror, a visage worn by the masquerade of normalcy he donned daily.

Sophie shifted in her sleep, a silent plea for his warmth, and he drew her closer, a gesture as reflexive as it was empty. He closed his eyes, feigning rest, while inside, the battle raged on. And there, in the quiet hours before morning, John Hawthorne grappled with the shards of a fractured heart, the echoes of his choices reverberating through the deafening stillness, reminding him of the path he had yet to choose.

Chapter 8: Confiding in Sam

John pushed open the door to the art cafe, a sanctuary of bohemian charm and aromatic indulgence, his entrance as unassuming as his neatly pressed shirt. The bell above the threshold chimed a soft welcome, yet its quaint cheer did little to ease the storm of emotions brewing within him. His gaze swept the space, each brushstroke of light and shadow on the walls mirroring the tumultuous dance of his thoughts.

The room hummed with the quiet symphony of life unfolding in real time: the clink of ceramic against wood, the murmur of voices weaving tales and secrets into the air, and the rich scent of coffee that caressed the senses like a promised embrace. John's pulse thrummed in his veins, a percussive counterpoint to the cafe's gentle rhythm.

His eyes found her then, Sam, ensconced in her corner kingdom where the world seemed to bend around her magnetic field. A halo of sunlight filtered through the window, crowning her purple-tinted hair with an ethereal glow that somehow managed to pierce through the heaviness in John's chest. He moved towards her, each step deliberate, navigating the sea of mismatched chairs and tables that hosted a tapestry of patrons—artists lost in thought, lovers entwined in whispered conversation, solitary souls seeking refuge in the pages of well-worn novels.

The closer John drew, the more the familiar cocoon of coffee and creativity wrapped around him, a velveteen shroud of warmth and complexity. The air was thick with the essence of roasted beans and sweet pastries, intermingling with the faintest hint of Sam's signature jasmine perfume—an olfactory whisper that beckoned him ever onward. As he approached, the soft exchange of ideas and laughter from the surrounding clientele seemed to fold into the background, the world narrowing to the tableau of anticipation before him.

With each footfall, John felt the weight of his secret press down upon him, a silent spectre that threatened to choke the easy charm from his demeanour. This was an arena of intimacy built upon brushstrokes and dreams, where truths were laid bare over steaming mugs and vulnerabilities shared under the guise of casual encounters. Here, in the presence of Sam's effervescent spirit, John knew the gravity of his confession would find no shadows in which to hide.

Sam's smile was a beacon amidst the art cafe's labyrinth of sensory impressions, her laughter a melody rising above the muted symphony of clinking cups and hushed conversations. John hesitated at the edge of her orbit, captivated yet daunted by the vivacity that radiated from her like sunlight through stained glass. She flicked her hand with an inviting flourish, motioning him to join her in the alcove carved out of the chaos.

"John," she greeted, her voice a vibrant note that cut through his apprehensions, "I was beginning to think you'd been swallowed up by one of the canvases on the wall."

Her jest carried a tone of amusement as he lowered himself into the chair opposite her. The quaint table bore the marks of countless confidences exchanged over its worn surface, the grain of the wood holding secrets as deep as its varnished scars. John's fingers found solace tracing these lines, a silent plea for courage to navigate the confession that clawed at his throat.

"Sam," he began, his timbre barely more than a murmur against the backdrop of the room's subtle noise. Shadows played across his features, the late afternoon light streaming through the window casting a mosaic of warmth and doubt upon his face. His eyes, usually pools of clear conviction, now wavered with an unspoken turmoil that seemed at odds with the gentle curve of his lips—a mask of humour and ease fracturing under the weight of his hidden truth.

"Is everything all right?" Sam's inquiry pierced the veil of unease, her head tilting slightly as she leaned forward, her curiosity painting her features with earnest concern.

The question hung in the air, a spectre of vulnerability between them. John wrestled with his resolve, the words he needed to utter ensnared by the thorns of hesitation. Each second stretched taut, a delicate balance of revelation and restraint, while the art cafe continued its indifferent serenade around them.

The subtle clink of porcelain disrupted the silence that had settled over them like a shroud. John's gaze, once adrift in the sea of his coffee, anchored itself upon Sam's expectant face. Her fingers paused mid-air, the vibrant tattoos on her wrist a stark contrast to the delicate China she cradled.

"Sam," John breathed out, each syllable heavy with an emotion he struggled to label. "There's something... about Jessica."

At the mention of the name, Sam's posture shifted, her spine straightening as if aligning itself with the gravity of his confession. The room seemed to lean in, the whispers of steam from their cups mingling with the soft jazz notes that floated lazily from a corner speaker.

"Jessica?" Sam prodded gently, her voice a lighthouse amidst the fog of his uncertainty.

Her eyes, bright and unyielding, held him in place—a demand for truth veiled in the comfort of her stare. The air between them thickened with anticipation, charged with the electric hum of unsaid words.

John swallowed, his throat tight. "I find myself drawn to her, in a way that's..." He faltered, the words tangling like wild vines within him.

"Electric?" Sam offered, her lips quirking upward in an effort to lighten the gravity of his admission.

"Exactly." John's nod was almost imperceptible, a confirmation cloaked in shadows.

"Life's too short, John," Sam said, her tone imbued with a boldness that seemed to dance along the edge of recklessness. Her hand reached across the table, hovering just above his own—a lifeline extended in the vast ocean of his disquiet.

"Sometimes, we stumble upon a passion so fierce it threatens to consume us," she continued, her words a siren song urging him toward the precipice of desire. "Shouldn't you explore what that means?"

Her question lingered in the air, punctuated by the distant sound of a coffee grinder roaring to life. Sam tilted her head, her purple locks catching the sunlight in a halo of defiance against the ordinary. Her playful smile, though tinged with sincerity, beckoned him toward an abyss lined with the intoxicating scent of possibility.

John's heart thrummed a frenzied rhythm against the cage of his ribs, each beat echoing Sam's call to embrace the fervour that Jessica ignited within him. It was a call to adventure, to the unknown, and it resonated with the part of him that lay dormant beneath years of carefully constructed normalcy.

"Perhaps," he murmured, the word slipping from his lips like a secret shared under the cover of dusk. His resolve wavered, a ship caught in the tempestuous waters of longing and loyalty, Sam's encouragement the wind that threatened to steer him off course.

John's inner turmoil cast a shadow over his usually affable features as he sat across from Sam, her earlier encouragement now mingling with the bitter taste of guilt in his mouth. The art cafe, with its mixture of vibrant canvases and the gentle clinking of coffee cups, seemed to recede into the background as he grappled with the gravity of his confession.

Sam observed him, her eyes no longer sparking with mischief but softening like the warm palette of colours that adorned the walls around them. "I know I said to chase your desires, John," she began, her voice a soothing balm against the cacophony of his thoughts. "But have you considered this might be about what's missing at home? With Sophie?"

The question hung between them, not as an accusation but as an invitation to introspection. "Communication, John. It's the lifeblood of love." Her words were like brushstrokes, painting a picture of understanding rather than judgment.

"Maybe it's not about Jessica," Sam continued, shifting her posture to one of reflective wisdom. "It could be that you're searching for something in yourself, something unfulfilled."

Her observations were a mirror reflecting back his own hidden depths, murky and yet to be fully understood. He pondered her counsel, feeling the seed of truth nestled within.

"Remember when I backpacked through Europe without a map or plan?" She leaned back, a wistful smile playing on her lips. "I thought I was looking for adventure, but I was really seeking myself. Found myself lost in Paris for days."

A chuckle slipped from John despite the weight on his chest. Sam's anecdotes often carried the dual gift of levity and insight. "Turns out, getting lost was the best way to find my path. It's all about asking the right questions, isn't it?" Her laughter was a light breeze that momentarily lifted the heavy drapes of his indecision.

"Did you ever find that little bistro again?" John asked, his voice steadier, clinging to the distraction she provided.

"Eventually," she replied with a spark of triumph. "Just had to follow the scent of fresh croissants."

The moment stretched comfortably as they shared a companionable silence, the cafe's atmosphere once more seeping into John's awareness—the faint aroma of oil paint mixed with the rich, earthy notes of coffee, the subdued hum of patrons lost in their own worlds offering a backdrop to his contemplation. The tension that had built up inside him ebbed away slightly, like high tide retreating under the pull of the moon.

In Sam's company, the world seemed less absolute, painted in shades of grey rather than stark black and white. And as he absorbed the essence of her free-spirited wisdom, John felt a reluctant smile form—a fleeting respite from his tangled web of emotions.

The last drops of coffee slid down the porcelain curve of John's cup, a bitter end to the swirling confessions that had filled the space between them. Across the table, Sam's hand emerged from the contrast of light and shadow cast by the flickering candle at their centre, her fingers coming to rest atop his with the delicate pressure of a falling leaf.

"John," she said, her voice a low murmur that seemed to resonate with the dark hues of the cafe walls, "whatever you decide, I'm here for you." In her touch, there was an anchor in the tempest of his heart—a promise not made lightly, given the tempestuous nature of the emotions they were navigating.

The air around them seemed to thicken, charged with the gravity of her words. He glanced up to meet her eyes, those vivid windows to a soul unafraid of life's tumultuous seas, and found within their depths a reflection of his own turmoil tempered by her unwavering certainty.

"Thanks, Sam," he breathed out, his reply barely audible over the soft jazz notes that now wove through the coffee-scented air like an insistent whisper. The warmth from her hand seeped into his skin, a balm to the confusion that had laced his veins with ice.

She withdrew her hand, the sudden absence of her warmth like the receding sun, and rose fluidly from her chair. Her suggestion floated towards him, carried on the wave of her spontaneous spirit. "Let's walk, clear our heads a bit."

The invitation hung between them, an ephemeral thread in the dimness of the cafe. His mind churned with the need for escape, for movement to mirror the racing of his pulse. With a nod that felt as though it required the effort of lifetimes, he stood, his muscles protesting the hours of tension they had endured.

Together, they emerged from the cocoon of the cafe, leaving behind the safety of its intimate corners and the refuge it offered from the world outside. The door closed with a soft click, sealing away the chapter of revelations, yet the story—his story—remained unfinished, pages fluttering in the winds of possibility.

As they walked through the threshold, John couldn't help but feel the seductive pull of the unknown path before him, with Sam at his side, a beacon amidst the fog of his conscience.

The golden haze of the afternoon sun wrapped around John and Sam as they exited the cafe, its warmth a gentle counterpoint to the turbulence that had churned in John's chest moments before. The street outside was bathed in an amber glow, the world momentarily tinged with the colour of nostalgia, as if encouraging them to slip away from the gravity of their earlier conversation.

They walked side by side, the clatter and melody of the city providing a rhythmic backdrop to their steps. A soft breeze carried the laughter of passersby and the distant aroma of street food, mingling with the less tangible scents of the waning day. As if by unspoken agreement, their discussion meandered into lighter realms, stories of shared memories and quips about the peculiarities of their surroundings danced between them, allowing a reprieve from the weighty matters that lingered just beneath the surface.

"Did you see that couple at the table next to us?" Sam's voice was playful, the tone in her words flirting with the edges of John's consciousness. "Matching sweaters. In this weather! It's a bold choice."

"Bold or a cry for help," John replied with a chuckle, his humour resurfacing like a trusted old friend. He found solace in the easiness of their banter, a delicate veil over the rawness of his confession.

As the sun began its descent, casting long shadows across the pavement, the moment came for them to part ways. They stopped beneath the spreading branches of an ancient oak, leaves whispering secrets above them. Sam turned to face him, her eyes holding his gaze with an intensity that belied the casual nature of their stroll.

"John," she said, her voice a tender caress against the symphony of the city, "you know you're not alone in this, right?"

He nodded, but the tightness in his throat prevented words from taking flight.

Without hesitation, Sam stepped forward and wrapped her arms around him, drawing him into an embrace that radiated a comforting heat. Her presence was a solid anchor, grounding him amidst the storm of his emotions. He felt the gentle pressure of her hands on his back, steady and reassuring.

"Follow your heart," she whispered, her breath warm against his ear, infusing him with a courage he hadn't known he needed. "But tread carefully, my friend. The heart is a wild creature—beautiful but untamed."

Her advice, woven with concern and wisdom, settled into the marrow of his bones. Sam released him from the hug, her fingers lingering just a moment longer than necessary, a silent promise of solidarity.

As they stepped back, her purple hair catching the dying light, she offered him a smile—a beacon of hope in the encroaching dusk. He watched her turn away, her vibrant figure retreating into the tapestry of the evening, leaving him alone with a heart full of questions and a horizon splashed with shades of uncertainty.

A shadow detached itself from the brickwork of neighbouring buildings, its form hunched and observational. Derek Thompson's eyes, magnified behind thick glasses, absorbed the scene with a ravenous curiosity typically reserved for the pages of an unfolding thriller. The intimate farewell between John and Sam was rich fodder for his insatiable appetite for neighbourhood intrigue. A knowing smile twitched at the corner of his lips as he catalogued this latest morsel, already anticipating the ripples it would send through their small community.

Meanwhile, John ambled down the sidewalk, the warmth from Sam's embrace lingering like a ghostly caress against his skin. It was a sensory balm that battled against the internal tempest churning within him. The fading sun threw long shadows across the pavement, mirroring the darkening tangle of his thoughts. Desire threaded through him—a yearning whisper, sinuous and invasive, tempting him toward pathways of forbidden fruit.

With each step, the weight of duty anchored his feet, cemented by a decade of commitment and shared history. His hand grazed the band of gold circling his finger, a tiny fortress against the siege of his unruly emotions. The encounter with Sam, so fraught with vulnerability and candour, had cracked open the fault lines in his carefully constructed facade.

The air held a hint of autumn's chill, a subtle reminder of change, of decay and rebirth. John breathed it in, hoping to find clarity in the crispness, but it eluded him, leaving only the taste of uncertainty on his tongue. The city around him whispered secrets in the sigh of wind through leaves and the distant murmur of traffic, but none offered a map for the labyrinth his life had become.

His heart, once sure of its rhythm and place, now beat an irregular cadence, syncopated with doubt and what-ifs. Could one follow their heart without losing themselves along the way? Sam's words echoed in the hollows of his mind, "beautiful but untamed." The dichotomy of risk and reward played out in the theatre of his psyche, a dance of shadows and light where every step could lead either closer to fulfillment or deeper into the abyss.

As John neared his home, the sanctuary of familiarity did little to soothe the restlessness that dogged his steps. The evening breeze carried whispers of lives lived boldly, of love pursued with reckless abandon, taunting the cage of his own indecision. He stood outside his front door, the key an icy promise in his palm, and paused. The threshold before him was more than a physical barrier; it was the line between the man he was and who he might become, between the safety of the known and the perilous allure of the unknown.

In the growing darkness, the streetlights flickered to life, casting pools of amber light that seemed to hold the secrets of the night. John's choice lay shrouded within them, a puzzle yet to be solved, a story yet to be told.

He took a deep breath, drawing in the crisp night air like a diver about to plunge into unknown depths. There was a heaviness in his chest, an ache that spoke of yearnings suppressed and choices yet to be made. The porch light cast a golden glow, illuminating the fine mist that had begun to gather, painting everything with a sheen of otherworldliness.

For a moment, John stood motionless, suspended in time, the key to his life as he knew it pressing cold and hard into his palm. The warmth of his home beckoned, the soft murmur of familiarity calling to him like a siren song. Yet, within its walls lay echoes of a life half-lived, of whispered conversations with Sam that had unveiled the depths of his restlessness.

With a resolve that belied his inner turmoil, John turned the key and pushed the door open. The familiar scent of his life—vanilla candles and fabric softener—washed over him, an olfactory anchor to the reality he had crafted. Stepping inside, he let the door swing shut behind him, the click of the latch a punctuation mark at the end of an unfinished sentence.

In the silence of his own foyer, John wrestled with the ghosts of possibility. The chapter of his day might have ended, but the story of his heart remained unwritten, a narrative pulsing with unresolved tension and veiled yearnings. As he shrugged off the constraints of his jacket, he couldn't shake the feeling that he was shedding more than just the trappings of the outside world—he was shedding the skin of complacency.

The house settled around him with familiar creaks and sighs, a symphony of domesticity that did little to quiet the cacophony in his mind. And as the mantle clock ticked away the seconds, John Hawthorne found himself standing at the precipice of the unknown.

Chapter 9: The First Kiss

John stood sentinel by the grill, the aroma of sizzling burgers mingling with the laughter and chatter of suburban camaraderie. He flipped a patty, the charred edges crisp and perfect, his motions practiced and easy. The smoke curled up into the summer sky, lazy and unhurried, much like John's outward demeanour. Yet beneath the veneer of his relaxed smile and neighbourly banter, a pulse of anticipation thrummed through his veins.

"Perfect day for a barbecue, huh, John?" one of the neighbours quipped, clinking his beer against John's spatula in a gesture of weekend solidarity.

"Couldn't ask for better," John replied, his voice smooth and affable. He laughed at the appropriate moments, nodding along to stories he barely heard, his gaze discreetly scanning the crowd. He was waiting, though none would be the wiser, for a ripple in the otherwise placid surface of the afternoon.

And then, like an answer whispered by fate, she arrived.

Jessica Sterling crossed the threshold of the Hawthorne's backyard with a grace that seemed to suspend time itself. Her sundress, a delicate kaleidoscope of summer blossoms, flirted with the breeze, hugging her silhouette before billowing out again like a sail catching wind. Heads turned, conversations paused mid-sentence, and even the children's playful shrieks dimmed as if the air itself were holding its breath.

From across the yard, John's eyes found hers. Emerald met earthy brown in a silent exchange that crackled with recognition, their shared secret folding into the space between them. For a moment, the world narrowed to the span of grass and garden that separated them, to the shared heartbeat of two souls amid the hum of suburbia.

Jessica's lips curved, the hint of a knowing smile crossing her features as she acknowledged him. Her walk was the slow pour of honey, measured and sure, each step a soft testament to the allure she carried as naturally as her own shadow. When she lifted her hand in a languid wave to the gathering, it was as though she ensnared the very sunbeams, her skin aglow with the light of late afternoon.

As she mingled, John returned to his task, tongs in hand, his movements automatic. But the heat from the grill was no match for the warmth spreading within him. Jessica had arrived, and with her, the promise of something intoxicatingly forbidden, a spark ready to ignite tinder into flame.

The laughter and chatter of the neighbours meshed into a symphony of suburban contentment as John worked the grill, his hands neatly turning the burgers with practiced ease. The aroma of searing meat filled the air, mingling with the scent of freshly cut grass and the faint hint of sunscreen. But amidst the casual revelry, John's senses were attuned to something far more compelling than the task at hand.

Across the yard, Jessica navigated the social waters with an effortless grace that belied the undercurrents tugging beneath her calm surface. Each time their gazes met, it was like a spark jumping across a gap, igniting something primal within them. Their eyes would lock for a fleeting moment, a silent conversation passing between them, before duty or interruption forced them apart. John's heart thrummed a steady rhythm, anticipation coiling tight in his chest with every clandestine exchange.

As the sunlight began to dip toward the horizon, casting long shadows upon the lawn, the opportunity they had been skirting around all afternoon presented itself. A neighbour called out, lamenting the dwindling supply of chilled beverages, and it was Jessica who responded with a melodic voice that seemed to resonate directly with John's pulse.

"Allow me," she said, her eyes finding John's with intent. "I could use a helping hand, though."

"Of course," John replied, setting down his tongs and wiping his hands on a nearby towel. The excuse was flimsy, transparent to anyone paying attention, but the crowd was too engrossed in their own enjoyment to notice.

They moved together, slipping through the clusters of chatting friends and families, their departure barely registering in the jovial atmosphere. As they rounded the corner of the house, the commotion of the party faded into a distant hum, replaced by the rustle of leaves and the occasional chirp of a bird settling down for the evening.

Their path took them past blooming flower beds and manicured hedges until they reached the old garden shed, its wooden slats weathered by countless seasons and standing sentinel at the edge of the property. They entered the cool, dim interior, where gardening tools hung in orderly rows on the walls, and the earthy scent of potting soil filled the air.

John's heartbeat quickened, thundering in his ears, as he closed the door behind them. The space felt smaller now, heavy with the weight of their proximity. Jessica stood mere inches away, her breaths shallow and quick, her chestnut hair cascading over her shoulders like a silken waterfall. He could nearly taste the wine on her lips from earlier, the desire to do so burning within him.

For a moment, neither spoke. The world outside ceased to exist, leaving only the charged silence and the palpable tension woven through the very air they shared. It was a precipice they teetered upon, each aware of the step they were about to take, one that could never be retracted.

The sun dipped lower, casting elongated shadows that danced upon the cracked earth behind the shed. As the laughter and clinking glasses from the party dimmed to a mere whisper on the breeze, John felt the world narrow until it held nothing but the space between himself and Jessica. The air, previously light with summer's touch, now seemed thick, charged with the electricity of their seclusion.

John watched as a droplet of sweat traced a path down Jessica's collarbone, disappearing into the valley between her breasts, accentuated by the cling of her sundress. He swallowed hard, feeling the dryness in his throat as if he too were crossing a desert of restraint. Around them, the garden was lush and alive, an intimate oasis set apart from the reality they had momentarily left behind.

Their eyes met, an unspoken conversation passing between them. His gaze, usually so steady and sure, wavered under the intensity of her emerald stare. In those depths, he found the wild and untamed currents he'd sought unknowingly, the promise of adventures he'd never dared to dream. Her eyes held stories, secrets that beckoned him closer, urging him to listen, to dive into those verdant pools and discover the depths for himself.

In that suspended moment, John's hand reached out, driven by a force beyond reason or logic. Like magnets, his fingers found hers, the contact sending a jolt through his veins. Their hands entwined, a lock and key of flesh and bone, fitting together in silent acknowledgment of the shared fervour that hummed beneath their skin.

The coarse texture of his palm against the softness of hers created a contrast as stark as their mingling breaths—a symphony of inhalations and exhalations that filled the void of words. Each breath was a note played only for the other, a quiet melody of desire that sang of the things they could not yet speak aloud.

In the sanctuary of the shed, time became a malleable thing, stretching and contracting with each heartbeat. Here, in the flecked light, the possibility of what could be loomed large, as intoxicating as the perfume of the nearby blooms that hung heavy in the still air.

The air was alive with tension, a palpable thing that danced between them like the shadows cast by the overhanging branches. John's gaze held Jessica's, a silent conversation flowing in the space of their joined hands. The world beyond the garden shed had ceased to exist; there was only the here and now, the charged silence and the warmth of her skin.

John's hand moved, almost of its own volition, to trace the contour of Jessica's cheek. His fingertips grazed her flesh, warm and inviting, and he felt the tremor of anticipation that coursed through him mirrored in the slight shiver that passed through her body. In that tender caress, an awareness bloomed within him, a recognition of the precipice upon which they teetered, the line they were about to cross. There was a moment—a heartbeat, a breath—when hesitation lingered, when the gravity of their actions hung heavy in the air.

But then, as if drawn by a force greater than themselves, they leaned in, closing the distance. The inevitable unfolded softly at first, a tentative brush of lips that spoke of questions and answers all at once. The kiss deepened, a slow unfurling of desire that had long been dormant. The taste of wine, sweet and heady, lingered on their lips, mingling with the promise of something forbidden and fiercely sought.

With urgency born of passion long denied, their bodies pressed together. There was no space for doubt as John pulled Jessica closer, his arms encircling her waist, anchoring her to him. The softness of her mouth against his was a revelation, each movement a discovery, each sigh a step further into uncharted territory.

Their kiss was a confluence of need and longing, of whispered dreams and unspoken confessions. And though the afternoon sun still warmed their secluded corner of the world, they were adrift in a place where time held no sway, where the only truth that mattered was the closeness and connection they found in each other's embrace.

The world contracted to the space between them, to the mingling of breaths and the slow dance of tongues. Jessica's hair was a silken cascade through John's fingers, a sensory ribbon binding him to her essence. Each strand slipped through his grasp, as if her very spirit were weaving around him, drawing him deeper into the labyrinth of their forbidden desire.

Their surroundings—the garden shed hidden by overgrown ivy, the muffled sounds of laughter from the barbecue—receded into a hazy afterthought. It was the scent of jasmine in Jessica's hair that filled his senses, the warmth of her skin against the coolness of the afternoon air that enveloped him. The quiet space around them pulsed with the rhythm of their quickening heartbeats, the only testament to the time slipping irretrievably by.

The thrill of secrecy, the tacit acknowledgment of lines being blurred and then crossed, heightened every touch, every sigh. Their embrace was a tightrope walk between restraint and abandon, each kiss a step further into the intoxicating void where only they existed.

Suddenly, the sound of approaching footsteps fractured the moment like a stone through glass. The intrusion jolted through them, a stark reminder of the world beyond their secluded haven. Adrenaline surged, casting a sharp light on the reality they had momentarily defied.

Their eyes met, wide with alarm. In that instant, they shared an unspoken pact, an understanding that skirted the edge of danger and consequence. They pulled apart hastily, hearts pounding against rib cages like caged birds desperate for freedom.

The footsteps grew louder, more distinct—a countdown to exposure that neither of them could afford. Breathless and flushed with the remnants of their stolen intimacy, they faced the imminence of discovery, the precarious balance between what had unfolded and what lay ahead.

John straightened his shirt with fumbling fingers, the fabric sticking to his skin in a telltale manner that made him all too aware of recent transgressions. He drew in a deep breath, trying to steady the rapid beat of his heart, each inhalation an attempt to cool the fire that

Jessica had ignited within him. Beside him, she smoothed the material of her sundress over her hips, the gesture deliberate, calming. Their eyes met, and in that silent exchange, they wove a wordless promise—a vow that this encounter was merely the beginning.

The air around them was thick with the scent of grilled meat and the laughter of unsuspecting guests, but as they stepped out from the shed, the atmosphere shifted. The world they re-entered now held a different texture, charged with the electricity of their secret. They moved through the crowd, a dance of avoidance and attraction, each step calculated to maintain an appearance of casual indifference.

Yet, every glance carried weight, laden with the memory of their clandestine touch. John's gaze flickered towards Jessica more often than he could control, each look a spark threatening to ignite the kindling of gossip among the neighbours. Her presence was a magnet, pulling at him with an intensity that felt both dangerous and inevitable.

Jessica's laugh, light and melodic, drifted across the yard, but it no longer seemed carefree. It was a siren call, laced with the huskiness of their shared whispers. She navigated conversations with an ease that belied the tremor John could sense beneath her composed exterior. Her emerald eyes betrayed a restless energy, a mirror to his own inner chaos.

Their relationship, once a blank canvas of neighbourly politeness, was now stained with shades of longing and the residue of forbidden kisses. There was a before, and there was an after, and they stood on the precipice of this new reality, acutely aware that their lives were irrevocably altered. The tension between them was a palpable thing, a serpent coiling in the grass, unseen yet poised to strike.

Though they mingled with the crowd, sharing smiles and exchanging pleasantries, the space between them thrummed with unspoken understanding. John's once confident demeanour was tinged with a restlessness that matched the sway of Jessica's dress in the gentle breeze—an echo of the yearning that continued to whisper through the fibres of his being.

Neither could deny the transformation that had occurred. The fabric of their connection had been pulled taut, straining against the confines of propriety. With each passing moment, the memory of their illicit embrace lingered like smoke, a spectre haunting the sunlit tableau of the afternoon barbecue.

The sun dipped lower, casting a golden hue over the backyard as the barbecue wound down. The laughter and chatter of the neighbours were mere background noise to John as he stood by the grill, the charred scent of cooked meat lingering in the air. His gaze wandered across the lawn, seemingly casual but with a predator's precision.

Jessica, her sundress now a silhouette against the waning light, moved among the guests with grace that belied the turmoil churning within both of them. She laughed, the sound airy and light, yet it reached John with the weight of all that remained unsaid.

He watched her, the way the fading sunlight played with her chestnut hair, turning it to shades of amber and flame. It was an ethereal sight that stirred something primal in him, a hunger that had been awakened and left unfulfilled. His fingertips tingled with the memory of her skin, and he clenched his hands to quell the rising urge.

As if feeling the intensity of his stare, Jessica glanced over, her eyes locking with his from across the yard. In that suspended beat, the world seemed to contract until nothing existed but the silent conversation between their gazes.

Her lips parted slightly, not in surprise but in recognition—of the shared secret, of the desires they had barely begun to explore. The corners of her mouth curved, not quite a smile but an acknowledgment of the electric current that buzzed through the space separating them.

John felt the moment stretch out, taut as a bowstring. The muffled sounds of the party faded into a hush, leaving only the rustle of leaves and the distant call of a bird heralding the approaching dusk. His heart thumped in his chest, a drumbeat syncing with the pulse he imagined dancing on Jessica's throat.

Then, as swiftly as their connection had flared, it was broken. Maggie's bright laughter sliced through the tension, and Jessica turned away, her skirt catching the breeze once more. John exhaled slowly, feeling the sharp edge of reality cut through the haze of yearning.

The future loomed before them, fraught with questions and the ghostly trails of forbidden touch. What lay ahead was uncertain—a labyrinth of desire and consequence—but in the gravity of their final exchange, there was an undeniable promise. It was a vow etched in the charged air, a silent declaration that the fire they'd ignited would not be easily extinguished.

With a last, lingering look at the spot where Jessica had stood, John took a steadying breath and turned back to extinguish the grill. The embers glowed defiantly for a moment before succumbing to the darkness, mirroring the smouldering intensity that refused to die within him.

Chapter 10: Jessica's Past Revealed

The door to the cafe creaked softly, a quiet herald for John and Jessica's entrance into the dimly lit sanctuary. They moved with an almost choreographed grace, their steps falling in time as if to a silent waltz that only they could hear. The low buzz of hushed conversations and the gentle clinking of cups against saucers wrapped around them like a shroud, concealing their presence from the outside world.

John's gaze swept the room, his eyes settling on a secluded corner where shadows danced across the walls, beckoning with whispered promises of privacy. There was an unspoken agreement between them as they navigated towards the table, each movement laced with a restrained urgency that belied the casual tilt of John's head and the fluid sway of Jessica's hips.

As they slid into their seats, the worn leather creaking faintly under their weight, the air between them thickened with anticipation. Jessica's fingers, long and delicate, found their way to her coffee cup, tracing the rim with a rhythmic precision that echoed the pounding of her heart. It was a dance she performed unwittingly, a tell-tale sign of the storm roiling beneath her calm exterior.

The steam from the dark brew rose in lazy spirals, carrying with it the rich, earthy scent that mingled with the fragrance of aged wood and paper from nearby bookshelves. The soft light cast from overhead lamps painted her features in shades of gold and amber, highlighting the slight furrow in her brow and the gentle bite of her lower lip—a portrait of vulnerability cloaked in silk and strength.

John watched her, the corners of his mouth twitching with the ghost of a smile that failed to reach his eyes. He recognized the play of emotions across her face, the subtle shifts too nuanced for any but those who cared to look closely. His own fingers curled around his cup, the warmth seeping into his skin, a stark contrast to the cool dance of unease in his gut.

Around them, the cafe continued its tranquil symphony, the melody of everyday life providing a backdrop to the intimate theatre unfolding at the corner table. For a fleeting moment, amidst the aromatic blend of coffee and pastries, they existed in a world apart—a world where the secrets yet unspoken hung heavy in the air, waiting to be unfurled like the petals of a night-blooming flower.

Jessica inhaled deeply, the subtle rise and fall of her chest barely noticeable beneath the smooth fabric of her dress. The air held a hint of trepidation as she exhaled, her voice steady but laced with the ghosts of memories past. "John," she began, her gaze anchored to the whirls of steam rising from her cup, "there's something about my history that I need you to understand."

She paused, gathering the threads of her story, weaving them into words. "Before I moved here, I was entangled with someone—Michael Archer." The name fell between them, a stone cast into still waters, ripples distorting their quietude. "It was intense, passionate... and ultimately, it scarred me in ways I'm still coming to terms with."

John's eyes widened imperceptibly, the muscles around his irises contracting with surprise. His mind reeled, grappling with the sudden revelation. Michael Archer—the same man whose reputation for charm and ambition had left indelible marks on the social landscape they both navigated.

This new knowledge sent a cascade of thoughts tumbling through John's consciousness. *She's been touched by the same fire that now threatens to consume us,* he realized, a sense of kinship threading through the shock. The parallels of their current liaison, so fraught with its own intensity and secrecy, began to sketch themselves against the backdrop of Jessica's admission.

He could feel the delicate balance they'd maintained begin to tremor, the lines of their relationship redrawn in this confessional light. Each word from Jessica's lips painted strokes of vulnerability and strength upon the canvas of her past—a past that now bled into the present, colouring their every interaction with deeper shades of complexity.

The soft murmur of the cafe swirled around them, a distant symphony to the intimate drama unfolding within John's heart. He sat motionless, save for the involuntary clench of his fingers around the ceramic handle of his coffee cup, anchoring himself to the moment as he navigated the treacherous waters of revelation.

The subdued clink of porcelain broke the hush that had settled over the secluded corner of the cafe, as Jessica's fingers absentmindedly traced the rim of her coffee cup. Her eyes, a rich tapestry of emerald and vulnerability, lifted to meet John's with an intensity that belied the tremble in her voice.

"Michael never understood... he couldn't," she whispered, her words spilling out like fragile birds taking flight. "I was a conquest to him, something to be won and then displayed." The honesty in her confession reverberated through the quiet space between them, raw and unfiltered.

John watched the subtle dance of emotions playing across Jessica's face, her every expression painting a picture of a woman who had walked through fire and emerged with the smoke woven into her soul. Each syllable that fell from her lips was an act of bravery, a testament to the courage it took for her to unravel her past before him.

He could see now, the scars that lay beneath her confident exterior, the secret history etched into her very being. It was as if he was glimpsing the undercurrents of a river that flowed beneath a smooth surface, tumultuous and full of hidden depths.

As she continued, the air around them grew thick with the scent of roasted coffee beans and unspoken truths. A faint warmth from the dim, amber lighting of the cafe graced their table, lending a soft glow to Jessica's features as they flickered with the ghosts of old wounds laid bare.

John felt his own pulse quicken, a rhythmic drumming against the inside of his wrist, echoing the unsettled storm of empathy and surprise that brewed within him. His grip on the coffee cup tightened imperceptibly, the ceramic cool and solid, a stark contrast to the fluid uncertainty of his thoughts. He could feel the faint ridges of the handle pressing into his skin, grounding him as he navigated the tempest of his emotions.

A surge of protectiveness washed over him, mingling with a dash of unease—a cocktail of reactions he struggled to reconcile. Here was a connection, taut and humming with potential, yet fraught with silent perils. The revelation of Jessica's past with Michael Archer, a man whose shadow loomed larger with each word spoken, wove a complicated web that threatened to ensnare them both.

The intimacy of the moment stretched out, filling the spaces between their words, entwining around them like a vine that held both beauty and thorns. John's throat felt dry, a desert amidst the oasis of the cafe, as he absorbed the weight of Jessica's admissions, each one a piece of her armour shed in trust.

In the quiet corner of the cafe, surrounded by the hushed murmur of other patrons, John realized the precarious ledge upon which they now stood. With every beat of his heart, with every breath Jessica took, the lines of their destinies blurred, intertwining with the silent language of understanding that passed between them.

The silence settled over their secluded table like a thick velvet curtain, muffling the distant clink of dishes and murmur of conversations. It was an empty canvas stretched taut between them, heavy with the brushstrokes of Jessica's confession. A shared gaze held fast, binding them in an unspoken pact that resonated deeper than words could fathom.

John's eyes, dark pools reflecting the dim glow of the cafe's antique chandelier, anchored Jessica's wavering spirit. The quiet was not awkward, rather it was reverent—an acknowledgment of the sacred ground now tread upon. In the stillness, Jessica's breath became the softest melody, her chest rising and falling with a rhythm that seemed to beckon John's own heart to sync with hers.

He finally broke the hush, his voice a low baritone, harmonizing with the underlying notes of trepidation and warmth that danced in the air around them. "Jessica," he said, each syllable deliberate, "the shadows of our past can be long, but they don't have to define the path we choose now."

His fingers released their vice-like grip on the coffee cup, the white ceramic stark against his flushed skin. He leaned forward slightly, closing the spatial divide between them, as if to bridge the gap of their shared uncertainties.

"Your honesty," he continued, his tone laced with a gravity that matched the depth of her revelation, "it's a gift. And I won't pretend I have all the answers or that I'm not feeling... overwhelmed." The word hung there, a testament to the labyrinth of emotions etched within him.

"But we're here now," John said, infusing a gentle firmness into his words. "Whatever complexity lies ahead, we'll face it together, won't we?" His question was rhetorical, yet it bore the weight of genuine enquiry, a tender probe into the fabric of their evolving connection.

In the ambiance of the cafe, amidst the rich aroma of roasted coffee beans and the faint scent of antiquated wood, John's reassurance mingled with caution. It was a delicate dance of sentiment, one foot in the safety of camaraderie, the other teetering on the precipice of the unknown.

The soft clinking of porcelain punctuated the silence that had settled over the corner table, where John and Jessica sat ensconced in their private haven within the cafe. The diffuse light from an overhead lamp cast a honeyed glow on their faces, painting them with warmth despite the coolness that threatened to seep through their connection.

John's hand moved first, a slight shift across the wooden surface, his fingers extending like tentative tendrils toward Jessica's own. Her eyes lifted from the contemplation of her coffee cup just as his touch grazed her hand, a fleeting contact that sent a ripple through the space between them. The corner of her lips quirked upward in a shared smile, the curve soft and vulnerable, echoing the subtle intertwining of their spirits.

"Jessica," he murmured, the name rolling off his tongue with an intimacy that was both exhilarating and unnerving. "We're flirting with fire, you know? It's impossible to ignore the... implications."

Her emerald eyes held his, alight with a flame that wavered between excitement and caution. "I know," she replied, her voice a melding of resolve and trepidation. "But don't you think some flames are worth the burn?"

The air around them seemed charged, electric with the pull of their mutual desire and the gravity of their situation. They were acutely aware of the others in the cafe, the low hum of conversation and the occasional scrape of chair against floor serving as a reminder that their cocoon of privacy was but an illusion.

"Perhaps," John conceded, feeling the heat of her gaze as if it were a tangible caress against his skin. "But we can't forget the cost. Not just to ourselves, but to... others." His thoughts strayed unbidden to Sophie, the image of her clear blue eyes suffusing him with a pang of guilt.

"Of course," Jessica whispered, withdrawing her hand with a grace that belied the tension coiling within her. "It's not just about us. There are lines we haven't crossed—yet."

"Yet," he echoed, the word laced with the intoxicating scent of possibility. They were skirting the edges of a precipice, the fall either a descent into chaos or an ascent to something transcendent.

"John," she began again, leaning in so that her breath fanned across his cheek, carrying the faintest hint of jasmine. "I'm not oblivious to the risks. But sometimes, life asks us to take a leap, doesn't it? To risk the fall for the chance to fly?"

He could feel the quickening of his pulse, the subtle tension that arched between them, taut as a bowstring. Every sense was heightened, attuned to the nuances of her presence—the way her hair fell over her shoulders, the richness of her perfume, the delicate timbre of her voice weaving through the air like music.

"Sometimes," John admitted, his words sinking into the quietude that wrapped around them. "But we must decide if the sky we're reaching for is worth leaving the ground beneath our feet."

Outside the cafe, the world continued its relentless pace, unaware of the silent storm brewing in the hearts of two souls ensnared by the gravity of their choices. Inside, the conversation hung suspended, a dance of potential and peril, each step measured against the backdrop of what might be and what should be.

As they lingered in the liminal space of decision, the afternoon sun filtered through the windows, casting long shadows that stretched across the floor like omens, their shapes mingling in a silent testament to the complexity of human longing.

The final whispers of their fraught conversation seemed to cling to the air as Jessica reached for her leather purse, her movements deliberate, each one an articulation of newfound purpose. The ambient hum of the cafe receded into a distant murmur as she clipped the fastener shut with a crisp snap, the sound punctuating the space between them. Her fingers curled around the strap, gripping it like a lifeline, betraying none of the storm that had raged moments before.

John watched her, the lines of her profile etched against the backdrop of the dimly lit room. She stood up, her posture straight, shoulders squared—a warrior donning invisible armour. The resolve in her stance spoke volumes; it was clear that Jessica was ready to march into the fray of her own life, to confront the dragons of her past with a courage that both awed and unsettled him.

He rose slowly, feeling the creak of his chair on the wooden floor echo within the cavernous chambers of his chest. John's mind churned, still ensnared by the tendrils of revelation that had unfurled before him. The knowledge of Jessica's previous entanglement with Michael Archer—and the scars it had left—loomed large, an uncharted territory now woven into the fabric of their connection.

His heart thumped a heavy rhythm, resonant with the tension that threaded through his veins. There was empathy, yes, but also an undercurrent of fear—a trepidation at the precipice of unknowns they were now poised to traverse. Each beat seemed to whisper a question: What now?

The scent of coffee lingered, a bittersweet reminder of the intimacy shared in hushed tones and furtive glances. It mingled with the faintest trace of jasmine from Jessica's perfume, a fragrance that had become a call to the depths of his soul. Yet, even as the aroma enveloped him, there was a chilling recognition that their shared secret had irreversibly altered the landscape of their relationship.

The emotional resonance of their exchange hung heavy, a tangible presence that wrapped around him, as suffocating as it was exhilarating. It was as if with each passing second, the stakes grew higher, the gravity of their situation more profound. John's grasp on his own cup tightened unconsciously, a futile attempt to anchor himself amidst the swirling currents of uncertainty.

"Jessica," he finally said, his voice a low rumble, "are you certain this is the path you want to take?"

Her eyes met his, emerald pools reflecting back at him not just conviction, but a plea for understanding. The silent communion between them was charged, a dance of unspoken fears and unarticulated desires.

With every fibre of his being pulled taut between longing and apprehension, John Hawthorne realized that the ground beneath him had shifted, and that going forward, every step would be upon new earth, rich with peril and promise.

They stepped through the door, leaving behind the cocoon of the cafe's murmured confessions and into an afternoon alive with deceptive normalcy. The outside world greeted John and Jessica with a familiar tableau—a pair of children chasing a frisbee, a dog lazily yawning under the shade of an oak—but it all seemed strangely distant now, as if they were actors who had stumbled off set into a reality that was no longer entirely their own.

The sunlight draped over them like a transparent veil, warm and golden, but its cheerfulness was at odds with the gravity that weighted their shoulders. They walked side by side in silence, each step away from the sanctuary of their secluded table marking the return to a life where the lines they had blurred remained boldly drawn for the rest of the world.

At the curb, the moment stretched taut—their parting, a silent accord that lingered in the shared space between them. John looked at Jessica, her emerald eyes shaded by the brim of her hat yet still vibrant with unspoken promises. There was a fleeting touch, fingertips brushing against the back of his hand, a whisper of connection that spoke volumes.

"Take care," he said, but the words felt trivial, a paltry offering to the enormity of what they'd shared.

"Always," she replied, her lips curving in a smile that didn't quite reach her eyes. It was a performance, a mask donned for the benefit of the unsuspecting world around them, but underneath the facade, John sensed the steel in her resolve.

He watched her walk away, her stride confident, the sway of her hips a silent song that echoed in the hollow left by her absence. The air around him was filled with the scent of blooming azaleas and the distant hum of traffic—everyday sounds that felt oddly foreign. The warmth of the sun caressed his skin, a stark contrast to the cool undercurrent of turmoil that churned within him.

As Jessica's figure grew smaller, blending into the throng of passersby, the reality of their conversation settled upon John with a weight heavier than before. The knowledge of their entanglement was a secret melody, haunting and sweet, that only they could hear above the noise of daily life.

Their shared confession lay between them like an invisible thread, tensile and vibrant, binding them together even as they moved apart. The sun dipped lower in the sky, casting long shadows that seemed to whisper of the hidden depths they had dared to explore—and the precipice on which they now stood, teetering between restraint and abandon.

John remained motionless, the last tendrils of Jessica's perfume lingering in the air as she vanished into the sea of anonymity. The world resumed its pace around him, a canvas of ordinary life that seemed surreal in the wake of their intimate exchange. He drew a deep breath, tasting the city's pulse—the tang of exhaust mixed with the sweetness of late spring blooms.

The cafe's door swung shut behind him with a soft jangle, severing the final physical tie to the space where truths had unfurled like delicate petals. John felt the texture of the moment, the roughness of the brick wall against his palm as he steadied himself, the grit under his fingernails—a stark reminder of the raw honesty they had shared.

His thoughts were a swirl of smoke, drifting and coalescing into shapes of longing and apprehension. He pondered the path ahead, each step mired in uncertainty and the intoxicating allure of the forbidden. The gravity of their conversation pulled at him, a current threatening to sweep him away from the safety of the shore he had known.

John's gaze followed the path Jessica had taken, the vibrant bustle of the street painting a vivid backdrop to his inner turmoil. The sun dipped further, shadows elongating like fingers stretching across the pavement, reaching for something just beyond grasp. In this shifting light, the line between reality and desire blurred, and John found himself straddling worlds.

He could feel the beat of his own heart, a rhythm at odds with the metronome of his structured life. The clatter of a nearby trash can lid, knocked askew by a stray cat, struck a chord with the dissonance within him. A breeze whispered past, carrying the remnants of conversations and the laughter of children playing in the distance—sounds muffled by the intensity of his introspection.

As the minutes ticked by, John's inner reflection grew more acute. There was a hunger, an ache that had been awakened, filling him with both dread and anticipation. The future loomed, a tableau yet to be painted, the colours of passion and consequence mixing on a palette not yet touched by the brush.

With a final glance toward the horizon—where the city's skyline met the tender embrace of dusk—John turned away. Each step was measured, a deliberate march back to the familiarity of his existence, but the echo of Jessica's words accompanied him, a siren's call that resonated through the core of his being.

Chapter 11: John's Inner Turmoil

John lay motionless, his gaze affixed to the expanse of white above him, as if the ceiling were a canvas for his festering thoughts. In the stillness of the night, each tick of the bedside clock seemed to echo the relentless churn of his restless mind. The pull of his conscience, the silent whispers urging him to seek refuge in the shadows of his study, could no longer be ignored. Carefully, he peeled back the sheets and placed his feet on the cold floor, feeling the chill creep up his skin like a premonition.

He moved with practised precision through the darkness, avoiding the creaky floorboard that sat like a traitor by the bed. Sophie's breaths remained deep and even, undisturbed by his quiet exodus. The tranquillity of sleep, untouched by the turmoil that plagued him, provided solace. As he closed the door behind him, the soft click felt like sealing away a part of himself, one that was reserved only for her gentle scrutiny.

The study welcomed him with the muted glow of moonlight filtering through the blinds, casting bars of silver over the leather-bound books and mahogany desk. John began to pace, the carpet hushing his footsteps to mere whispers against its plush surface. Once an escape into the world of words and wisdom, the room now felt like a confessional, waiting for him to reveal his soul.

Unbidden memories of Sophie surfaced with each step, enveloping him like the warmth of sunlight through autumn leaves. He reminisced about the laughter that once filled rooms similar to this one, the shared glances that conveyed profound meaning among friends, and the gentle caresses of hands that promised more in the solitude of the night. The early days of their marriage were a tapestry woven with threads of passion and companionship, a masterpiece they had created together.

He paused by the bookshelf, trailing his fingers over the spines, each title a fragment of the life they had built. The scent of aged paper and ink swirled around him, mingling with the ghost of her perfume that lingered in the fabric of the armchair where she often read. How effortlessly their lives had intertwined, how fervently he had believed in the simplicity of love and the sanctity of vows.

Yet here he stood, a man adrift in his own home, the certainty of his existence slowly unravelling. Doubt casts long shadows across the room, turning familiar objects into spectres of what once was. It was in this sombre twilight zone of recollection and remorse that John Hawthorne grappled with the duality of his desires, the weight of longing and loyalty entwined in a delicate dance of fate.

The moon cast a pale glow over the room, and in its light, John's eyes sparkled with an illicit fire. He sat motionless at the mahogany desk, his fingers absentmindedly tracing the polished surface that gleamed like obsidian under the night sky's watchful eye. A rush of images invaded his mind, each one a vivid brushstroke painting a portrait of forbidden desire.

Jessica Sterling – her name alone was a siren song, a melody laced with temptation. In the quiet of the study, John could almost hear her laughter, a sound as melodic and intoxicating as the finest wine. It rolled through the corridors of his memory, echoing off the walls, filling him with a longing that was at once both exhilarating and terrifying.

He closed his eyes, surrendering to the fantasy. The feel of Jessica's skin against his own was electric, igniting every nerve ending with a symphony of sensation. Silk upon steel, her touch was gentle yet insistent, a paradox that mirrored the complexity of their clandestine encounters. Her scent enveloped him—a heady mix of jasmine and something uniquely her own – a fragrance that seemed to whisper secrets meant only for him.

With a start, John's eyes snapped open. He rose from the desk and made his way to the window, the coolness of the glass a stark contrast to the heat coursing through his veins. Outside, the world lay bathed in silver, the streets empty and hushed, as if holding its breath in anticipation of dawn's arrival.

His reflection stared back at him, a haunted visage that bore the marks of inner conflict. The guilt enveloped him like a shroud, a tangible presence. His betrayal was more than just an act; it was a chasm that threatened to engulf the life he had meticulously crafted, fragment by fragment.

As he gazed out into the moonlit street, John grappled with the gravity of his actions. The weight of his duplicity pressed heavily on his chest, an anchor dragging him down to depths where the light of reason grew dim. With Sophie asleep in their bed, a mere shadow away from the truth, the sharp sting of remorse lanced through him.

Yet, even in this moment of self-reproach, the allure of Jessica's enigmatic pull was undeniable. She was the question to which he had no answer, the puzzle whose pieces he yearned to fit together, even as they cut into the very fabric of his being.

John stood there, his forehead resting against the cool pane, a man caught between the seductive dance of what could be and the solemn vows of what should be. The night held him in its embrace, a silent witness to the war raging within – a war where every battle left no victors, only casualties of the heart.

The hush of the house enveloped John as he stood at the threshold of the kitchen, his resolve to forge a path back to Sophie firm in his chest. He stepped onto the cool tiles, their chill seeping through the soles of his feet and climbing his spine—a stark contrast to the warmth that swelled within him, fuelled by the desire to mend the frayed edges of their bond.

John set about preparing breakfast with a precision that defied the chaos of his thoughts. John measured each movement, a silent hymn to the life he had vowed to cherish. The sizzle of butter as it hit the pan whispered secrets, while eggs cracked against the rim of a bowl with the crisp finality of decisions made. The golden yolks spilt forth, their rich colour a promise of new beginnings as he whisked them into submission.

He transformed the kitchen into a place of devotion, pouring his intentions into each deliberate gesture. Coffee beans ground between the burrs of the machine, releasing their heady fragrance into the air—a scent that spoke of comfort and shared mornings. Water hissed and bubbled as it transformed the grounds into a dark elixir, the steam curling upward like spirits seeking absolution.

John watched the bread turn a perfect shade of golden brown in the toaster, the quiet pop marking another small victory in his quest for redemption. Each slice on the plate represented a layer of hope, and each dollop of jam served as a comfort for hidden wounds.

He arranged the meal with care, the clatter of cutlery a gentle symphony to accompany his silent prayer. Here, in the half-light of dawn, with the aroma of coffee lingering like a tender caress, John endeavoured to rekindle a flame that flickered beneath the weight of his yearning—a yearning for both the woman who lay sleeping in their bed and the siren whose call still echoed in the chambers of his heart.

Dawn's tentative fingers of light caressed the horizon, spilling a soft luminescence through the bedroom curtains. John cradled the breakfast tray in his arms with the delicacy of one bearing an olive branch, the China whispering secrets of his intent as he stepped over the threshold. His heart thrummed a staccato rhythm, anticipation and dread mingling like bitter and sweet flavours on the tongue.

The room was bathed in the hesitant glow of daybreak, the shadows retreating to their corners as if wary of the peace offering that John presented. He approached the bed, where Sophie lay in repose, her breathing a gentle hush against the silent confession of his presence. With a hopeful smile tempered by the gravity of unspoken truths, he reached out, his touch a feather-light prompt nudging her from slumber.

Sophie stirred, the quiet rustle of sheets accompanying her ascent from the depths of dreams. Her eyelids fluttered open, revealing the blue pools of her gaze, brightening with each passing second as the reality of her husband's gesture dawned upon her. A sleepy surprise etched its way across her features before melting into a warmth that bloomed like the first blush of spring. She propped herself up against the pillows, the morning light casting a halo around her, touching her blonde hair with a painterly stroke.

John observed her transformation, every nuance of her expression a canvas he longed to preserve in the gallery of his memory. The love that bound him to this woman and this life twirled within him, its waves crashing against the cliffs of regret lining his heart. In her smile, he found both sanctuary and torment, each stirring echoes of what had been and whispers of what might never be again.

Between them, an invisible thread woven through the silence carried the scent of coffee and the promise of shared moments. John, the perennial arbiter of charm, felt the weight of his duplicity heavy upon his shoulders, even as the lightness of hope flickered in his chest like a candle struggling against the wind.

"Good morning," he murmured, his voice the anchor in the vast ocean of his emotions. "I thought we could start the day together... like this."

Sophie's answering smile was the lighthouse guiding him back to shore, but the rocks beneath the surface remained, unseen yet perilously sharp. As she accepted the tray, her fingertips brushed his, a current of connection that sent ripples across the still waters of his resolve.

John pierced a strawberry with his fork, the crimson fruit bursting against the steel prongs as he lifted it to his lips. The sweetness should have been a delight, but it soured in his mouth, tainted by the acrid guilt that gnawed at him from within. Sophie talked of mundane things—of meetings and memos—and John nodded where appropriate, his replies laced with the practised ease of years spent together. Yet, his mind was adrift, caught in the riptide of memories: Jessica's laughter, a melody that once made his heart dance now felt like a requiem for fidelity.

The room seemed to shrink around him, every word from Sophie's lips tightening the invisible noose of his secrets. He was here but not present, a spectre at the feast of their love. The sound of cutlery clattering on China punctuated the silent cacophony in his mind, with each click serving as a reminder of the duplicity that clung to him like a shadow.

A chuckle escaped Sophie, light and genuine, and for a brief moment, John anchored himself to that sound. It was a life raft in the stormy sea of his conscience. They shared a glance, a quirk of her lips inviting him to partake in the private joke. He did, the laughter bubbling up from some untainted wellspring within him, and their eyes met—a connection forged in mirth, strong enough to eclipse the shadows. She reached out, her hand covering his, her warmth a balm to the chill of his transgressions.

"Remember when we first tried making omelettes?" Sophie said, her voice tinged with nostalgia. "We ended up with scrambled eggs, but it didn't matter because we were together."

John squeezed her hand, the gesture a lifeline, throwing him back to a time before whispers of temptation had slithered into their bed. Her touch was tender, soothing, yet beneath it lay an abyss—the knowledge of how close he stood to the edge of betrayal.

They finished their breakfast, the conversation meandering through safer waters. But even as Sophie's presence enveloped him, the siren song of desire called from across the chasm of his choices, the image of Jessica's emerald gaze burning behind closed lids. His heart, a battlefield of longing and loyalty, bore the scars of a war he had never wished to wage.

John's hands moved with a mechanical grace, scrubbing the breakfast dishes as Sophie rinsed and placed them in the rack. Water droplets caught the light, casting prismatic refractions across the chrome faucet—a fleeting display of domestic serenity belying the tempest raging within him. Their routine was a dance they had performed countless times, a testament to the life they had built together, yet it did nothing to soothe the restlessness that gnawed at his soul.

Sophie's hair brushed against her cheek as she leaned forward, a stray lock falling into her line of sight. John's fingers itched to tuck it behind her ear, to reclaim the intimacy of such simple gestures, but he hesitated. The ghost of another, the memory of chestnut waves cascading between his fingers, held him captive.

"Thanks for breakfast," Sophie said, her voice a melody that usually calmed the disquiet in his heart. Today, though, it was a bittersweet symphony, each note reminding him of both what he cherished and what he yearned for beyond the confines of their orderly existence.

"Anytime," he replied, the words tasting like a promise on his tongue—a vow to be better, to do better. But promises were fragile things, easily shattered by the weight of unspoken truths and concealed desires.

After placing the last dish and restoring the kitchen to its pristine state, Sophie dried her hands and reached for her briefcase. "I'll see you tonight." Her smile was still the same, but it now masked the growing gap between them.

John followed her to the door, his gaze trailing the familiar curve of her spine. He watched as she stepped out into the crisp morning air, the day greeting her with the promise of possibilities he feared he no longer shared. He stood there, framed by the doorway, the very picture of the devoted husband—yet beneath the surface, a frenzy of emotion threatened to pull him under.

"Have a good day," he called out, the words hollow, echoing against the walls of the home they had made.

Sophie turned, her eyes catching his for a heartbeat—an eternity—before disappearing, leaving a void that beckoned dangerously to fill. John's resolve wavered, a brittle thing on the verge of breaking. He wanted to be the man she believed him to be, the one she deserved, but Jessica's siren call played a relentless chorus in his mind, tempting him toward the jagged rocks of ruin.

He shut the door, leaning against it as if it could support the weight of his guilt. The silence of the house wrapped around him, a tangible reminder of the solitude that awaited. And somewhere, just beyond the veil of fidelity, the thought of Jessica lingered—intoxicating, undeniable, a tantalising whisper that spoke of the forbidden.

John closed his eyes, the image of her emerald gaze imprinted behind his lids. It was a vision that promised ecstasy and agony in equal measure, a harbinger of the torment that lay ahead should he succumb. Torn between the comfort of his familiar life and the allure of a passion he had never dared to explore, he found himself engulfed in an exquisite torment.

The clock ticked on, indifferent to his internal struggle, and the sun climbed higher, its rays creeping across the floorboards like a slow-burning revelation. John stood motionless, poised at the brink of unmade decisions, resisting the relentless pull of unquenchable desires.

John's return to the study felt like stepping into a different world, one where the morning light played tricks with the shadows, casting an ethereal glow on the walls that seemed to pulse with unspoken secrets. The aged material creaked under his weight as he settled into the leather chair behind the desk, its comforting embrace at odds with the turmoil churning within.

His hands found refuge in his hair, fingers weaving through the short strands as if they could untangle the knotted thoughts that plagued him. He grappled with the image of Jessica—a vision so vivid it threatened to shatter the veneer of his composed life. The memory of her laugh, a sound that seemed to resonate with the very strings of his soul, mingled with the scent of her hair, a fragrance that now lingered like a ghost in the corners of his mind.

He was both thrilled and terrified by the realization that he was falling for her. The realization beckoned him with the thrill of the unknown, promising a passion that ignited his heart, yet it also whispered warnings of destruction, of lives upended by the reckless pursuit of desire.

John's gaze drifted to the window, the glass cool beneath his touch. Outside, the suburban utopia was slowly stirring, the first signs of life appearing as neighbours embarked upon their daily routines. The scene was a tableau of normality, a stark contrast to the internal chaos that raged within him.

As he watched a lone jogger navigate the winding path, John felt the pull of two worlds—the one he had built with Sophie, grounded in love and shared history, and the other, a seductive dance in the dark with Jessica, full of promises yet unspoken. The ambiguity clung to him, leaving his future as uncertain as the shifting patterns of clouds above.

The neighbourhood was waking up, but John remained frozen, caught between the warmth of the sun's rays and the shadow of doubt that clouded his judgment. At this crossroads of longing and obligation, he stood silent—a man ensnared by the call of what could be—while grappling with the stark reality of what should be.

Chapter 12: Close Call

John glanced at Jessica from across the room, his brown eyes a silent signal amid the mundane proceedings of the community meeting. As if on cue, they both rose discreetly, their chairs quietly scraping back. The chatter around them provided cover as they slipped away, leaving the droning voice of the chairman to fade into the background. They moved with a purposeful grace, John's casual attire blending into the rows of books, and Jessica's sundress a whisper of colour in the dimly lit library.

The plush carpet underfoot cushioned each step, an unspoken pact forming with every stride. An electric charge permeated the air, a mutual understanding brewing between them like a simmering storm. They navigated through the maze of bookshelves, towering sentinels of knowledge that now bore witness to their clandestine intentions.

Reaching a secluded corner cloaked in shadows, Jessica leaned back against a bookshelf, her posture casual yet charged with anticipation. The spines of countless novels pressed against her, like the silent audience to her racing heart. The faint scent of aged paper and leather-bound promises filled the space between them, a heady perfume that spoke of secrets and stolen moments.

John closed the distance, his movements deliberate, the subtle tension of his well-muscled arms evident beneath his clothes. He stepped closer until he stood mere inches from Jessica, the proximity sending a current of awareness through them both. His fingers traced the curve of her hip before brushing against hers, so light it could have been accidental, but the spark it ignited was intentional—a fiery prelude to the forbidden dance they were about to begin.

Jessica's breath caught as John pressed himself against her, his growing arousal evident. Her emerald eyes flickered with vulnerable excitement as she met John's steady gaze. Risk pulsed in the quiet corners of this literary sanctuary, making her heart race and her skin tingle with anticipation.

Desire hung heavy in the air as John began to unbutton her blouse slowly, revealing hints of lace beneath. Their suspended moment shattered as she reached for him in turn, boldly unbuckling his belt and reaching inside to tease him with her skilled hand.

The hush of the library wrapped around John and Jessica like a velvet cloak, a charged atmosphere cradling them in their secret tryst. As John pressed Jessica firmly against the shelves and claimed her mouth with a fervent hunger, a silent plea for something transcendent wove into the kiss.

Jessica responded with equal fervour, arching her back and pressing her chest to meet John's hands. He eagerly cupped and caressed her lace-clad breasts before tugging down the fabric to take one taut nipple into his mouth. She gasped as he grazed the sensitive flesh with his teeth, sparks of pleasure racing through her veins.

John's fingers trailed down, dancing along the hem of Jessica's skirt before slipping beneath the fabric. As his touch found the damp heat between her thighs, she shuddered in response—a secret spoken in the language of touch. His fingers traced circles around her clit before plunging inside her, each thrust eliciting a soft moan from Jessica's lips.

Her fingers tangled in his hair, pulling him closer as if to weave him into her very being. Their whispered exchanges were breathy and broken. The air thrummed with lust as they succumbed to their secret desires, every gasp a testament to the intensity of their illicit dance.

The warmth of Jessica's breath mingled with the musty scent of aged paper as they lost themselves in the fervour of their embrace. Just as John deepened the kiss, a voice cut through the air, sharp and clear, slicing into their moment like a blade.

"John? Are you in here?" Sophie's voice echoed softly, reverberating off the library walls with an unsettling clarity.

Panic ignited within John's chest, and he broke away from Jessica, their connection severed with a jolt. Jessica's wide eyes mirrored his shock, both of them frozen in the urgency of the moment. Time seemed to stretch, heavy with the weight of an impending discovery. Heartbeats raced in unison, a frantic drumbeat that drowned out the whispering shelves around them.

"Quick," John urged, his voice barely above a whisper, breathless with adrenaline. They disentangled themselves as if drawn apart by an invisible force, hastily stepping back into the shadows cast by the towering bookshelves.

Jessica smoothed her skirt, fingers trembling slightly as she adjusted the fabric that had ridden up during their heated encounter. John ran a hand through his hair, attempting to tame the dishevelled strands that mirrored the chaos in his mind. The silence of the library felt suffocating, amplifying every rustle and breath, each minute sound echoing like a warning bell.

"Just act natural," he murmured, trying to steady himself against the overwhelming rush of fear and desire still coursing through him. The thrill of the forbidden lingered in the air, but now it was laced with the bitter tang of anxiety.

Jessica nodded, her composure gradually returning, but the wild pulse of emotion beneath her calm facade was evident in her eyes. She tucked a loose strand of hair behind her ear, a gesture that seemed almost instinctual yet laden with significance.

"Okay," she replied, her voice steady but low, carrying the weight of shared secrets. She took a breath, the scent of old leather and dust swirling around them, grounding her amidst the chaos.

As the footsteps grew closer, John caught a glimpse of the narrow aisle leading to their hiding place, the light filtering through the high windows casting long shadows across the floor. He glanced at Jessica, who leaned against the bookshelf, her heart pounding visibly in her throat, a delicate pulse of vulnerability beneath her composed exterior.

"Remember," he said, forcing a smile that felt more like a mask than a genuine expression, "we're just two regular patrons of this fine establishment." The words felt hollow, a fragile shield against the reality of their situation.

Jessica's lips twitched in a semblance of a smile, but the tension hung thick in the air, a tangible reminder of their risky liaison. As they prepared to face the unexpected intrusion, the atmosphere crackled with unspoken implications, a lingering question hanging between them: How much longer could they keep playing this dangerous game?

John's hand shot up, a swift and purposeful motion that ended with his fingers grazing the spine of an ancient book perched on a high shelf. It was an old trick from a forgotten play, but under the heavy curtain of tension, it seemed like the most natural act in the world.

"Ah, this volume," he said, drawing it down with feigned interest, his voice a practiced melody of calm. "You were looking for this, weren't you, Jessica?"

His smile, as Sophie rounded the corner into their secluded nook, was one of those perfectly sculpted expressions—warm, disarming, as if they were merely two friends engaged in idle banter among the rows of literary antiquity. The adrenaline that thrummed through his veins was masterfully concealed behind the facade of casual ease, the vibrant pulse muted by the stillness of his composed features.

Sophie approached, her steps deliberate, her eyes sharp as flint, scanning the scene before her. There was a flicker of something in her gaze—a question unasked—as she looked between John and Jessica, who stood with her back to the books, her own face a mask of serene attentiveness.

"Finding everything okay?" Sophie's words were casual, but they carried an edge, cutting through the air with surgical precision.

"Absolutely," John replied, his tone light, airy, like dandelion seeds floating on a summer breeze. He held the book up, brandishing it as though it were a shield that could ward off any lingering doubt. "Just helping Jessica here. You know how these old collections can be—full of hidden treasures."

The humour in his voice danced like a shadow across the room, ephemeral yet potent enough to lift the corners of Sophie's mouth into a hesitant smile. It was a deft touch, a stroke of charm wielded with the finesse of a maestro conducting an orchestra of emotions. For a moment, the space between them, charged with unsaid words and unreadable thoughts, softened under the weight of his levity.

"Indeed," Sophie conceded, her attention briefly ensnared by the title of the book in John's hand, allowing the moment to pass and with it, the spectre of suspicion that had momentarily clouded her eyes.

With Sophie's gaze momentarily captured by the ancient script on the spine of the book, Jessica seized the moment, her voice a velvet ribbon winding through the tension. "Thank you, John," she purred, each syllable infusing the air with an allure that was as natural to her as breathing. Her gratitude was laced with an underlying current of intimacy that only John could detect, a private acknowledgement of their shared secret.

"Of course," John responded, his eyes meeting Jessica's for a fleeting instant before flicking back to Sophie. The book in his hand felt like a talisman, a prop in the elaborate play they were all unwitting performers in.

As Sophie turned away, reassured or simply choosing not to dwell on the matter, John and Jessica exchanged a look that was a silent concerto of emotion. A wave of relief swept over them, blending with the simmering embers of unquenchable desire. The thrill of their narrow escape caused their breaths to come a little faster and their chests to rise and fall.

The danger they had flirted with lingered in the charged space between them, a reminder of the precipice they balanced upon. The library, with its shadows nestled between the wisdom of ages, held them in a momentary embrace, acknowledging the gravity of the risks they dared to take.

In the quiet aftermath of Sophie's departure, the musty scent of books was like incense in a sacred temple where they'd nearly succumbed to their sacrilegious fervour. They stood, statuesque, until the echo of Sophie's footsteps faded into the labyrinth of shelves and corridors beyond.

Finally, alone again, yet acutely aware of the fragility of their situation, John and Jessica allowed themselves one more silent communion—a promise, a warning, a yearning—before the veneer of composure settled back upon them like a cloak. With the spell broken, each step they took thereafter was measured and deliberate, a dance with danger neither was ready to forsake.

With the ghost of their indiscretion still hanging in the air, John and Jessica parted. He meandered through the rows of chairs, his return to the community meeting as unobtrusive as a shadow slipping across the floor. The library had reclaimed its tranquil guise, the hushed murmurs of the gathering a soothing relief to the storm that had raged between them. However, the memory of their encounter clung to him like a subtle fragrance that persists long after the flame has faded.

John's hands felt oddly empty without the warmth of Jessica's skin beneath his fingertips, the absence akin to a missing note in a familiar melody. As he took his seat among his peers, the room's stale air seemed to thicken with unspoken words and half-caught glances. Each interaction carried a veneer of normalcy, but beneath it there was an electric current of tension that only he could feel, sending tremors through the facade of his composure.

The exhilaration of their secret and the looming image of consequences oscillated in his mind. The conversations around him faded into the background, and the voices of his neighbours became mere whispers amidst his racing thoughts. John laughed at the appropriate moments, his charm instinctual, but his laughter lacked its usual resonance, tinged instead with a hollow quality that betrayed his inner conflict.

His decisions weighed heavily on him, akin to a verdict awaiting delivery. Every smile he offered was an effort to keep the dam from breaking, every nod an attempt to anchor himself in the reality he had so recklessly jeopardised. His heart, usually so sure of its rhythm, now beat an erratic dance, syncopated by the dual drums of desire and dread.

As the meeting droned on, John found himself longing for the quiet corner of the library where time had ceased to exist, if only for a stolen moment. But here, amidst the humdrum of civic duty, the clock ticked unforgivingly forward, reminding him that every second was another step away from the precipice they had dared to approach—and yet, also a step closer to the next time they might dance along its dangerous edge.

Jessica slipped back into the fold of the community meeting with the grace of a shadow folding into night. Her pulse still thrummed with the electricity of their forbidden touch, each beat a reminder of John's hands tracing paths of fire beneath her skin. She listened to the neighbours' discussions on mundane affairs— zoning in and out of conversations about town budgets and park renovations. The words felt distant, muffled by the noise of her inner tempest.

Her emerald eyes flickered intermittently towards John, observing his performance in this suburban theatre with a polished ease that concealed the turmoil she knew churned within him. Jessica's own heart waged a silent war, caught between the exhilaration of what had transpired against the stark shelves and the sobering complexity of their entanglement. The risk—their risk—was intoxicating and dangerous, a potent cocktail that left her heady and apprehensive.

As the meeting concluded, Jessica rose with the others, her movements fluid and deliberate. She exchanged pleasantries, her voice smooth like velvet, betraying none of her inner disarray. With each step towards the exit, she felt the duality of the life she led—one where she was the enigmatic newcomer with a past shrouded in whispers, and the other, a woman whose desires could set her world ablaze.

The library doors opened, and the cool night air embraced her, a stark contrast to the lingering warmth of John's touch. She hesitated momentarily on the threshold, feeling the invisible thread that connected her to him pull taut. Then, Jessica stepped out into the night, the darkness swallowing her figure as she began the solitary walk back to her reality.

John emerged moments later, the weight of their secret encounters pressing heavily upon him. He took a deep breath, the crisp air filling his lungs, cleansing yet not absolving. He took measured steps that softly echoed against the pavement, each footfall serving as a reminder of the precipice they danced upon.

Their paths diverged, two silhouettes moving away from each other under the canopy of an indigo sky. The heat of their earlier encounter seemed a world away now, replaced by the cool indifference of the night. Streetlights cast long shadows as they retreated into their separate lives, the choices they had made—and those that lay ahead—etching themselves into the fabric of their fates.

The library stood silent behind them, a vault of stories untold, holding the echo of their passion within its walls. As they disappeared into the night, the chapter of their secret affair remained open, the pages rife with the ink of possibility and the smudges of peril.

The night stretched on, a shroud of velvet darkness pierced by the occasional glimmer of starlight. Sophie and John walked alone, his footsteps muted against the soft earth of the path that led away from the library. The air was cool and carried the scent of impending rain, a sharp contrast to the heated embrace he had shared with Jessica among the quiet whispers of ancient books.

He could still feel the ghost of her touch against his skin, a sensation that both tormented and exhilarated him. With each step, the memory of their encounter replayed in his mind, a relentless wave of longing and regret. The thrill of their secret and the rush of desire were an intoxicating cocktail that left him dizzy with need and fear. He could feel the risks they took, with the potential consequences haunting him like a presence lurking just beyond his vision.

Jessica moved through the shadow-draped streets, her heels clicking a steady rhythm on the pavement. The chill in the air caressed her bare arms, raising goosebumps, a stark reminder of the warmth she had relinquished upon leaving John's embrace. The afterglow of their closeness filled her senses, with the musky scent of old paper mingling with the faint trace of his cologne in her nostrils.

Her mind whirled with conflicting emotions. The excitement of their forbidden moments was undeniable, each secret rendezvous igniting a fire within her that she feared might consume her entirely. Yet there was an undercurrent of trepidation, a knowing whisper that cautioned her of the precipice on which they so recklessly danced.

Both John and Jessica walked their separate paths, the silence around them a stark canvas for the turmoil within. A dangerous melody, promising both devastation and ecstasy, pounded their hearts. The cloak of night wrapped around them, a confidante to their secret love yet also a harbinger of the shadows that lurked in the corners of their affair.

As the first drops of rain began to fall, dotting the ground with darkened spots, the unresolved tension between what they desired and what they stood to lose swelled within them. Each drop was a reminder of the delicate balance they maintained, a dance between passion and discretion, between reckless abandon and the harsh light of day that would soon expose them.

Their connection, a thread spun of fervour and fraught with danger, lay taut between them, unseen yet unbreakable. As the rain fell harder now, washing over the world in a cleansing torrent, John and Jessica retreated into the solitude of their separate existences, the choices of the night lingering like a promise—or a curse—whispered by the wind.

Chapter 13: Sophie's Suspicion

Sophie Hawthorne sat at the kitchen table, the porcelain rim of her coffee cup smooth under the pads of her fingers. Her gaze lingered in the periphery, where John stood with his back turned, a figure haloed by the soft morning light that filtered through the gauzy curtains. There was something about the way he glanced at his phone—a furtive darting of his eyes—that scraped against the quiet harmony of their routine.

She breathed in the rich aroma of her coffee, a fleeting comfort against the chill of suspicion that crept along her spine. Each time his thumb swiped the screen, her heart marked the rhythm—an arrhythmic beat that spoke of secrets whispered in silence.

In the days that followed, Sophie witnessed the man she knew so well transform into an enigma clad in casual attire. His laughter still filled the spaces between them, but it was edged with a restlessness that had never before disturbed the air of their suburban cocoon.

Once, she found him in the study, the glow of his phone casting shadows across his face as he angled the device away from her approach. "Just work," he said, his voice a lighthouse beam cutting through fog—steady, yet somehow distant. She nodded, feigning indifference, while the taste of doubt settled bitterly on her tongue.

She observed him, her analytical mind cataloguing each new habit like evidence in an unseen trial. He would hesitate before tapping out a message, as if weighing each word. How he'd step outside to take calls, his chuckle drifting in through the half-open window, mingling with the scent of freshly cut grass and leaving her with a gnawing hunger for clarity.

Sophie's thoughts twisted around themselves, a silent tempest that raged behind her composed exterior. She wanted to believe in the foundation they had built together, each stone laid with care and intention. Yet the signs, though whisper-soft, were relentless as the tide, eroding her certainty with every clandestine glance he cast toward his digital confidant.

At night, she lay beside him, tracing the familiar lines of his profile against the pillow. In sleep, he seemed untouched by the complexities that shadowed their days. She yearned to wake him, to demand truths that would soothe or sear her soul, but fear rooted her in place—a statue in a garden of thorns.

And so she remained, suspended in a liminal space where trust and trepidation danced a tightrope waltz. The walls of their home, once a sanctuary, now whispered of hidden depths and unseen currents, and Sophie could not help but wonder what lay beneath the surface of John's placid smile.

The golden light of the late afternoon suffused the living room, with sunbeams dancing across the polished surfaces and casting long, elegant shadows. Sophie moved through the space like a ghost, her fingers brushing over the mantelpiece, straightening the cushions on the couch, each movement a silent testament to the restlessness that gnawed at her insides.

As she neared the armchair by the window, John's jacket—draped carelessly over the backrest the night before—caught her attention. She reached for it, the fabric cool and smooth beneath her touch. As she lifted it, something slipped from its pocket and tumbled to the carpet—a soft thud that seemed to reverberate through the quiet room.

Sophie froze, staring down at John's phone. It lay there, an innocuous rectangle of technology that suddenly felt as heavy as a leaden secret. Her heart began a slow, deliberate pounding, echoing in her ears like distant drums heralding an uncertain fate.

She bent down, her movements hesitant, as if the device might shatter under the weight of her trepidation. The phone felt alien in her palm, vibrating with potential revelations. Every rational fibre in her being screamed to put it back, to respect the sanctity of privacy, but the seed of doubt had rooted deeply, sprouting tendrils of curiosity that she could no longer restrain.

With a trembling hand, she unlocked the screen, the familiar swipe of her thumb betraying an intimacy that now seemed tainted by suspicion. The phone's glow illuminated her face, a pale canvas tainted by the flicker of emotions too tangled to name.

And then she saw it—a message that glowed like a beacon amidst the mundane notifications. Jessica's name was a whisper against the silence, the text beneath it a siren's call wrapped in casual words that held an undertone of something far more intimate:

"Can't stop thinking about last night..."

Sophie's breath hitched in her throat, the air in her lungs turning to ice. Last night, John had mentioned that he was working late. When he'd come home with a smile that didn't quite reach his eyes and a kiss that tasted of apologies yet unspoken.

The phone dropped from her nerveless fingers, landing once more on the carpet as if eager to escape her grasp. Around her, the room seemed to close in, the walls pressing with unseen eyes, the sunlight dimming to the quality of a fading dream.

Sophie stood at the edge of a chasm, the text on the screen unfolding like a path into darkness. The man she knew—the man she loved—was slipping through her fingers like grains of sand, leaving her grasping for answers in a reality that had shifted beneath her feet, treacherous and unknown.

The evening air clung to the walls of the Hawthorne residence, thick with the scent of unease as the front door clicked shut. John, unaware of the storm brewing within, shrugged off his jacket and let it hang loosely from his fingers. Sophie's eyes followed him, piercing through the silence that had wrapped itself around them like a shroud.

"John," she began, her voice barely above a whisper, but laden with the weight of her apprehension. "We need to talk about... a message I saw." The last word lingered between them, a ghost of accusation.

His face, a map of easy-going charm, crinkled into confusion. "A message?" he echoed, searching her face as if trying to gauge the depth of the waters he was about to wade into.

"From Jessica," Sophie pressed on, the name tasting of betrayal on her tongue. Her heart pounded fiercely against her chest, each heartbeat a pulsating harbinger of impending truth. His eyes, always so full of laughter, now darted away—an instinctive flinch from the blow yet to be delivered.

"Jessica?" John repeated his words, pretending to be innocent, but his voice betrayed him, revealing a crack in his armour. He set down his jacket, his movements suddenly deliberate, a magician preparing for an act of misdirection. "She's just a friend, Soph. Nothing more."

Sophie studied him, looking for the man she married within the unfamiliar contours of his deflection. She longed to find solace in his explanations, to believe in the foundation they had built together. However, uncertainty persists relentlessly, and words intended for someone else had already eroded her trust.

"Is that why you're thinking about her late at night?" Her question hovered in the air, laden with implications, her blue eyes searching for the harbour of his truth amidst the turbulent sea of his evasion.

John's jaw tightened, the line of his mouth a barricade against the onslaught of her probing. "You're reading too much into it," he said, his tone steady but his gaze faltering, skimming over her features as if to smooth over the ripples of her suspicion.

Her senses heightened, detecting a subtle shift in his posture and a subtle tension in the air that conveyed more than his dismissive words.

In the quiet of the kitchen, the hum of the refrigerator seemed to underscore the disconnect between them, a monotonous reminder of domesticity disrupted.

"John, I—" Sophie started, but the words tangled in her throat, fear and longing weaving a complex tapestry that muted her voice.

"Let's not do this," he interrupted, a plea veiled as a command. "Trust me, there's nothing going on."

However, rebuilding trust can be a challenging task. And as John reached out, his hand brushing hers in a gesture meant to console, Sophie withdrew ever so slightly—a dance as old as time, where touch becomes a language of its own, and even the smallest distance speaks louder than words.

The air crackled with the latent storm of their discord, as Sophie's fingers coiled into fists upon the cool surface of the kitchen table. The dim light from the overhead fixture cast shadows that seemed to play out the drama unfolding between them.

"John, I need you to be honest with me," she said, her voice taking on a steely edge that belied the tremor beneath. Her heart was a rapid drumbeat against her chest, each thud echoing her growing fear of betrayal.

He let out a heavy sigh, his eyes reflecting a mingling of exasperation and something darker, unspoken. "I am being honest, Soph," he replied, but the familiar warmth that usually laced his words had vanished, leaving behind an unsettling chill.

Sophie's frustration surged, cresting in a wave that broke the facade of calm she struggled to maintain. "No, you're not!" Her voice rose sharply and clearly, piercing through the oppressive silence that enveloped the room like a protective layer. "Don't do this—don't make me question what I feel, what I know."

John's laughter was short, devoid of humour—a shard of glass shattering against the tile. "You think you 'know'? That's rich, Sophie."

He stepped closer, his presence oppressive. "You're being paranoid. That's all this is."

"Paranoid?" The word hung between them, a spectre of accusation that painted her as the villain in her own story. It wounded deeper than any knife could reach, severing strands of trust with its serrated edge. "Is it paranoia when your husband hides messages from another woman?"

"God, you're impossible!" John's control snapped, his voice a thunderclap that reverberated off the walls. His hands balled at his sides, knuckles pale. "When did you become so insecure? So suspicious?"

"Maybe since you started giving me reasons to doubt you," she shot back, her words fuelled by a hurt that had been simmering, unacknowledged, beneath the veneer of their everyday life.

The space between them was charged, a live wire of tension that neither dared to touch. Their voices, once tender whispers shared in the dark, now were weapons brandished in the harsh light of accusation. They stood on a precipice, the ground crumbling beneath their feet, each harsh word a step toward an abyss from which there might be no return.

The tempest of their words finally broke, leaving Sophie gasping in its wake, tears forging hot paths down her cheeks. The air seemed to solidify around her, holding the echoes of their anger like a malevolent spectre. It was a silence that screamed louder than any decibel they had reached, a thick, choking fog of unspoken fears and unrealised truths.

John's figure, once a source of comfort, now loomed as a dark silhouette against the backdrop of the open doorway. Stormy with conflict, his eyes locked with hers one final time before he abruptly turned on his heel. The door slammed behind him with a finality that seemed to suck the oxygen from the room.

Sophie's chest heaved, her sobs the only sign of life in the desolate kitchen. She clutched at the edge of the table, the wood grain pressing into her palms, anchoring her to the moment even as her world threatened to spin out of control. The sharp tang of betrayal stung her nostrils, mingling with the comforting aroma of coffee that now sat cold and forgotten.

Outside, John's car cut through the stillness of the suburban night, tires whispering secrets to the asphalt as he navigated the familiar streets. The quiet houses stood like sentinels, their windows dark and inscrutable, mirroring his own tumultuous thoughts. He drove mechanically, the muscle memory of routine guiding him more than conscious thought. He parked several streets away to ensure that Sophie would not be aware of his location.

The cool night air, tinged with the scent of jasmine and the impending autumnal decay, brushed against his skin as he hesitated on Jessica's doorstep. A shiver ran down his spine, not from the chill but from the anticipation of crossing yet another line—one he could never uncross. Her house loomed before him, its facade both inviting and foreboding, a siren's call to the shipwreck that was his conscience.

In his pocket, his phone lay silent, a heavy reminder of the fracture he had left behind. Guilt gnawed at him like a relentless pest, yet there was something intoxicating about the danger of this secret indulgence. The moon hung above, a silent witness to the countless tales of human folly.

For a brief moment, John Hawthorne hovered between desire and duty, the night's shadows providing a fleeting respite from the decision he knew he had to make.

A soft click echoed through the tense silence as Jessica's door swung open, the hinge's whisper a stark contrast to the roar of John's heartbeat. Her silhouette framed by the warm glow of the entryway, Jessica's eyes widened for a fleeting second before her lips curved into a knowing half-smile. It was as if she had sensed the tumultuous storm that raged within him, her gaze cutting through his defences with surgical precision.

"John," she said softly, her voice carrying clearly in the stillness of the night. The word hovered between them, teeming with unsaid vows and mysteries yet to reveal.

He hesitated, the threshold underfoot a chasm between two worlds—the one he knew, bound by vows and veiled in familiarity, and the one that whispered of forbidden pleasures. She stepped aside, her movements graceful and deliberate, an invitation wrapped in moonlight and shadows. The air shifted as he crossed into her domain, charged with an electric current that hummed along his skin, awakening every nerve.

Inside, Jessica closed the door with a soft but final click, sealing away the outside world. Her emerald eyes locked onto his, their depths holding a magnetic pull that tethered him to this moment— to her. The space between them crackled with the energy of untold desires; with each breath they drew, threading them tighter together.

John found himself enveloped in her presence, the subtle fragrance of her perfume mingling with the faint scent of antique wood from her home. Their bodies moved with a practiced familiarity— two celestial bodies drawn into an inevitable orbit. His hands found the curve of her waist, fingers tracing the lines of her form as if committing every detail to memory.

There was solace in her embrace, a temporary balm to the raw edges of his conscience. But it was a treacherous comfort, for with every touch and shared breath, guilt crept in like a shadow at dawn. It gnawed at him, a relentless reminder of the life that lay in pieces even as he sought refuge in the warmth of her arms.

As they swayed to a rhythm only they could hear, Jessica's head tilted back, exposing the elegant line of her throat. Her chestnut hair cascaded down, a waterfall of silk against the pale canvas of her skin. John's resolve wavered, the sight of her vulnerability stirring something primal within him.

"Are you sure?" Her voice was a whisper, barely audible above the thrumming of his own blood in his ears.

"Never been less sure of anything," he admitted, his words a confession torn from the depths of his turmoil.

Her low and intimate laughter wrapped around him, offering a strange mix of absolution and condemnation. As they continued to move together, lost in the dance of what could never be undone, John felt the weight of his choices pressing against his ribs, a burden he was willing to bear—for now.

John lay motionless, the soft rustle of satin sheets beneath him a stark contrast to the tumult raging in his mind. In the dim glow of the moonlight filtering through gauzy curtains, he stared at the ceiling—a blank canvas upon which his regrets painted themselves in endless loops. The night's silence was suffocating, thick with the residue of whispered promises and the echo of Jessica's sighs.

The room smelt faintly of her jasmine perfume, an intoxicating scent that clung to him, a reminder of their entanglement. His heartbeat, steady and relentless, was a drumbeat in the quiet, each pulse marking the seconds slipping away into the abyss of his choices. The weight on his chest felt like stone, cold and immovable, as he grappled with the duality of his existence—caught between the warmth of home and the fire of Jessica's allure.

He could still feel the imprint of her lips on his skin, a branding that seared deeper than flesh, questioning the very fabric of his being. The remnants of their union lingered on his body, a testimony to the passion they had shared and the forbidden path he tread. The passion he felt drew him into its depths, even as it threatened to drown him.

Outside, the whisper of leaves brushing against the window pane sounded like hushed warnings, urging him to consider the precipice on which he teetered. But within these walls, time seemed suspended, reality blurring at the edges, allowing him to indulge in the fantasy of the moment while the truth lay just beyond reach.

John turned his head, glancing beside him where Jessica lay. He wanted to believe in the simplicity of their connection—to immerse himself in the depths of what they had found in each other—but the image of consequence loomed large, casting shadows over any semblance of peace.

His thoughts drifted back to Sophie, to the life he had promised to build with her, now fracturing under the strain of his secrecy. The image of her tear-stained face, her voice trembling with hurt, haunted him. He understood that he was the mastermind behind her suffering, meticulously building the groundwork for a future filled with fractures and rifts.

With a heavy heart, John rolled over, burying his face into the pillow. He closed his eyes, willing sleep to come and grant him a few hours' reprieve from the relentless grip of reality. Yet sleep proved elusive, dodging his grasp like a thief in the night, leaving him ensnared in the web of his own making—a web woven from threads of desire, deceit, and the intoxicating danger of the illicit.

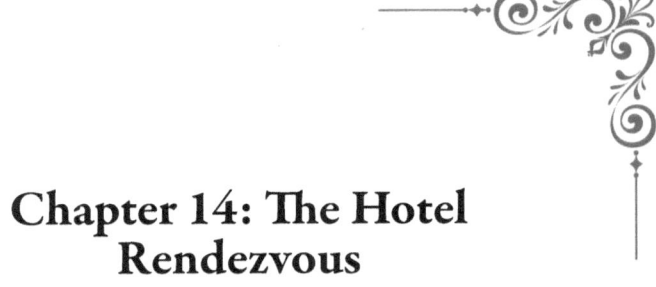

Chapter 14: The Hotel Rendezvous

John's heart thrummed a frenetic rhythm against his ribcage as he strode into the grandeur of the hotel lobby, its marble floors and gilt-edged opulence contrasting sharply with the chaos churning within him. An expensive scent filled the air, seeming to whisper secrets from every shadowed corner. He approached the front desk with a feigned nonchalance, belying the adrenaline pumping through his veins, weighed down by anticipation and trepidation.

"Checking in," John murmured, his voice steady despite the internal maelstrom. He leaned slightly forward, ensuring the name he offered remained for the clerk's ears alone. "Jameson. Mark Jameson."

The pseudonym effortlessly slipped off his tongue, the anonymity it afforded adding an illicit thrill to the rendezvous. As the clerk nodded and handed him a key card, a flicker of excitement sparked behind John's calm facade, mingling with the undercurrent of danger threading through the night's promise.

With each step toward the suite, the plush carpet swallowed the sound of his movements, as if the hotel itself conspired in the silent symphony of their impending affair. The door clicked open, yielding to John's touch with an almost imperceptible sigh, revealing the inner sanctum where the night would unfurl its hidden splendours.

The room exuded a decadent charm, swathed in shadows and soft, dim lighting that cast an intimate glow over the lush furnishings. Heavy drapes ensured the sanctity of their private cosmos, while a velvety chaise lounge beckoned with its curved promise. But it was the king-sized bed that ensnared John's gaze—a beacon, a symbol, an altar to the passions soon to be unleashed.

He stood there, a man caught between two lives, on the precipice of the known and the uncharted. For a brief moment, the room felt like a tangible reflection of his soul—opulent yet secretive, perched on the brink of revelation. The air itself seemed to pulse with potential, charged with the electric hum of what was to come.

As John's eyes lingered on the bed, its sheets turned down just so, the crisp linens whispered promises across the distance. The pillows, plump and virginal, held the indentations of dreams he had yet dreamed, and in their softness, he saw the contours of a desire he had long sought to articulate.

In this suite, time paused, the world outside muted to a distant hum, and John Hawthorne found himself enveloped by a seductive ambiguity—a slow-burn tension that wound its way around his heart, squeezing with both plea and warning. Here, amid the opulence and the hushed tones, lay a path to the grand adventure he had craved, shrouded in the velvet drapes of intrigue and the intoxicating perfume of a life less ordinary.

John retreated to the refuge of the ensuite bathroom, his reflection in the mirror a spectre of both anticipation and doubt. The cool marble beneath his fingertips grounded him as he leaned into the sink, the water's icy kiss jolting him from his reverie. Droplets cascaded down his face, the chill stark against his flushed skin—a physical manifestation of the internal chaos that threatened to consume him.

He studied the man staring back at him; the contours of his face were familiar, yet he searched them for signs of the reckless abandon that had led him here. In the steamed haze, John's visage seemed to waver, as if caught between the steady life he knew and the whispered promises of the unknown. His hands, steady and sure in the daylight hours, now trembled with the weight of his decision. They were traitors to his resolve, revealing the fissures in the facade he presented to the world.

With a deep breath, he straightened his posture, his habitual gesture of confidence feeling more like armour he strapped on to face the battle within. The scent of his cologne hung in the air, a tangible cloud of propriety that fought against the raw, unbridled yearning that beckoned him forward.

The click of the door announced her arrival before she even crossed the threshold. Time constricted around John, every second bloated with significance as he turned to behold Jessica stepping into the room like a vision conjured from his most secret dreams.

With their eyes locked, they acknowledged the intangible swirl of passion and risk between them in a silent communion. Their gaze, filled with secrets and silent understandings, resonated deeply in the quiet space of their shared breaths. Her emerald gaze bore into him, fierce and unflinching, a challenge and an invitation entwined in their depths.

"John," she uttered, her voice a velvet caress that seemed to trail fingers down his spine. Jessica's presence filled the room with an energy that was palpable, a magnetic pull that rendered the space between them charged and expectant.

Her lips, with their sensuous curve, tantalized him with a promise of both sin and salvation, ensnaring him in their spell. The very air shifted around her, heavy with the perfume of intrigue, infusing the room with a heady blend of danger and desire.

They faced surrender in the opulent suite, each to the other, the night, and the smouldering hunger that had drawn them together. As reality and fantasy intertwined, John Hawthorne teetered on the edge, bewitched by the woman who held the power to unravel him completely.

With a determination that belied the quivers within, John stepped forward, eliminating the gap between himself and Jessica in strides that felt both inevitable and treacherous. The air between them crackled with the electrifying energy of unspoken desires, a dance of shadows and whispers on the brink of becoming physical.

As they drew near, the world outside the suite's walls seemed to dissolve, leaving only the intimate cocoon of dim lights and the faint hum of the city beyond. Time itself held its breath as their bodies met in an embrace that was timid, tender—a silent exploration before the storm.

John's hands, those of a man who had built a life on certainties, now ventured into unknown territory. They found the silken cascade of Jessica's chestnut hair, slipping through his fingers like strands of night. As he exhaled a breath he hadn't realized he'd been holding, her arms encircled him, pulling him closer into the enigma she embodied.

A deliberate caress replaced the tentative touch, tracing the architecture of her body—a map of curves and secrets yet to uncover. Each stroke of his fingertips against her skin was a wordless poem; every glance exchanged a sonnet of silent promises.

As their lips met, the world outside faded into oblivion. The kiss was a conflagration of emotions—tender and desperate, clandestine and all-consuming. It spoke of secretive glances, covert texts, and the bravery of stepping into a deep chasm.

Jessica's tongue teased against his teeth, a bold invitation to surrender further. She nipped at his bottom lip, drawing forth a gasp that echoed in the vast expanse of their hearts. They both lost themselves in the haze of desire, blurring the line between reality and fantasy with each passing moment.

Burning curiosity fuelled John and Jessica's morphing movements into a sensual dance. As they approached the bed, garments fell to the floor, revealing vulnerable flesh, flushed with excitement. They halted at the edge of the mattress, gazes locked in anticipation, breathing heavily.

Whispers of seduction and promises of ecstasy rang in their ears as they came together on the bed. Jessica's back arched against the soft sheets as John buried his face in her neck, a mixture of relief and yearning evident in their sighs. In that moment, they were one – bodies intertwined as they explored each other's forms.

The atmosphere pulsed with lascivious energy as John trailed his fingertips across Jessica's smooth skin. He caressed her breasts, thumbs grazing erect nipples before descending to her inner thighs. Jessica writhed beneath him with every touch, fingers gripping the sheets tightly while her other hand slid through John's hair.

Heart pounding, John could feel sweat forming on his brow as he continued his erotic journey along Jessica's body. Her hips bucked involuntarily when he reached her swollen mound. Applying gentle pressure to her clitoris, he revelled in her ecstatic gasps. Her legs quivered in response, encircling his waist and drawing him closer.

Feeling an irresistible urge to taste her, John lowered his mouth to Jessica's slick wetness, tongue swirling around her clit before plunging into her eager depths. She trembled beneath him, gripping his hair tighter while moaning in approval. Their eyes locked; the raw lust conveyed wordlessly between them further ignited their passion.

As they reached a fever pitch, John positioned himself over Jessica and entered her with a deep thrust that evoked cries of pleasure from both of them. They found their rhythm quickly, thrusts becoming more frenzied and deliberate as their moans echoed off the walls. Their chests heaved with every gasp, sweat mingling as their bodies met in feverish desperation.

Jessica's nails dug into John's back, urging him onward. His hands gripped her hips firmly, guiding their movement as their bodies collided with desperate abandon. The sound of skin-on-skin permeated the air, punctuated by increasingly intense grunts and cries of delight.

As their ecstasy escalated, John and Jessica clung to one another, locked in a passionate embrace. The heat between them swelled like an unstoppable wave, ready to crash at any moment. Finally, they reached the ultimate crescendo, their shared orgasm overtaking them as they cried out in unison.

In the aftermath, they lay breathless, entwined in each other's arms. The world beyond the bed seemed distant and insignificant compared to the electric connection they shared. As the night enveloped them in darkness, whispers and sighs faded into silence—a true testament to the intensity of their passion and the intimate secrets revealed in the hours before dawn.

John lay still for a moment, the drum of his heartbeat slowly retreating to the quiet postlude of their union. Jessica's breaths, soft and rhythmic against his chest, were the gentle lullabies that lulled her into a contented sleep—her body a warm silhouette against the cool sheets that whispered tales of their recent entanglement.

He observed her closely, her chest's rise and fall a pulsating rhythm to his racing thoughts. With a tenderness that contradicted the storm within, John extricated himself from the cocoon of limbs and linen, his movements deliberate, calculated not to stir the serene figure beside him. The room was suffused with the scent of their mingling—the musk of desire clinging to the air like a second skin he was hesitant to shed.

Silently, he padded across the plush carpet, the rich fibres pressing between his toes as he approached the balcony doors. Easing them open, he stepped out, the chill of the night caressing his bare flesh—a stark contrast to the warmth he had just abandoned. The city sprawled below him, a tapestry of twinkling lights and distant murmurs, each luminescent dot a life, a story, a choice that wasn't his—at least not tonight.

John leaned on the balustrade, the cold metal biting at his palms, grounding him in the reality of this covert escape. He gazed outward, letting his eyes blur the lines between the city lights and the stars above, seeking refuge in the vastness. The breeze carried whispers of lives unfolding beyond his reach, tales of love and loss that drifted up to him, wrapping around his conscience like tendrils of mist.

The sky was a canvas of deep blues and purples, the dark hues mirroring the shades of secrecy that coloured his own actions. He closed his eyes, taking in the crispness of the air, allowing it to fill his lungs, hoping it might clear the fog of emotions that clouded his judgement.

But the night held no absolution, only questions that echoed through the canyons of his mind, reverberating against the walls he had meticulously built around his life. The piercing thrill of the unknown now punctures a life once punctuated by predictability.

John lingered there, a solitary figure framed by the backdrop of the city's endless dance, a man caught between two worlds—one of comfort and constraint, the other of risk and rapture. As he stood in quiet solitude, the night seemed to hold its breath, waiting for a choice to be made and a path to be taken.

And though he knew the dawn would soon paint the sky with the first light of consequence, for now, he existed in the limbo of twilight, where all truths remained veiled and every touch was a memory carved into the night.

John's fingers curled around the wrought-iron railing of the balcony, the metal cool and unyielding under his touch. Below, the city unfurled like a tapestry of light and shadow, each glimmering streetlamp and neon sign a testament to lives moving forward in blissful ignorance of his turmoil. The soft murmur of distant traffic, a lullaby of normalcy, carried the air, a world away from the tempest raging within him.

The guilt was a spectre in the night, its cold fingers tracing down his spine. He had betrayed Sophie, the woman who loved him with a quiet constancy, whose trust he'd shattered with every whispered promise to Jessica. Her image, blonde hair catching the sun, blue eyes bright with shared secrets, flickered in his mind's eye—a stark contrast against the heat of Jessica's emerald gaze, which promised oceans of depth and currents of wild abandon.

A shiver ran through him, not from the chill of the night but from the realisation that he could no longer see his reflection in either pair of eyes. The allure of Jessica's touch lingered on his skin, an intoxicating blend of jasmine and desire that seeped into his very bones. It was undeniable, the way she ignited something primal within him, something that Sophie, with all her steadfast love, had never awakened.

John turned his gaze skyward, where stars blink indifferently at his plight. He could easily lose himself in their vastness, forgetting the intricate web he had woven. He considered the path that had led him here— to this precipice of corruption and deceit. There had always been a restlessness in him, a hunger for more than the neatly trimmed lawns and polished routines of suburban life.

He acknowledged the thrill, the exhilarating pulse of life that coursed through him whenever he was with Jessica. However, this acknowledgement was accompanied by a shadow of potential fallout, looming over him like a storm cloud poised to explode. Could the thrill justify the impending deluge of consequences?

The fabric of his life, once so tightly woven, was fraying at the edges, threads of loyalty and longing pulling apart in silent defiance. The night whispered of secrets and sins, of a man who danced on the knife-edge of morality, each step a precarious balance between two contrasting desires.

In the sombre embrace of the evening, John stood alone, grappling with the complexity of his own heart—a heart divided by the safety of the known and the call of the forbidden. As the darkness deepened, wrapping him in its ambiguous veil, he wondered if the dawn would bring clarity or further entangle him in the seductive snare of twilight's last shadows.

John's silhouette merged with the shadows as he slipped back into the suite, the door closing behind him with a whisper of finality. The room lay drenched in moonlight, silver beams spilling across the plush carpet and up the opulent curtains, casting the world in ethereal half-light. His gaze found Jessica, a serene figure amidst the tangled sheets, her chestnut hair a dark cascade against the pale linens.

The sight of her, so vulnerable in slumber, stirred something in John—a mixture of tenderness and turmoil. He approached the bed, each step measured, his eyes tracing the gentle rise and fall of her breathing. In sleep, she was a siren's song personified, lulling him closer with the promise of peace yet underscoring the cacophony of his desires.

The weight of his indecision immobilized him as he stood there. The thrill of their connection resonated within him, a hum of electricity that defied silence. But it was more than physical allure that bound him to her; it was the glimpse of something untamed, a shared recognition of souls seeking refuge from the monotonous symphony of everyday life.

With a breath that felt like surrender, John allowed himself to sink back into the bed, the mattress yielding to their collective warmth. Gingerly, as to not disturb her dreams, he wrapped an arm around Jessica, pulling her close. Her body, instinctively attuned to his touch even in sleep, curled into him, a perfect fit that made his heart ache with poignant longing.

The night stretched taut around them, filled with the resonance of unsaid words and unacknowledged truths. As John nestled against her, the soft rhythm of her breath became his anchor in the tempest of his emotions. He closed his eyes, hoping to find solace in the quietude of the moment, yet the storm within raged on—a silent maelstrom of guilt and desire.

Outside, the city whispered its nocturnal secrets, each distant sound a reminder of the life he had momentarily stepped away from. Yet here, in the embrace of paradox, with Jessica's warmth seeping into his very bones, John found himself at the precipice of something profound—a place where love and lust intertwined, where right and wrong blurred into a tapestry of human complexity.

As dawn's first light threatened to breach the horizon, John remained awake, cocooned in the ambiguity of his choices. Everything and nothing seemed possible in the shroud of predawn greyness, the future an enigmatic puzzle whose pieces he held yet couldn't quite place.

In the stillness of the room, time lost meaning, and for a fleeting moment, John allowed himself to simply exist—caught between the remnants of yesterday's promises and the uncertain whispers of tomorrow.

John's fingers trailed over the smooth expanse of the sheets, the fabric a cool contrast to the lingering warmth where Jessica lay beside him. The faint light from the city beyond the curtains painted shadows across her face—shadows that seemed to dance with the secrets he kept nestled deep within his chest.

A car horn sounded in the distance, a solitary beacon in the night's embrace, and John's thoughts scattered like leaves in the wind. He pondered the silent streets below, empty avenues that mirrored the hollow feeling taking root in his gut. The opulent room around them felt like a gilded cage, splendid yet suffocating, as if the very air they breathed was charged with the electricity of their transgression.

He listened to the hum of the city, a steady pulse that beat in time with his own heart—a heart that was now a battleground for loyalty and longing. In the back of his mind, a song of what-ifs and maybes played on, a haunting melody that promised ecstasy tinged with the bitterness of betrayal.

The texture of Jessica's hair between his fingers was silk and fire, and he knew that with every caress, he wove another thread into the intricate web of deceit. As she shifted in her sleep, murmuring softly, a wave of tenderness washed over him, followed by a surge of remorse.

The combination left him breathless, trapped between the tide's pull and the shore's salvation.

He lay there motionless, each tick of the clock a hammer against the walls of his resolve. The taste of forbidden fruit still lingered on his lips, sweet and damning, and John realised the morning would bring no absolution, only the sharp sting of reality.

The predawn sky burst with colour, a canvas of purples and blues whispering of endings and beginnings. The vast ocean of his emotions isolated John in the quiet before dawn. The world outside beckoned with its mundane certainties, yet the enigma of the room held him captive.

As he lay beside Jessica, her breath a gentle cadence against the storm of his inner turmoil, John Hawthorne was a man adrift. With the first light of day peeking through the curtains, his future remained shrouded in mist, an intricate dance of shadow and light that promised nothing but the complexity of the human heart.

Chapter 15: Jessica's Ultimatum

John's hands roamed over Jessica's body with a fervour that belied the calm suburban life he embodied by day. Their limbs tangled on the edge of her bed, two silhouettes blurred into one by the urgency of their movements. The heat of their skin melded together, a silent testament to the smouldering tension that had been building between them for weeks. This room, dimly lit and draped in shadows, became their world—a world where the electric air pulsed with each ragged breath and stolen kiss.

The scent of lavender from the sheets mixed with the musk of their desire, creating an intoxicating blend that seemed to wrap around them, thick and heady. The faint creak of the bed frame sang a rhythm to their dance, a siren's call to sink deeper into the depths of their forbidden embrace.

But as John deepened the kiss, angling his head to claim more of Jessica's mouth, there was a sudden stillness. Her lips, which had been moving against his with such insistent hunger, paused—a fleeting hesitation that felt like a crack in the glass.

Jessica pulled back slightly, breaking the seal of their intimacy. Her emerald eyes, usually so full of fire and challenge, searched John's face. They shimmered with a vulnerability that seemed out of place amidst the bold strokes of her usual confidence. In those eyes, a storm brewed—a tempest of unspoken words and hidden depths that John found himself inexplicably drawn toward yet equally afraid to navigate.

The change was subtle; the shift in atmosphere was barely noticeable at first. But it was there—the lingering question in her gaze, the tremble of uncertainty that whispered through the charged silence. It was as if she sought an answer in his eyes, trying to read the story that lay within the man whose laughter rang easy but whose soul simmered with restless longing.

John could feel the weight of her scrutiny— the delicate balance teetering on the precipice of something undefined. The warmth of her breath against his skin contrasted sharply with the sudden coolness of doubt that threaded through the sultry air between them.

Jessica inhaled sharply, the sound slicing through the thick veil of desire that had moments ago enveloped them. Her voice, when it came, trembled on the edge of a precipice, barely louder than the rustle of the sheets beneath their entangled limbs. "John," she whispered, her words quivering like the surface of a still pond disturbed by a single drop. "I love you."

Her confession hung suspended, an echo resonating into every corner of the dimly lit room. The air seemed to thicken with her admission, time pausing as if the universe itself was holding its breath for John's response. The shadows cast by the soft glow of the bedside lamp appeared to lean in closer, drawn by the gravity of her vulnerability.

John's heart stuttered, his mind a whirlwind of chaos and disbelief. The taste of Jessica's passion lingered on his lips, now tinged with the bittersweet flavour of her sincerity. He felt the press of her body against his own, the heat that radiated from her skin now competing with a cold dagger of panic that lodged itself within his chest.

The subtle hues of doubt and longing painted across Jessica's features beckoned him, demanded he acknowledge the depth of what she offered—a depth he recognized all too well within himself. Yet the memory of another face, one framed by golden locks and expectations, flashed before his eyes, casting a pall over the incandescent moment they shared.

John searched for words—any words—that might bridge the chasm that her love had opened between them. His throat constricted, each possible utterance dissolving before it could reach his trembling lips. A torrent of emotions clashed within him: elation, guilt, fear—a turbulence threatening to uproot the carefully constructed life he had always known.

His silence stretched, the seconds piling upon one another like heavy stones, building a wall of uncertainty that threatened to separate them forever. In that prolonged quiet, filled only by the sound of their mingled breaths, John Hawthorne stood at the crossroads of his existence, torn between two worlds—the safe harbour of his past and the tempestuous sea of a future with Jessica.

The air in the bedroom, once thick with desire, now quivered with a desperate urgency as she clutched at John's shoulders. Her emerald eyes, usually so commanding and sure, flooded with a raw need that stripped away any pretence. "You must leave her, John," she breathed, her voice a melodic insistence that resonated with an intensity he'd never heard from her before.

She searched his face for signs of acquiescence, for the shared passion to manifest into life-altering decisions. The soft curve of her mouth, which had so recently explored his with unbridled enthusiasm, now trembled with the enormity of her request. It was as if the words themselves were sacred, a plea that reached beyond the confines of the room, demanding more than stolen moments and whispered promises.

John felt the seismic shift in her tone, a departure from the tender whispers that had danced between them mere heartbeats ago. Her hands roamed over his back, pressing him closer as though she could meld his indecision into resolve through sheer will. However, navigating the labyrinthine corridors of his heart proved to be more challenging.

He hesitated, a silent statue save for the ragged rise and fall of his chest, the pulse in his throat betraying the chaos within. His hands, which had roamed the valleys and peaks of Jessica's body with confident fervour, now betrayed him; they slid from her waist reluctantly, as if his skin mourned the loss of contact. He watched his own fingers graze the hem of her blouse, the delicate fabric a stark contrast to the rough storm brewing behind his ribcage.

John's gaze dropped to the floor, unable to bear the piercing light of Jessica's expectancy. The plush carpet underfoot seemed to swallow the sound of his faltering heartbeat, and the walls echoed back none of the reassurances he sought. Each second that ticked by loomed large, a pendulum marking the inexorable passage toward a decision he wasn't ready to make.

John Hawthorne stood on the brink of two diverging paths, in the dimly lit room where shadows played across their entwined forms like whispered secrets. One, a path paved with the warm familiarity of commitment and routine; the other, a tempestuous journey that promised the kind of fervour he had only dared to dream of.

But dreams have a way of dissipating upon waking, and as the silence stretched taut between them, the dreamlike quality of their connection began to fray, pulling them back to a reality where every choice bore weight and every whisper held consequence.

Jessica's features, previously soft with longing and vulnerability, suddenly solidified into a mask of stoic resolve. The fiery passion that had blazed in her emerald eyes dimmed, replaced by the cool glint of hurt that recognized the silent rejection standing before her. She turned from John, her back an elegant barrier, her arms crossing over her chest in a self-protective embrace that felt as much like armour as it did a balm for her wounded spirit.

The room, once alive with the heat of their fervour, now seemed to contract, the air thinning as if it were struggling to breathe through the tension. Shadows grew bolder in the dimness, stretching across the walls and floor, reaching toward the pair like dark fingers eager to trace the contours of their discord. The faint hum of the city beyond the window was a low lament, a soundtrack to the unravelling tableau within.

The faint glow of the bedside lamp threw a golden hue onto Jessica's hair, turning the chestnut strands into a cascade of burnished copper that fell just shy of touching the cold space that yawned between them. The silence bore down oppressively, each second ticking away on the clock by the door, feeling like a pronouncement about the death of what might have been.

In this stillness, the world outside faded to nothing more than a distant echo, leaving only the palpable ache of choices unmade and words unsaid. John stood frozen, the chill of indecision wrapping around his heart like creeping ivy, insidious, and cold. He watched her guarded figure, the curve of her shoulders revealing the fortress she had built against him in mere moments.

And so they remained, two figures ensnared in the twilight of their own making, a dance of shadows and light playing upon the walls, an elegy to the passion that once promised to consume them both.

John extended a hand, the tremble in his fingers betraying the turmoil that roiled within him. "Jessica, I—" His voice, usually so sure and steady, fractured under the weight of his confession, each syllable thick with the gravity of their predicament.

The room seemed to contract around them, the air growing denser, as if suffused with the tangible essence of his internal conflict. The soft, apologetic cadence of his words hovered in the space, an offering laid bare, yet insufficient to bridge the chasm of Jessica's expectations.

"Please understand, it's not that simple," he said, his voice a low murmur, as though speaking any louder would shatter the delicate balance of the moment. But the answers she sought—a clear-cut path, a promise sculpted in certainty—remained elusive, dancing just beyond the edge of his reach, obscured by the shadows that now crept along the walls, encroaching upon the remnants of their closeness.

Jessica's breath caught, a silent counterpoint to his stammering attempts at explanation. Her eyes, once alight with desire, now held the sheen of unshed tears, their emerald depths darkening with the pull of something more profound. She cut through his faltering speech with a voice honed sharp by resolve, a blade forged in the fires of vulnerability turned to steel.

"John, you need to leave." Her command sliced through the heavy air, each word laced with a sorrowful finality. It was a declaration born not of anger but of self-preservation, the intonation ringing with the muted chime of a heart encasing itself behind protective walls.

Her figure, backlit by the lambent glow of the lamp, seemed to draw the very light into herself, casting her resolve in stark relief against the encroaching darkness. It was a portrait of strength etched in shadow and sorrow, a woman reclaiming her own narrative amidst the wreckage of what could have been.

John's heart clenched, a visceral response to the resolute set of her jaw, the way her silhouette seemed to brace against the storm of emotions that had surged between them. He recognised in her stance the quiet power of a siren calling forth the will to navigate treacherous waters, to emerge from the tempest intact, if not unscarred.

In that moment, amidst the whisper of fabric as she turned from him and the faint scent of jasmine that lingered like a ghost of their intimacy, John understood the irrevocable shift. The hesitant touch of his hand retracted, leaving behind only the echo of contact and an indelible mark on the canvas of their shared history—a history that was now folding in upon itself like the closing petals of a flower at dusk

John's fingers trembled slightly as he reached for his jacket, draped haphazardly across the back of a chair. The fabric, still warm from their entanglement, felt like a betrayal against his skin. He slid it on— the act heavy with the finality of a curtain falling after the last act.

Each deliberate and measured motion echoed the urgency that had propelled them to the brink of reason just moments before.

He paused at the door, the silence humming in his ears. There was a gravity to the air, thick with the unsaid and the undone. His eyes found Jessica's figure one last time, her posture a stark sculpture of resolve and regret. John felt the weight of his choices—each one a leaden stone in the pit of his stomach—as he memorized the contours of her silhouette, a sight he knew he'd carry with him long after tonight.

The door behind him clicked, severing the fragile connection that held them together. Stepping into the cool night, John made his way to his car, which was an island of solitude amidst the sea of suburban twilight. Inside, the quiet was deafening, a stark contrast to the noise of passion and pleading that had filled the hotel's bedroom.

As he drove, the streetlights played over his features, casting his expression in a flickering tableau of torment. They painted his face with strokes of amber and shadow, each passing beam like a spotlight on his inner conflict. The soft hum of the engine was a lullaby sung too late, a soothing sound that could not ease the tempest churning within him.

His hands steady on the wheel belied the chaos of his thoughts. John's mind replayed the evening—a tapestry of desire and despair woven together in a pattern that offered no clear path forward. The taste of Jessica's lips lingered, a bittersweet reminder of what could have been, of the precipice upon which he teetered between loyalty and longing.

Each mile that unfurled beneath the tyres was a marker of distance and decision, the road stretching out before him like the narrative of his life, full of twists and turns, some taken and others forsaken. In the rearview mirror, the lights of the city receded until they were nothing more than a constellation of possibilities, twinkling with the allure of the unknown and the comfort of the familiar, both equally out of reach.

The cool leather of the steering wheel under his grasp anchored John to the present, to the inescapable truth of his actions. As he pulled into his driveway, the facade of his house loomed—a spectre of normalcy that now seemed a foreign land. John Hawthorne, with a sigh that held the remnants of fractured dreams, steeled himself for the days ahead, prepared for the reckoning that awaited within the walls that had once signified sanctuary.

His heart beat a staccato rhythm, each pulse a cacophony of emotions that surged and receded like the ebb and flow of a dark sea within him. Jessica, with her emerald eyes and unspoken stories, had kindled a fire in the hearth of his soul—a blaze that threatened to consume the very foundations of his being. However, Sophie's unwavering presence served as a beacon, guiding him home, and her unwavering trust served as an anchor, stabilizing his vessel amidst the turbulence of existence.

A sigh escaped him, fogging the windscreen momentarily with the warmth of his breath, a ghostly testament to the turmoil inside. He loved them both, in ways that defied reason, their visages etched upon the chambers of his heart—Sophie's blonde serenity and Jessica's chestnut vibrancy, a chiaroscuro of affection and desire that painted his reality with conflicting shades.

The weight of his decision pressed down upon him, like the gravity of a judgment passed. In that moment of stillness, with the air thick with the scent of impending rain, John realized that the world he knew had completely changed. The man who had left that morning was not the same man who returned; this truth seared into him as irrefutably as the changing patterns of the stars overhead.

With a breath that felt like the first or perhaps the last, John opened the car door, stepping out into the crisp morning air that no longer promised solace but whispered of the inexorable consequences yet to unfold.

John's hand lingered on the brass knob, the cold metal a stark contrast to the warmth of his palm. He turned it slowly, the soft click of the latch yielding to his unsteady resolve. The door swung open with a muted creak, the sound slicing through the silence of the house like a subtle admonition.

He stepped inside, the familiar scent of lavender and lemon polish failing to greet him as it once had. Instead, the air felt stagnant, heavy with unsaid words and the ghosts of laughter that no longer danced in the corners of the rooms. The dim light from the streetlamps outside filtered through the sheer curtains, casting elongated shadows that seemed to stretch towards him, as if seeking to envelop him in their sombre embrace.

The plush carpet hushed his footsteps, echoing the rhythm of his racing heart. The house, once a sanctuary of domestic bliss, now loomed around him with an oppressive presence. It was as though the walls themselves bore witness to his transgression, their silence a judgement he could neither escape nor refute.

The living room, bathed in the soft glow of twilight, held remnants of his other life—the framed photographs smiling with frozen joviality, the neatly arranged throw pillows, the bookshelf lined with titles that spoke of shared interests and quiet evenings. Yet these tokens of conjugal harmony now seemed like artefacts from a bygone era, relics of a simplicity he had willingly shattered.

John paused, allowing the weight of his surroundings to settle upon him. He breathed in deeply, the air cool and devoid of the warmth that human presence imbues.

A part of him longed for the comfort these walls once offered, but another part—a restless presence that thrived on whispered promises and forbidden touches—recoiled at the thought of confinement within them. There was a desolation in the silence— a forlornness that clung to the fabric of the space, weaving itself into the tapestry of his reality.

With each step he took toward the staircase, John felt the delicate balance of his world tilting precariously. The ascent seemed laborious, each stair a milestone marking his descent into a labyrinth of emotional turmoil. At the landing, he stopped, gazing back at the living space that now felt like a stranger's abode.

There would be no turning back from here; the die had been cast, the dice tumbling in a game where there were no winners, only survivors. In the stillness of the night, John grappled with the inevitable confrontation that awaited: the looming discourse with Sophie that would unravel the final threads of pretence.

He stepped down the hallway, the soft carpet muffling his passage, the hushed tones of the house whispering secrets he could not yet divulge. As he pushed open the bedroom door, the emptiness of the room embraced him—a prelude to the coldness that might soon replace the warmth of a shared bed.

Chapter 16: Derek's Blackmail

John stepped onto his porch, the late afternoon sun dipping into an opulent sea of burnt oranges and purples as it cast long shadows across the manicured lawns of suburbia. His mind was a tempestuous whirlpool of thoughts about Jessica—her captivating emerald eyes, the intoxicating scent of her perfume, the sinuous way she moved—that had stirred something dormant within him. It was a dangerous reverie, one that was abruptly shattered by the sight of Derek Thompson approaching with a stride that seemed all too purposeful.

"Good evening, John," Derek greeted him, his voice slicing through the tranquillity of the suburban tableau. The smile that curled the corners of his thin lips held a conspiratorial edge, and the gleam in his magnified eyes suggested the thrill of having unearthed a treasure trove of secrets.

"Evening, Derek," John replied, his own tone guarded as he sought to mask the tumultuous undercurrents of emotion roiling beneath his calm exterior. He leaned against the wooden railing of his porch, the rough texture grounding him to the moment as Derek ascended the steps to join him.

"Quite the day, isn't it?" Derek remarked casually, gesturing toward the horizon, where the sun continued its descent, painting the sky with strokes of impending darkness. "The kind of day that makes you think... about life, about... hidden desires."

The words hung heavy in the air between them, laced with an insinuation that sent a shiver down John's spine despite the balminess of the evening. There was a slow-burn tension simmering, one that John felt acutely as Derek's presence encroached upon his personal space, that familiar eagerness in his demeanour now taking on a more ominous shade.

"Hidden desires, Derek?" John ventured cautiously, feeling the weight of those words like stones in his stomach. He could sense the intricate plot Derek was weaving, one that threatened to ensnare him in its complex web.

Derek's chuckle was a low rumble, akin to distant thunder forewarning of a storm. "Oh, we all have them, don't we, John? And sometimes, those desires have a way of... surfacing, despite our best efforts to keep them submerged."

The veiled threat in Derek's tone was as clear as the crisp evening air itself. The seductive undertones of their conversation were not lost on John, nor was the subtle but unequivocal message: Derek knew something he shouldn't, and this knowledge empowered him with a disquieting leverage.

As the sun's last rays surrendered to twilight's embrace, casting the neighbourhood in looming shadows, John realized with a sinking heart that the placid surface of his life might soon be disrupted by the ripples of a secret laid bare.

John's fingers traced the grain of the wooden railing, a hollow echo to the erratic beat of his heart. The late afternoon light splintered into prisms around Derek's silhouette, casting an otherworldly glow that seemed to crown him with a halo of forbidden knowledge.

"Beautiful evening, isn't it?" Derek mused, letting his eyes roam over the horizon where the sun began its descent, painting the sky in shades of fire and regret.

"Sure is," John replied, but his voice faltered, strangled by the tightening grip of unease. Derek's casual remark felt like the prelude to a darker symphony, each note resonating with a hidden intent. John's gaze flickered back to Derek, searching for a sign, a clue to the man's true purpose.

"Especially when evening shadows unveil more than just the night," Derek continued, his smile never reaching his eyes, which remained locked onto John's with unsettling intensity.

A shudder rippled through John's spine, his skin tingling as if brushed by unseen whispers. He fought to keep his composure, to maintain the facade of ignorance, but Derek's words prickled at his consciousness, unravelling the tightly wound coil of his thoughts.

"Shadows can be... deceptive," John managed, his tongue feeling thick and clumsy in his mouth.

"Indeed." Derek paused, tilting his head ever so slightly, as if contemplating a particularly juicy morsel of scandal. "But sometimes they reveal truths we'd rather keep hidden. Secrets between... lovers, perhaps?"

The world seemed to contract around John, the air growing dense and suffocating. His laugh, meant to be light, came out as a choked gasp. "I'm not sure what you mean, Derek."

"Come now, John," Derek chided softly, the satisfaction oozing from his voice like molasses. "Let's not play coy. It doesn't suit you."

With those words, Derek reached into his jacket, producing an envelope that seemed benign yet brimmed with menace. He extended it toward John, who took it as if it were a serpent coiled to strike.

"Photographs can be so... illuminating, don't you think?" Derek whispered, the sound grating against John's ears like sandpaper.

John's hand trembled as he extracted the contents, his pulse hammering against his temples. The images within were damning—a secret embrace, a stolen kiss, each captured moment a further blow to his carefully crafted life.

"Jessica..." The name escaped his lips before he could swallow it down, a whisper of utter despair.

"Ah, so you do recognize her," Derek said, his tone dripping with venomous triumph.

Shock immobilized John, causing his mind to spiral into a state of panic and disbelief. How had it come to this? He was cornered, trapped by the consequences of his own reckless desires. He looked up, meeting Derek's gaze, and saw nothing but cold calculation staring back at him.

"Everyone has their secrets, John," Derek stated, a dark prophet revealing an unwanted truth. "And every secret has its price."

In that moment, under the oppressive weight of Derek's scrutiny and the incriminating paper clenched in his fist, John knew his world was about to fracture. The façade of respectability and the illusion of normalcy were all in danger of collapsing.

And as the sun bled out its last rays, surrendering to the encroaching night, John Hawthorne stood on his porch, a man teetering on the precipice of ruin.

The silence that followed Derek's chilling revelation was pregnant with the unspoken threat, a thin wire stretched taut between them. John watched as Derek folded the photographs with meticulous care, the soft rustle of paper slicing through the stillness. The late afternoon sun spilled its golden light across the porch, casting shadows that seemed to whisper of the darkness encroaching upon John's life.

"John," Derek began, his voice assuming a businesslike timbre that belied the malice beneath. "You're a man of influence, connections. I'm merely asking you to lend a hand to an old neighbour."

John's gaze lingered on Derek's expectant face, noting the slight upturn of his lips—part salesman, part serpent. There was no mistaking the unyielding intent in the older man's eyes; they held the glint of a predator who had cornered his prey. "What do you want?" John managed to ask, his throat dry, the words tasting like ash.

"Nothing too burdensome. Just a few introductions, some favourable words whispered into the right ears," Derek replied, outlining a plan that would entwine John's professional reputation with

Derek's nascent real estate ambitions. "Refusal isn't wise, John. Think of it as... mutual assistance."

The air around them grew thick with the scent of freshly mowed grass and the distant aroma of barbecues igniting—the suburban idyll clashing grotesquely with the undercurrent of coercion. John stood, grappling with the ramifications of Derek's demands. Thoughts tore at his mind with the intensity of a squall. Fear gnawed at the edges of his resolve, guilt clawed at his conscience, and anger simmered like a dangerous undertow, threatening to pull him under.

He could almost hear the murmur of his wife's voice, feel her trust in him—a trust now as fragile as a spider's web glistening with morning dew. How could he face Sophie, knowing that the truth might shatter their world? Yet, the alternative was to become complicit in Derek's scheme, a puppet dancing on strings of blackmail.

"Of course, we wouldn't want any... unfortunate details to find their way to Sophie, would we?" Derek said, his voice as sharp as a velvet-coated dagger. "A happy home is a precious thing, after all."

John's heart pounded against his ribcage, a drumbeat echoing the turmoil within. He fought to maintain the facade of calm, aware that any crack in his demeanour would only embolden Derek further. He forced a nod, a gesture that felt like conceding to the enemy in a war he didn't know he was fighting.

"Good, good," Derek murmured, satisfaction oozing from every syllable. "I knew you were a reasonable man, John."

As Derek turned to leave, his footsteps assured and unhurried, the setting sun dipped below the horizon, surrendering the world to twilight. Shadows lengthened and converged, enveloping John in a gloom that seemed to mirror the dread curling inside him.

The decision lay heavy on his shoulders, a mantle woven from threads of deceit and desperation. John's mind raced with the possibility of confession, the harrowing thought of coming clean to

Sophie. But the path ahead was fraught with uncertainty, each step a potential plunge into an abyss from which there might be no return.

Standing alone, John's silhouette cut a solitary figure against the backdrop of an indigo sky. The night's first stars blinked into existence, indifferent witnesses to the turmoil of one man's soul. As the evening chill settled in, John braced himself for the storm he knew was coming—the tempest that would test the very foundations of his existence.

John's voice, once a bastion of confidence, now quivered like a leaf caught in a tempestuous wind. "I'll... see what I can do," he managed to say, the words scraping against his throat as though they were shards of glass. The act of uttering them felt like a betrayal, not only to his wife, Sophie, but also to himself and the life he had meticulously built.

"Of course, you will," Derek replied, his tone smooth as silk, yet edged with something darker, something that sent a shiver down John's spine. He watched, nearly paralysed, as Derek's lips curved into a smile that didn't quite reach the cool calculation in his eyes.

As Derek turned on his heel and strode away, John's legs felt rooted to the wooden planks of the porch, each grain and knot beneath his feet suddenly hyper-detailed, as though mocking his predicament. His hands, those deft instruments that had penned love letters to Sophie and sealed business deals with firm handshakes, now trembled uncontrollably at his sides.

He was conscious of every breath, each inhale sharp and jagged, and every exhale a whisper of despair. The fabric of his shirt clung to his back, damp with the perspiration of fear. John lifted his gaze to the horizon, where the sun's final embers flared defiantly before succumbing to the encroaching night. The sky was painted in bruises of purple and orange; beauty contrasted with the ugliness of the secret now festering between him and Derek.

The neighbourhood, once a sanctuary of manicured lawns and friendly waves, had transformed into a stage for his potential undoing.

John could almost hear the whispers behind closed doors— the rustle of curtains as unseen eyes watched and waited. With each beat of his heart, the walls seemed to close in around him, the air thick with the scent of impending ruin.

Derek's footsteps faded into the distance, the quiet patter a grim lullaby for the innocence lost. John's chest tightened, a silent scream lodged within as he contemplated the next day, fraught with deceit and the weaving of web after intricate web. The cost of his silence weighed heavily upon him, a debt that promised to compound with interest until it crushed him beneath its unforgiving ledger.

In the twilight gloom, John stood alone, a man adrift in a sea of turmoil, his resolve tested by the siren call of a simple, devastating truth.

John's silhouette stretched across the porch, a dark line blurring the boundary between respectability and the shame clenching his gut. His thoughts churned like storm clouds in his mind, a tempest of panic and guilt colliding with the cold realization that caving to Derek's demands was tantamount to shackling himself to an endless cycle of manipulation.

The scent of jasmine from Sophie's carefully tended garden wafted through the air, a cruel reminder of the purity he stood to soil with his silence. He could see her now, her blue eyes wide with hurt, the trust they held shattering like delicate crystal against the brutal truth. The image pained him—a visceral throb that resonated more deeply than any physical wound.

John swallowed hard, the taste of fear bitter on his tongue. The thought of confessing to Sophie and witnessing the dawning horror on her face made his knees weak. But as the haunting hues of twilight enveloped him, a glimmer of resolve ignited within him. It was faint, flickering with uncertainty, but it was there—a beacon guiding him toward the treacherous path of honesty.

He closed his eyes, summoning the memory of their vows, the weight of the gold band encircling his finger suddenly heavy with significance. Sophie deserved more than a facade, more than a husband ensnared in deceit. Love, the kind that had bound them together beneath a sky much like this one, demanded sacrifice. And perhaps—just perhaps—the embers of that love could survive the inferno he was about to ignite.

He let out a breath he hadn't realized he'd been holding, the cool air caressing his skin like a lover's touch—a touch he longed to deserve once more. With each pulsing heartbeat, his decision crystallised, the fear mingling with an unexpected surge of relief. There was no turning back; the road ahead loomed, fraught with peril, but it was a path he knew he must walk. For Sophie. For himself.

John found his courage fragile and untested. Tomorrow, he would face the consequences, whatever they may be. For now, he stood alone, bracing against the gathering darkness, the whispering leaves echoing his newfound determination.

John's hand closed around the doorknob, the metal cool and unforgiving against his skin. He turned it slowly, the faint creak of the hinges a solemn prelude to the resolution hardening in his chest. The door shut behind him with a soft click, a punctuation mark at the end of one chapter, and the tentative beginning of another.

The decision to confess lay before him, stark and undeniable, like the line dividing shadow from sunlight. Fear gnawed at the edges of his mind, a beast he could neither tame nor fully understand. Yet intertwined with that terror was an unexpected sense of relief, the kind that comes from shedding a burdensome mask.

He'd been adrift on a sea of lies, swept along by currents of forbidden desire and easy complacency. But now, John resolved to take the helm, to navigate the stormy waters he had helped to churn. Each throb of his heart was a steady rhythm, a drumbeat of purpose that drowned out the whispers of doubt.

He would confess to Sophie. He would lay bare the truth, however it may strike. John understood, perhaps for the first time, that the path to healing must traverse the jagged landscape of honesty, no matter how perilous the journey.

He knew that tomorrow would bring its trials—the look of heartbreak in Sophie's eyes, the possibility of losing everything he held dear. The very thought sent a shiver down his spine, a cold trail that settled in his bones. However, he could no longer turn back; the truth, like a spectre haunting him, demanded its release.

Within John, a light flickered to life, fragile and defiant. He would face the consequences of his actions with only the hope of forgiveness and the will to repair what went wrong. Tomorrow would come, and with it, the reckoning.

Chapter 17: The Pregnancy Scare

The shrill ring of John's phone cleaved the stillness of his living room, a jarring intrusion that yanked him from the cocoon of his thoughts. He reached for it, the smooth surface cold against his palm, an ominous prelude. As he brought the phone to his ear, Jessica's voice cascaded through the line, each word laced with a sharp edge of panic that pricked at his skin.

"John... I—I think I might be pregnant," she stammered, her breaths hitching in a rhythm that spoke of spiralling fears.

A chill skittered down John's spine, an icy finger tracing the outline of his orderly life. His heart stuttered, then pounded with the force of a trapped bird against its cage as shock and urgency flooded his senses, mingling with a dark undercurrent of excitement.

"Stay where you are, Jessica. I'm coming over," he said with a steadiness that belied the tumult inside him.

Without hesitation, John rose from the cushioned safety of his sofa, the fabric grazing his fingertips like a whisper of the normalcy he was leaving behind. The room seemed to contract around him, the walls pressing in with silent judgement, the air thick with the scent of lavender and lemon polish—scents that once soothed but now seemed suffocating.

He strode toward the door, his movements brusque, the soft click of the lock loud in the hush. Each step was heavy with the gravity of Jessica's revelation, his mind a whirlwind of conflicting emotions.

The world beckoned outside, but inside, John Hawthorne grappled with the potential consequences of this new reality, his existence on the verge of irreversible change.

The world outside blurred into a watercolour of suburban idyll as John raced down the sun-drenched sidewalk, the midday air clinging to his skin like a second, warmer layer. Each footfall was a sharp punctuation against the quiet of the neighbourhood—a stark contrast to the turmoil churning within him. His thoughts, once neatly filed away in the recesses of his mind, now erupted in rapid succession, each more alarming than the last. The jittery possibility of fatherhood and the piercing fear of scandal created a maelstrom that uprooted the very foundations of his predictable life.

The drone of distant lawn mowers and the occasional bark of a dog did little to silence the cacophony of scenarios playing out in his head. What if she were pregnant? What then?

The charming facades of the neighbouring houses offered no comfort, their shadows lengthening across the pavement like silent omens. John's hand hovered over the brass knocker on Jessica's door, the metal cool and unyielding beneath his touch. He hesitated, the heartbeat in his throat a drum beat to the tension wrapping around him like a shroud.

In the moment before he could announce his presence, the door swung open, revealing Jessica Sterling, her emerald eyes wide with apprehension. The sunlight caught in her chestnut hair, igniting fiery strands that danced in the gentle breeze. Her face, usually the picture of composure and allure, was now a canvas of worry.

"John," she breathed, her voice barely above a whisper, yet it sliced through the stillness, laden with a gravity that pulled at him with an almost physical force.

With a trembling hand, she reached out, her fingers brushing lightly against his forearm as if to reassure herself of his reality. She stepped aside, wordlessly beckoning him into the sanctuary—or perhaps the precipice—of her home. Crossing the threshold, John felt the subtle shift, as though the act of entering this space marked the crossing of an imperceptible line. The door closed behind them with a soft click, sealing away the world outside and enveloping them both in the uncertainty that lay ahead.

The hush of Jessica's living room wrapped around John like a shroud, the world outside her window muffled and distant. The only sound that dared to pierce the silence was the rhythmic ticking of an antique clock perched on the mantel, its hands marking time in merciless progression.

Jessica paced, her movements restless and jagged against the backdrop of stillness. She would occasionally glance at John, her emerald eyes flickering with silent questions and fears they both shared but couldn't voice. They existed in this moment as two islands adrift in a sea of tension, close enough to sense each other's turmoil, yet worlds apart in their isolation.

"Shall I—?" John began, his voice trailing off into nothingness, the offer to help hanging suspended between them.

Jessica only nodded, her lips pressed into a thin line. Her fingers fumbled with the box containing the test, her usual grace replaced by a clumsy urgency. John watched, feeling simultaneously intrusive and necessary, caught in an intimate dance where every step was fraught with consequence.

She turned on her heel, the hem of her dress swaying lightly, and disappeared into the bathroom, closing the door behind her with a soft click that seemed to echo in the cavernous quiet of the room. Left alone, John was suddenly acutely aware of the space she had vacated, the absence of her presence like a cold draught sweeping through him.

His gaze settled on the delicate trinkets that adorned her bookshelves. There was a tiny glass figurine of a dancer caught mid-pirouette, its form crystalline and perfect—a stark contrast to the chaos unfurling in their lives. Next to it stood a photo frame, the image within it a captured laugh from a time before he knew the weight of consequences, before their choices had led them here.

He ran a hand through his short brown hair, a gesture of frustration and helplessness that had become all too familiar. His thoughts churned with the possible futures that might be shaped within the confines of the bathroom—the walls now seeming to hold the power of judgment over everything he thought he knew about himself, about Jessica, about the life he'd so meticulously constructed.

John's eyes drifted to the window, where tendrils of sunlight clawed their way through the blinds, casting long, slanted shadows across the floor. Although the light was warm, it failed to dispel the chill that had deeply penetrated his bones. It was as if the very air around him was waiting, holding its breath for the verdict that would ripple through the fragile tapestry of their intertwined existences.

And there, amidst the opulence of Jessica's carefully curated sanctuary, John Hawthorne stood—a man teetering on the edge of an abyss, the threads of his reality fraying with each tick of the clock.

The door to the bathroom creaked open, and there stood Jessica, her silhouette framed by the dim light spilling from within. In her hand, the future oscillated between the stark white of the pregnancy test and the tremble of her fingers. John's breath caught in his throat as she approached, her footsteps muted against the plush carpet.

They sat together on the suede couch, shoulder to shoulder, yet miles apart in their own private turmoil. The air between them was electric with anticipation and dread, each second elongating into a lifetime. Outside, the world continued its indifferent spin, but within these walls, time seemed to have congealed— thick and suffocating.

Jessica's hand found John's, her grip both a plea for support and a lifeline to something tangible amidst the chaos. His fingers closed around hers, and their other hands clutched the harbinger of fate, an artefact that held power beyond its size.

The clock on the mantel ticked on, indifferent to the human drama unfolding beneath it. Sunlight danced lazily through the room, touching upon the fine China displayed in the cabinet, casting a golden glow over the half-drunk cups of tea, abandoned in their haste.

Finally, the appointed minutes passed, and they leaned toward the test as if drawn by an invisible force. They locked eyes for a brief, intense moment before turning their attention to the digital display that captured their collective breath.

"Negative," Jessica whispered, her voice a blend of disbelief and relief.

John felt the tension drain from his body, the tightness in his chest easing as he exhaled a sigh. The feeling was akin to receiving a reprieve from the gallows, a temporary suspension of their sentence.

Yet, as they sat there, the initial rush of relief began to fade, replaced by a sober reflection on the razor's edge upon which they balanced. The negative result did not erase the tangled web of their affair or the shadow it cast on their future—a future fraught with hidden dangers and silent accusations.

John's heart continued its erratic dance, the echo of its beats resonating in the quiet room as he and Jessica looked at each other, their shared relief palpable yet laced with a silent tension. The moment hovered between them, a delicate bubble of respite poised to explode at any moment, unleashing the myriad consequences of their relationship. His gaze lingered on her face, reading the complex tapestry of emotions that played across her features—a mirror to his own inner turmoil.

"Jess," he began, his voice barely above a whisper, as if afraid to shatter the delicate peace they had momentarily carved out from the chaos. "We... we need to talk about this."

The words fell into the space around them, heavy and laden with significance. She nodded, a small gesture fraught with an understanding that went beyond the syllables he had uttered. They moved to the living room, sinking onto the plush sofa that suddenly felt too stiff, too formal for such a conversation.

"John, I..." Her voice trailed off, betraying the confidence she usually wore like armour. He could see the strain behind her emerald eyes, the uncertainty that flashed within their depths.

"We can't ignore what happened," John said, his tone attempting steadiness. "This scare—it's been a wake-up call."

Jessica's hands clasped tightly in her lap, knuckles whitening. "I know. It's just—I've never felt this way before." Her admission hung between them, vulnerable and raw.

He reached out, his fingers brushing against hers, offering comfort and seeking it in return. Their relationship, built upon whispers and stolen moments, now faced the unyielding light of reality. The touch was electric, a reminder of the fire that had drawn them together, but now it also burnt with the knowledge of their recklessness.

"We have to be more careful," he murmured, the words feeling inadequate to describe the labyrinth of choices and potential pitfalls that lay ahead.

"Careful," she echoed, a bitter chuckle escaping her lips. "Is that all we can be?"

"Jess, we..." John's voice faltered, his easy going charm dissolving under the gravity of their situation. The humour that so often coloured his conversations felt out of place, a foreign language in this new context of whispered fears and unspoken promises.

"Let's just take this one day at a time," Jessica suggested, her usual assertiveness replaced by a tentative hope, a lifeline cast into uncertain waters.

They sat there, side by side, the ticking of the clock now a metronome to their thoughts—each tick a step further into the unknown, each tock a reminder of what they stood to lose. The afternoon sun dipped lower, shadows stretching across the floor like dark fingers ready to pull them under.

John watched Jessica's lips move, the cadence of her voice weaving a tapestry of vulnerability and undeniable strength. Each word was a silken thread, binding him to this room, to this moment of stark honesty that lay between them. Her emerald eyes shimmered with a sheen of unshed tears as she spoke of fear, of longing, and the precarious ledge upon which they now found themselves. He absorbed her every syllable, a symphony that stirred the depths of his soul, resonating with the silent war raging within him.

His life—a well-orchestrated sonnet of suburban predictability—clashed with the wild, uncharted melody that Jessica embodied. The decision he faced represented a significant shift, a leap from the familiar comforts of routine into the thrilling depths of the unknown. John's heart beat a rhythmic drumroll against his ribcage, each pulse humming with the electricity of their concealed connection. Yet, in the stillness of the room, he felt the gravity of consequence tethering him to reality.

As their conversation waned, the space around them seemed to contract, heavy with words left unsaid and futures untold. The tension hung like a thick fog, a silent witness to the complexity of emotions entwined within their exchange. A clock ticked somewhere in the distance, its steady rhythm mocking the chaos of John's thoughts.

Preparing to leave, John felt the weight of the day's revelations press down upon his shoulders, a mantle woven from threads of relief and regret. The atmosphere in the room crackled with the static of their lingering touch; the memory of their closeness was both a balm and a blade to his conflicted spirit. He stood, feeling the pull of his mundane world outside these walls, a siren call to the man he was expected to be, even as part of him yearned to stay, to dive headlong into the tempest that Jessica represented.

"Take care, Jess," he said, his voice a mere whisper, the echoes of their shared turmoil reflected back to him in her gaze. Their goodbye was a quiet collision of souls, a brief confluence of what was and what could never be. With a last look, he stepped over the threshold, leaving behind the cocoon of their secret space, carrying with him the haunting melody of their forbidden liaison, a song that would play on, muffled yet insistent, beneath the veneer of his everyday life.

John closed the door behind him, the click of the latch a crisp punctuation to the chapter they had just lived. His footsteps on Jessica's porch were soft, hesitant, as if each tread was an effort to distance himself from the chaos of emotions he left smouldering in the room behind him.

He descended the steps, the wood beneath his feet releasing faint groans, like whispers of the secrets they concealed. The scent of jasmine from a neighbour's garden wafted by, a fragrant reminder of moments too tender to touch yet too potent to ignore. It wrapped around him, a sensory shroud evoking images of Jessica's trembling hands, her eyes—a tempest of hope and despair—locked onto his. An undercurrent of what-ifs seemed to pulse through the world around him, a symphony of might-have-been played out in the rustle of leaves and the distant bark of a dog.

He walked, his stride infused with purpose, yet every step felt laden, as though he trod through the thick molasses of his own trepidation. He grappled with the duality of relief and longing, each battling for dominance in the quiet theatre of his mind.

John paused, the decision looming large before him, a spectre born from the intimacy he and Jessica shared, now a ghostly presence at his side. In his chest, his heart drummed a staccato beat, echoing the internal cacophony of choices that beckoned with seductive whispers.

With one last glance back at the house that held so much of him within its walls, he turned away, the taste of uncertainty bitter on his tongue. He walked home, his future an unwritten stanza in the poetry of his life.

Chapter 18: John's Confession

John stood at the threshold of the living room, a silent sentinel framed by the dying light that filtered through gauzy curtains. The steady throb of his heart was a drumbeat to the confession that lay heavy on his tongue, a bitter fruit that had ripened past due. Shadows played across the walls, mirroring the turmoil that twisted within him as he drew in a breath laden with the scent of beeswax polish and the distant aroma of garlic and basil wafting from the kitchen. There was a thickness to the air, an anticipatory pause that seemed to hold even time captive. He exhaled slowly, the decision cementing itself within him; there would be no retreat from this precipice.

"Sophie," his voice cut through the stillness, a singular note that held more weight than a whisper but less assurance than a shout. In the kitchen, the rhythmic chop-chop of a knife against the cutting board ceased abruptly, the silence that followed as jarring as a scream in the quiet of their suburban sanctuary.

Sophie turned, her figure haloed by the warm glow of under-cabinet lighting, her hands still poised to resume their task. Her blue eyes found John's, and in them, he saw the flicker of unease stir to life. She was attuned to the nuances of his tone, the uncharacteristic gravity that pulled at the corners of his words like a shroud. A crease formed between her brows—not yet the furrow of betrayal, but the prelude to a symphony of emotions he was about to conduct.

"Is everything alright?" she asked, her voice a melodic contrast to the disquiet that hummed beneath the surface of their conversation. She wiped her hands on a towel, leaving streaks of moisture that darkened the fabric, as if foreshadowing the tears that might soon follow.

John's feet felt rooted to the hardwood floor, a forest of doubt thickening around him. He opened his mouth, the aperture a gateway for the truth he had harboured, but the words clung to his tongue like reluctant leaves on an autumnal tree. His voice trembled, an unsteady vibration that betrayed the internal tempest he could no longer quell.

"Something has happened," he managed to say, each syllable a battle won against the silence. The words hung in the air, heavy with the gravity of their meaning, yet they lacked the precision of confession; they were the brushstrokes of a larger, darker painting yet to be revealed.

Sophie's arms wrapped protectively across her chest, a subconscious fortress erected against the unknown. Her eyes, pools of analytical thought, searched John's face for clues, the furrow deepening upon her brow as she pieced together the fragmented implications of his hesitant speech.

"John, you're scaring me," she said, her voice laced with concern that spiralled into fear. The questioning tilt of her head and the slight narrowing of her gaze were manifestations of her mind racing to outrun the possibilities. Every pause between John's words was a chasm into which her imagination plunged, conjuring spectres of disaster.

He swallowed hard, the guilt and remorse constricting his throat like a vice. "I need to tell you something important," John continued, his voice barely more than a whisper now, as if volume could somehow lessen the impact of his revelation. The shadows cast by the setting sun stretched across the room, entwining with the tension that filled the space between them.

In the kitchen, the scent of simmering herbs and spices became an ironic backdrop to the bitterness welling up inside him. How could he disrupt the sanctuary they had built with a confession so sordid? However, the truth echoed loudly in his heart, compelling him to confront the sin that threatened to silence him.

Sophie's hand reached out, as if to grasp some tangible evidence of his words, before retreating to the sanctuary of her crossed arms. The security of their shared history seemed to shudder on its foundation, awaiting the full force of John's admission. Her lips parted in preparation for a question, yet it remained unspoken, hovering on the brink of understanding and dread.

John's confession spilled out, a stark contrast to the soft hum of the refrigerator and the gentle clink of dishware in Sophie's hands. "I've been unfaithful," he murmured, his voice fracturing under the weight of his transgression.

Sophie's body went still. The knife she had been using to chop vegetables lay forgotten beside a half-sliced tomato, its vibrant red a jarring splash of colour against the sterile white of the cutting board. A sharp intake of breath filled the void, her chest rising and falling with the sudden shock of his words. In that moment, the air seemed to thicken, silence wrapping around them like a shroud, suffocating and impenetrable.

The kitchen, once filled with the comforting aromas of cooking, now felt like an alien landscape as Sophie turned to face her husband. A storm of emotions clouded her blue eyes, usually so clear and composed, with disbelief etching lines of confusion across her forehead.

"John," she whispered, her voice splintering as if the single syllable carried the entirety of her pain. "How long?"

That question hung between them, heavy with implications yet naked in its simplicity. It was a query that sought not just the span of time but the breadth of betrayal, a measure of distance between heartbeats where trust had faltered and love had stumbled into the shadows.

John, who was always tall and exuded an effortless charm, appeared to diminish before her gaze, his shoulders bowing inward as if bracing against a powerful wind of judgment. His mouth opened, then closed—no immediate answer forthcoming, only the palpable pulsing of a broken vow reverberating through the room.

John's voice, once a soothing baritone that filled their home with laughter and warmth, now trembled like a leaf caught in an unforgiving breeze. "Sophie," he began, his words laced with a remorse so palpable it seemed to seep into the walls, "it started as nothing... just conversations, but..." The confession stumbled from his lips, fragmented and raw, each syllable a testament to his internal war.

The shame was evident, shadowing his usually bright eyes, turning them into darkened pools of regret. He reached out, not to touch, but to find the right words, suspended between them. "I love you, Soph. I always have. But with Jessica, there's this passion—an intensity I can't explain. It's like I'm lost to it." His admission hung heavy, a shroud of sorrow draping over the remnants of their shared dreams.

Sophie's back stiffened, her muscles coiling as if preparing to strike. She paced the length of the kitchen, her every step a silent drumbeat echoing her escalating fury. Her fists clenched at her sides, knuckles whitening—a physical manifestation of her heart being squeezed by betrayal.

"Passion? Intensity?" Her voice echoed, sharpening like a knife's blade, cutting through the dense tension. "And what of loyalty, John? Of integrity?" Sophie halted her pacing, turning to him with a glare that could shatter glass. "You wear your charm like armour, but beneath it, you're just...chaos."

The very air seemed to vibrate with the force of her anger, charged particles colliding in the fading light of their love. She stood rooted, a pillar amidst the storm of emotions threatening to tear down the life they had meticulously built together.

Sophie's anger, once a furious inferno, began to ebb away, leaving behind glowing embers of heartache. Her breaths, drawn through the jagged shards of their fractured life together, came slower and sharper in the quiet aftermath. Her hands unclenched, no longer weapons of wrath but trembling testimonies of vulnerability.

John watched, his own heart a leaden weight in his chest, as tears welled in Sophie's eyes. They brimmed, lingered, and then spilt over, tracing paths down her cheeks like rivers reshaping a barren landscape. The depth of his betrayal was mirrored in those silent tears, and the pain of shattered trust was etched deep into her elegant features.

"Leave," she whispered first, the word barely a ripple in the charged atmosphere. Then, louder, "Leave, John!" Now, her command cut through the thick air, slicing what remained of their brittle connection. The finality of it resonated with the determination that had always underpinned her voice, even now as it trembled with the strain of suppressed sobs.

The tension in the room spiralled, tangling around them like ivy, tightening with each second that passed. It clung to the walls, draped over the sparse furniture—a tapestry of unresolved emotions, heavy and suffocating.

There they stood, two silhouettes cast by the dying light that filtered through the gauzy curtains, caught in a tableau of desolation. The setting sun threw shadows across Sophie's face, painting her anguish in hues of orange and red, as if even the day mourned the end of their union.

John felt the wordless plea rise in his throat, an instinctive urge to bridge the chasm that had opened between them. But the silence spoke louder than any apology could, and he swallowed the futile gesture back down into the hollow space where his resolve used to be.

John silently walked upstairs to their bedroom. His hand hovered over the brass handle of their shared closet, an emblem of a life built side by side. As he opened it, the scent of Sophie's perfume wafted out like a ghost of intimacy past, wrapping around him in a cruel reminder of what was slipping through his fingers.

With each garment he selected—a neatly folded sweater, the tie she'd given him last Christmas—his movements grew more hesitant, as if the very fibres were woven with memories. The soft textures whispered against his skin, echoes of times when clothing had been discarded in the throes of passion rather than packed away in the sombre silence of departure.

His hands trembled slightly as they brushed over the sleeve of her favourite shirt, one she often wore on their lazy Sunday mornings at home. John let his fingers linger, tracing the delicate buttons, each one a testament to the domestic tranquillity that now felt like a mirage.

As he laid his choices on the bed, a canvas of regret, his mind swirled with introspection. The bag lay open, a gaping maw ready to swallow the remnants of his life with Sophie. He recognised the sharp pangs of loss cutting through him, a clear signal that the fabric of their relationship was tearing, irreparable, after his betrayal.

He sat on the edge of the bed, the mattress dipping under the weight of his burdened frame. In the quiet, John could hear the echo of laughter that once filled the room, now replaced by the heavy breaths of his own remorse. The walls appeared to enclose him, adorned with images of smiles and embraces, each one piercing his heart.

"Is this what I wanted?" he murmured into the void that answered with oppressive silence. He grappled with the paradox of his desires, the yearning for something undefined that had driven him into another's arms, versus the profound love he held for Sophie. The contrast cut through him, a schism too wide to mend.

The realisation settled upon him with the weight of a verdict; he had wounded the one person who had stood steadfastly by his side. The understanding was complete and shattering, fracturing the illusion of contentment he'd so carefully curated.

In the waning light, the shadows danced across the room, playing out scenes of a past untainted by transgression. John's eyes followed the shifting patterns, seeing in them the intricate plotting of his mistakes, the slow-burn tension that had simmered beneath the surface of their lives, now ignited into an inferno that consumed all it touched.

Finally, he zipped the bag closed, an act that seemed to seal his fate. With the soft click of interlocking teeth, the chapter of John and Sophie, woven together by love and daily ritual, was coming to its close. Hefting the weight of his choices upon his shoulder, he stood, a man ensnared by the consequences of his own making, about to step into the pervasive sense of intrigue that was his uncertain future.

John re-entered the living room, the air thick with tension as he clutched his duffel bag—a physical manifestation of his inner turmoil. The dimming evening light filtered through the curtains, casting elongated shadows that seemed to play out the silent drama unfolding between him and Sophie. A muffled stillness hung over them, a charged silence punctuated only by the subtlest of sounds: the distant hum of traffic, the ticking of the grandfather clock, the furtive breaths that escaped their lips, betraying the storm of emotions swirling within.

Sophie stood rooted to the spot where John had left her, her posture rigid yet fragile, as if the slightest touch could shatter her composure. Her arms were no longer crossed defensively; they hung limply by her side, mirroring her sudden resignation. John hesitated, the weight of his packed bag pulling at his shoulder like an anchor, tugging him toward the precipice of a future devoid of her.

Time seemed to compress as he made his final steps toward the door, extending the moment into an eternity. With each footfall, memories seeped from the walls—their shared laughter, whispered confessions, moments of tender vulnerability—each one a ghostly spectre of what they had built together, now crumbling into dust.

John's gaze lifted, meeting Sophie's for one long, aching instance. Her face was a canvas of raw emotion; tear tracks glistened on her cheeks, her blue eyes awash with a tempest of betrayal and sorrow. The sight cleaved through him sharper than any spoken reproach. It was as if he could see the fragmented pieces of her trust, once whole and unyielding, now scattered irretrievably across the hardwood floor.

In that glance, a silent apology passed from him, a futile attempt to bridge the chasm his actions had wrought. His lips parted, but no words came forth—they would be but hollow echoes in the vast emptiness between them. There was a palpable finality in the way she looked back at him—a resigned knowledge that this was the end of their story.

The latch clicked, a sound so mundane yet laden with significance, as John pulled the door open. He paused on the threshold, casting one last look over his shoulder. Sophie remained motionless, a figure of stoic grace amidst the chaos of her heartache, a poignant reminder of all he had forsaken.

The door thudded shut, the sound reverberating through the empty spaces of the house like a solemn drum heralding the end of an era. The vibration of the wood meeting frame seemed to carry with it the weight of all that had been said and left unsaid, resonating in the stillness with a haunting finality.

John stood outside, enveloped by the night's cool breath, the scent of jasmine from Sophie's garden mingling with the crisp air, a cruel reminder of the domestic haven he had shattered. Shadows clung to him, wrapping around his shoulders like a shroud, as the faint glow from the living room window cut a stark contrast against the encroaching darkness.

Inside, the silence felt alive, a tangible presence that settled over the house, oppressive and thick. The silence clung to the walls, seeping into the crevices of the life they had built together—a life now irreparably fractured. The echo of the closing door lingered, a ghostly whisper that spoke of irreversible choices and the harrowing void they leave behind.

Sophie's breath hitched in the quiet aftermath, her blue eyes reflecting the tumultuous storm of emotions that raged within, casting shadows across the contours of her face. She remained where John had left her, rooted to the spot by the gravity of betrayal, her heart splintering silently in the absence of her husband's retreating footsteps.

The uncertainty of their future hung palpable and dense, a fog that clouded both heart and mind. For Sophie, the path forward was obscured by the mist of tears and the ache of wounded love, while for John, the road ahead lay shrouded in regret, each step away from the life he knew a descent into the unknown.

With the door now separating them, the barriers were not just physical but emotional, a chasm that stretched wide and deep, filled with the debris of broken vows and the chill of lost warmth. As the night wrapped itself around him, John's internal turmoil mirrored the chaos of the darkened skies above, the stars veiled by the same sombre cloak that enshrouded his spirit.

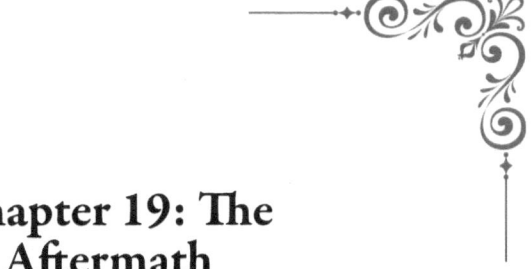

Chapter 19: The Aftermath

-Six Months Later-

John Hawthorne lingered in the threshold of his new apartment, the scent of fresh paint and old wood lingering in the still air like ghosts of a life not yet begun. His gaze drifted over the sea of cardboard boxes, each one stamped with cryptic scribbles of marker that promised a misplaced fragment of his former existence. The room hummed with an emptiness that echoed the hollow feeling resonating within his chest—a stark contrast to the vibrant home he had woven together with his wife, now unravelled by silence and space.

The walls, barren and indifferent, rose around him, a gallery of blank canvases that refused to whisper the secrets of previous occupants. The sparsity of furnishings—a couch still stiff with unfamiliarity, a lamp casting a cold glow—accentuated the starkness of his new reality. He stood rooted, a man unmoored, adrift between the remnants of a life once lived and the uncertainty of one that lay ahead.

Reluctance tugged at his limbs as he navigated through the quiet chaos, ultimately resting on the edge of a bed that had not yet experienced the weight of his dreams. The mattress creaked softly beneath him, a testament to its newness and his own discomfort. In his hand, John cradled his phone, an artefact of connection in a world where he felt increasingly disconnected. His thumb hovered over Jessica's number, a sequence of digits that held the potential for solace or further upheaval.

The dim light from the window painted shadows across his features, revealing the contours of conflict etched into his brow. Hesitation danced with desire in his eyes, the need to hear her voice warring against the fear of what it might awaken. His heart oscillated between hope and trepidation, each pulse echoing in the quiet room.

John exhaled slowly, the breath leaving his lips laden with the weight of decisions yet made. He could almost feel the warmth of Jessica's enigmatic presence at the other end of the line, her voice a siren call luring him toward the rocks of forbidden emotion.

With a resolve that trembled like a leaf in the wind, John summoned the courage to bridge the distance between solitude and possibility. His finger pressed down, and the phone came to life, its ring cutting through the quietude of the apartment like the first drop of rain upon a drought-stricken land. As he waited for her answer, every second stretched into eternity, charged with the electricity of anticipation and the gravity of choices yet to unfold.

"Hello?" Jessica's voice, a velvet ribbon in the static air, wound through the line.

"Jessica, it's John." His words stumbled into the phone, each syllable taut with the strain of emotions held back like floodwaters behind a fragile dam. The silence that followed was thick, charged with the current of their shared history and the weight of words unsaid.

"John," her warmth radiated through the receiver, a sunbeam on his storm-grey mood. "It's been a while."

"Indeed," he said, a laugh attempting to disguise the tremor in his voice. "I just wanted to hear your voice."

"Is everything alright?" Her question, genuine and tinged with concern, seemed to reach through the phone and press gently against his chest.

"Everything's... in transition," he replied, vagueness wrapping around his heart like a shroud. The tension-laden pause that followed was too fragile to cross.

"John..." she began, her initial warmth retreating into the shadows of hesitation. "We need to be careful."

"Of course," he agreed, the word a stone sinking fast through the depths of their delicate rapport.

The conversation dwindled, a dance of avoidance against the backdrop of their unspoken yearning. As they bid their goodbyes, the click of disconnection echoed the closing of a door, leaving John to face the silence alone once more.

As John stepped outside, he entered the embrace of the evening, the neighbourhood surrounding him heaving in the twilight. The air, thick with the scent of jasmine and approaching rain, clung to his skin as he wandered aimlessly along the sidewalk.

Derek Thompson stood there, his presence as enduring as the oak tree's long shadows across his lawn. Despite his casual stance against the white picket fence, his eyes pierced John's with an intensity that defied his casual demeanour.

"Evening, John," Derek called out, his voice lilting with a neighbourly inflection that couldn't quite mask its probing nature.

"Good evening, Derek," John replied, forcing a smile to his lips as he approached. The older man's gaze felt like a spotlight upon John's private stage, where the drama of discretion played its silent act.

"Nice night for a stroll," Derek observed, his words fishing for something below the surface, hungry for a nibble of gossip.

"Sure is," John agreed, his reply noncommittal, a deft sidestep from the snare of prying questions. The light from Derek's porch flickered, casting both men in a dance of alternating shadow and revelation as the evening grew bolder in its descent.

"Interesting lady," Derek mused aloud, his words hanging in the air like ripe fruit, tempting but untouchable.

"Isn't everyone around here?" John countered with a wry chuckle, deflecting with humour as he always did.

"Suppose you're right," Derek agreed.

John excused himself, continuing down the path as the afterglow of sunset faded to dusk. With each step, the whispers of the neighbourhood seemed to recede, leaving him alone with the night's embrace, a companion as enigmatic as the conversations left trailing in his wake.

The evening's cool breath whispered against John's neck as he continued his walk, the unsettling cadence of Derek Thompson's probing behind him. The air was a perfume of wilting jasmine and impending rain, a stark contrast to the sterile scent lingering in his new apartment. He walked with the unsettled energy of a man who could feel the eyes of the neighbourhood on him, alight with speculation.

John's relief at reaching the safety of Maggie Wilson's home was palpable, the warm glow from her windows offering a temporary sanctuary. Maggie's house always seemed to hum with a life of its own, the walls steeped in solace and secrets. Tonight, though, as he stepped through the threshold, the atmosphere held a tang of citrus and silent scrutiny.

"John!" Maggie's greeting was a beacon amidst the storm of sideways glances. Her smile was genuine, but it didn't quite reach her eyes, which held a shimmer of something akin to sorrow or maybe betrayal.

"Hey, Maggie," he managed, his voice rough like gravel underfoot. "Thanks for having me over."

"Always," she assured, guiding him into the fold with a touch that was both tender and telling. The room swelled with the murmur of conversations pausing as he passed, whispers cloaked in clinking glasses, and forced laughter.

"Can we talk?" Maggie asked, her voice laced with the honey and sting of candied lemon peel. She led him to the seclusion of her plant-laden sunroom, where the ambiance was thick with humidity and unspoken words.

"Everyone's worried about you," she began, her tone a careful blend of concern and reproach. "This thing with Jessica—it's not like you, John."

"Maybe I'm not who everyone thinks I am," John retorted, the smile he wore brittle as autumn leaves. His humour was a shield, thinning with each gentle thrust of Maggie's honesty.

"Or maybe you're exactly who you've always been—just... lost right now." Maggie's hand rested lightly on his arm, a grounding force amid the chaos.

"Perhaps," he conceded, his gaze skirting past her to the verdant tendrils of ivy pressing against the glass, yearning for escape. Shadows danced between them as the evening sighed into night, leaving John ensnared in a web of his own making, Maggie's disappointment a silent spectre in the space they shared.

The hush of the sunroom wrapped around them like a shroud, Maggie's words weaving through the stillness with a tenderness that belied their piercing intent. "John, your heart's tangled in a thicket," she murmured, her gaze soft yet searching, "and it's hurting those who care for you."

A wry smile flickered across John's lips, the humour not quite reaching his eyes. "Isn't life just one big bramble patch?" He quipped, the levity a flimsy barrier against the weight of her concern.

Maggie sighed, the sound as mournful as the wind whispering through autumn leaves outside. "Don't make light of this. We're here for you, but you need to face what you've done."

"Facing things head-on was never my forte," John admitted, his voice threaded with a rueful honesty. The silence stretched between them, filled with a tension that was as palpable as the humidity clinging to the air.

———— ❦ ————

The next day at his desk, John sat adrift in a sea of paperwork, the rhythmic tapping of keyboards from adjacent cubicles a mocking reminder of productivity. He glanced at the screen before him, its contents blurring into indecipherable glyphs that taunted his lack of focus. A sigh escaped him, ruffling the neat stack of reports he had yet to touch.

His distracted gaze wandered to the window, where the city sprawled beneath a sky tinged with the promise of dusk. The fading light cast long shadows across his hands— hands that seemed disconnected from the man who once wielded them with confidence and purpose.

Another sigh, deeper this time, betrayed his internal disarray. Each breath felt like an admission of defeat, each exhalation a further unspooling of the tightly wound persona he had cultivated for so long. The office buzzed with the undercurrents of ambition and success, yet John sat marooned at his island of desolation, surrounded by reminders of a life that seemed increasingly alien to him.

Colleagues passed by with fleeting glances, their expressions a blend of curiosity and unease as they observed the once-impeccable John Hawthorne reduced to a figure of abstracted despondency. The whispers that followed felt like tendrils of fog, curling around him with cold insinuation.

As the day waned, the shadows deepened, mirroring the murky thoughts that clouded his mind. John Hawthorne, the man who once moved with easy charm and certainty, now sat paralysed by the intricate webs of choices spun from his own desires—a man haunted by the spectres of what could have been and what was spiralling beyond his control.

The office's fluorescent lights hummed a dull requiem for the day as John Hawthorne slipped his phone into his pocket, its screen dark and still. He stood, shrugging on his jacket with the mechanical movements of a man whose thoughts were miles away from the emptying cubicles and the soft clack of keyboards yielding to silence.

He walked in the dusky street with a sense of purpose, each step echoing a routine that had lost its meaning. The evening air was crisp, laced with the scent of rain yet to fall, and it filled his lungs with a chill that seemed to seep into his very bones.

He found himself outside a bar, its sign a muted beacon in the twilight. The door opened with a jangle of bells, ushering him into a realm of dimly lit refuge. Here, the world seemed to exist in half-tones and whispers. Amber light pooled on worn wooden tables while shadows played at the edges, offering anonymity like a cloak. John claimed a corner seat, a silent spectator to the low murmur of conversations and the clink of glassware.

It was in this subdued haven that Michael Archer materialised, his arrival marked by the subtle shift in energy, like the prelude to a storm. He approached John's table with measured steps, the picture of refined composure. His dark hair was touched with silver, each strand seemingly in perfect agreement with its place in the world.

"John," Michael greeted, his voice smooth—a velvet ribbon unfurling in the hushed atmosphere. "Mind if I join you?"

"Michael," John replied, masking surprise with a casual nod, gesturing to the empty chair opposite him. His voice exuded a practiced ease, yet beneath it, a taut wire of tension pulsed with the currents of unspoken history.

"Long day?" Michael asked, the corners of his eyes crinkling slightly as he settled into his seat, a well-tailored suit hugging his frame like a second skin.

"Something like that," John said, his words skating over the surface of truths he wasn't ready to dive into. He took a sip of his drink, relishing the burn as it travelled down his throat—a fleeting distraction from the weight pressing on his chest.

"Sometimes I find these places have a way of making all that fade... if only for a little while," Michael observed, motioning to the bartender with a familiarity that bespoke many such visits.

"Perhaps," John murmured, glancing around the bar, where shadows danced with secrets of their own. He felt the gaze of his companion, probing yet not intrusive, a dance of conversational foreplay that promised more than idle chatter.

Their exchange continued, a delicate balance of pleasantries woven with an undercurrent of something darker, something that neither man was willing to voice just yet. In the pregnant pauses and exchanged glances, there was a recognition of the game they were playing—one of evasion and revelation, each waiting for the other to show his hand.

The clink of ice against glass punctuated the stillness, a gentle chime that seemed to echo through the dimly lit space. John watched droplets race down the side of his tumbler, each a silent testament to the passage of time. Across from him sat Michael Archer, who nursed a neat whisky with a contemplative air. The bar's ambient jazz infused their silence with a smoky cadence, a backdrop to the unfolding drama.

"Jessica Sterling," Michael began, the name rolling off his tongue with a precision that felt both calculated and casual. "She's quite the enigma, isn't she?" His question hung between them, a lure cast into murky waters.

John's fingers tightened around his glass, the chill seeping into his bones. "That's one way to put it," he replied, his voice betraying none of the maelstrom brewing within.

"Affairs are curious things," Michael continued, locking eyes with John in a gaze that seemed to strip away pretence. "They start as a spark, a whisper of 'what if', but they tend to burn hotter and faster than we anticipate."

John felt the words coil around him, tightening with an uncomfortable truth. He swallowed, the liquor no longer offering the solace it had minutes prior. "And usually end in ashes," he added, the taste of regret bitter on his tongue.

"Exactly." Michael's nod was slow, deliberate. "They're cyclical, you see—intoxicating descent, exhilarating secret worlds, until reality comes crashing back. And it always does. The aftermath is..." He trailed off, allowing the weight of unspoken consequences to settle in the air.

A visceral understanding began to press against John's ribs, the realization of his own cycle—a relentless pursuit of something just beyond reach, a mirage of fulfillment that now left him parched in its wake.

"Nobody escapes unscathed," Michael murmured, almost to himself, as though he were recalling a distant memory rather than discussing a present dilemma. "Not the ones who stray, nor those they return to."

The words wrapped around John, a shroud woven of truths he'd tried to ignore. Jessica's siren call that led him astray, the allure of her confidence, her mystery—it all seemed so hollow now. The pain of betrayal, the jagged edge of guilt; they were his companions in the night, flickering shadows cast by the fire he'd stoked.

Michael's presence, both unsettling and oddly comforting, served as a mirror reflecting a future John had yet to acknowledge. The man before him, a mentor in many ways, now offered a sombre lesson not found in any boardroom or strategy meeting.

"Think carefully about your next move, John," Michael said, the finality in his tone suggesting the close of a chapter rather than offering advice. "This game has higher stakes than you're accustomed to."

John nodded, and the silence enveloped them once more. In the dim light of the bar, surrounded by the scent of aged wood and lingering whispers of other patrons' secrets, he understood the gravity of his choices—each one a step in a dance that promised no clear end, only the certainty of its toll.

John sat motionless, the last syllables of Michael's cautionary counsel reverberating in the close air of the bar. A single ice cube clinked against the glass in his hand, a poignant reminder of the passage of time and a metaphor for the gradual erosion of his once steadfast certainties. The murmur of conversations around him dwindled into obscurity as he grappled with the labyrinthine path that lay ahead. His thoughts resembled a turbulent ocean, with each wave crashing into the next, leaving behind a trail of foam-flecked confusion.

He glimpsed his reflection in the polished surface of the tabletop—a spectral version of himself, distorted and dimmed by the patina of countless others who had come before, seeking solace or absolution in amber liquid and hushed tones. Michael's words, potent and piercing, cut through the fog of John's indecision, insisting he acknowledge the shards of lives he had splintered—his own included.

The bartender began to lower lights, signalling an end to the refuge of darkness. With a sigh that seemed to carry the weight of his world, John pushed away from the table, his movements heavy with unspoken regret. The chair legs scraped softly against the wooden floor, a subdued farewell to the sanctuary of shadows.

Stepping out into the night, the chill air embraced him like an unwelcome confidant, whispering truths he was reluctant to hear. The street lay barren, the glow of streetlamps casting long, spectral fingers across his path. He wrapped his coat tighter around himself, warding off more than just the evening's cold embrace—the biting breeze felt like the collective exhalation of every mistake that trailed behind him.

As he walked, his footsteps echoed against the pavement, the rhythmic tap-tap-tapping of a metronome ticking away the moments of solitude. The familiar houses loomed on either side, their windows dark and secrets held tight within walls that might once have whispered of comfort but now murmured of judgement and lost chances.

The ambient light from the bar's windows faded with each step, leaving John enshrouded in the penumbra of the nocturnal world. The subtle scent of dying leaves mingled with the earthy dampness of the night, carrying with it the pungent reminder of life's cyclic decay and renewal. It was in this solitary trek that John found himself truly alone, not just in company but in the daunting expanse of his soul—a man disjoined from the tapestry of connections that once defined him.

With each block traversed, the bitter sweetness of introspection settled deeper into his bones, a constant companion alongside the spectre of his crumbling personal life. For a brief moment, he stood motionless, his silhouette contrasting with the apathy of the cityscape, a man at the nexus of his personal story, with the stars serving as silent witnesses to the turmoil within.

Chapter 20: Therapy and Self-Reflection

John Hawthorne sat rigid in the plush chair, the muted tones of the therapist's office wrapping around him like a cocoon he couldn't escape. His fingers drummed an erratic rhythm against the supple leather armrest, betraying his attempt at composure. The room was still, save for the soft hum of the air conditioner and the faint scent of lavender that did little to soothe his fraying nerves.

The walls, adorned with abstract paintings, seemed to close in on him, their colours swirling in his peripheral vision as if mocking his internal chaos. He avoided the therapist's gaze, his eyes flitting from the diplomas lining the wall to the elegantly potted Ficus in the corner. Each glance was a silent plea for something, anything, to distract him from the impending confession.

"John," came the gentle prompt, a voice both calm and disarming slicing through the tension. The therapist's tone was the auditory equivalent of a warm blanket, offering comfort yet smothering him with its weight. "Whenever you're ready, I'm here to listen."

A knot tightened in John's chest, the secrets he harboured pressing down like lead upon his lungs. He shifted in his seat, the fabric whispering against his chinos in quiet reproach. It wasn't just the telling that petrified him—it was the unravelling of the carefully constructed facade, the threat of exposing the yearning that gnawed at his soul.

"Sometimes," John began, his voice barely above a whisper, "I feel like I'm living someone else's life." The words hung heavy in the air, each syllable laden with the restlessness that shadowed him. They were the first drops of rain in a long-overdue storm, the beginning of his own undoing.

John's fingers ceased their nervous dance along the leather armrest, steadying as though anchoring him to the present. "I've been feeling...trapped," he admitted, his voice trembling like the first tentative leaf in a tempest. The word felt unfamiliar on his tongue, yet it was incredibly precise, like an arrow pinpointing its target with unnerving accuracy.

With each subsequent breath, the trembling in his voice subsided, as if the truth he spoke fortified him internally. "It's as if I'm walking through a fog, seeing the outline of my life but never grasping it." John's analytical mind sought refuge in logic, dissecting his emotions as one would a complex puzzle, arranging and rearranging the pieces in search of a fit that eluded him. Yet beneath the veneer of composed reasoning, a storm brewed—a chaotic maelstrom of desire and discontent that defied order or explanation.

The room blurred before John's eyes as a memory surged forward, unbidden but vivid as lightning against a night sky. He was back in the warmth of a summer evening that smelt of jasmine and whispered promises. The sun had dipped below the horizon, painting the sky in hues of fiery orange and dusky rose, the fading light casting long shadows on the path where he walked.

Jessica Sterling appeared as if conjured by his deepest yearnings, materialising from the twilight with a grace that left his heart stuttering. Her chestnut hair unfurled in the gentle breeze, each strand catching the last kiss of sunlight, transforming her into a siren born of the golden hour. The air around her vibrated with a subtle energy, an electric current that beckoned him closer with every pulse.

"Hey, neighbour," she greeted him, her voice a melody that played upon the strings of his restraint. Her emerald eyes locked onto his, gleaming with secrets and silent laughter—a challenge and an invitation all at once.

"Jessica," he replied, the name rolling off his tongue, tasting of sweet danger and the lure of the unknown. The world seemed to tilt on its axis, bringing them into an orbit defined by the magnetic pull between them.

She laughed, a sound that trickled down his spine, awakening a dormant hunger for adventure, for the thrill of the illicit. It was a laugh that hinted at shared confidence and unspoken desires. There, in the waning light, Jessica offered a glimpse of a life less ordinary—a promise wrapped in the soft curves of her sundress, which clung to her body like a second skin.

John remembered the way his gaze traced the silhouette of her figure, each curve a siren's call, each movement a tether drawing him irrevocably into her world. The subtlety of her perfume—a blend of vanilla and wildflowers—wrapped around him, a sensory shroud that dulled the edges of his reality.

In that pivotal moment, beneath the stars that blinked lazily above, the restlessness that gnawed at John's core found its mirror in Jessica's allure. The dissatisfaction that shadowed his days morphed into an intoxicating thrill that coursed through his veins, promising respite from the persistent monotony of his existence.

"Care to walk with me?" she asked, her lips curving in a smile that held both innocence and knowing. It was an offer laced with temptation, a single question that upended the careful architecture of John's life.

As the memory receded, leaving behind the sterile calm of the therapist's office, John exhaled slowly, the confession spilling from him not as an admission but as an acquiescence to the tangled web of his own making. He could still taste the phantom sweetness of that summer air; he could feel the ghost of that yearning that had led him astray.

The silence in the therapist's office clung to John like a shroud, a stark counterpoint to the cacophony of his racing thoughts. He gazed at the innocent pattern on the rug, tracing its intricate patterns as if they could guide him out of the maze of his emotions. The once vivid images of Jessica had faded, leaving behind the dull ache of emptiness that gnawed at his insides. A sense of hollowness echoed through his chest, reverberating with the truth he could no longer deny: his affair was nothing more than a misguided quest to fill the void within himself—an abyss carved by unmet desires and unacknowledged dreams.

Later, as John sat in the couples counselling session, the room seemed compressed by the weight of unspoken words. The air was thick with tension, an invisible fog that made it difficult to breathe. Sophie's silhouette was rigid against the backdrop of the nondescript office, her posture betraying a fortress of self-control. Her eyes, two cerulean pools reflecting a stormy sky, held a tumultuous blend of hurt fiercely battling with resolve. She exuded a quiet strength, yet her hands, folded neatly on her lap, betrayed a slight tremor—a subtle testament to the chaos swirling beneath her calm exterior.

John felt the fissures in his heart widen with each silent heartbeat, aware that the woman he loved, the woman he had wounded, was a mere arm's length away yet miles apart. In that fraught space between them, he grappled with his own contradictions—the yearning for connection battling the fear of exposure, the desire for adventure locked in combat with the need for security. The man who had laughed so easily, who had charmed his way through life, now found himself disarmed by the gravity of his choices.

The clock on the wall ticked away the seconds, each one a sombre reminder that time, indifferent to its turmoil, marched relentlessly forward. John knew that beyond this room, beyond this painful crucible of honesty, lay the possibility of redemption or the finality of loss. As he stood on the brink of everything, he realized that healing required not only facing his demons but also facing the intimacy he had so desperately avoided.

The counsellor's soft voice sliced through the heavy silence, "Sophie, would you like to begin?" Her nod was almost imperceptible as she inhaled a controlled breath.

"John," Sophie's voice emerged, the single syllable holding a galaxy of hurt within its confines. "I believe in us, or I did. But that trust... it's shattered now." She measured each word, trying to control the floodwaters behind her eyes. Her hands, hidden from John's direct view, clenched into fists beneath the table, white-knuckled anchors in a sea of tumultuous emotions.

She paused, gathering the fragments of her composure. "What we built together," she continued, her voice steadier but still resonating with the tremor of betrayal, "felt sacred. And you stepped outside of it, as if it were nothing." The air around them grew dense, heavy with the weight of unspoken words and the shadow of infidelity that loomed over their marriage.

John swallowed hard, feeling the constriction of his own throat as he bore witness to her pain—a pain he had authored. "Sophie, I'm so sorry," his voice cracked under the burden of regret. It was a frail thing, his apology, fluttering in the vast space between intention and action. He hesitated, then plunged onwards, driven by the need to make her understand. "I got lost," he confessed, his tone laced with a raw vulnerability that felt foreign on his tongue. "I was chasing something, some elusive depth I convinced myself was missing."

His gaze, which had danced around the room like a cornered animal, now fixed upon her. "But I realize now, the void I thought existed out there," he gestured vaguely, encompassing the outside world, "was really within me. I've been afraid—terrified, actually—of diving in too deep, of what true intimacy could mean." His confession hung in the air, thick with the scent of vulnerability and the bitter tang of honesty, as enigmatic as the man who uttered it.

The counsellor observed them both, allowing the words and silences alike to occupy the room, each one potent with the possibility of healing or further heartbreak. John and Sophie sat, two souls adrift in the aftermath of a storm, surrounded by the remnants of their fractured serenity.

Sophie's gaze lingered on John, a silent sentinel amidst the chaos of his confessions. As if through a haze, she watched the man who had shared her bed and life, now stripped bare of pretences. His words, raw and unrefined, seeped into the room's stillness, each one laden with the gravity of their shattered trust. Her blue eyes, once icy with hurt, softened like the thawing of a long winter's frost, revealing a glimmer of the warmth that had guided her heart before the tempest.

Sophie's fingers, once clenched in silent protest against the pain, now relaxed upon her lap, a delicate surrender to the weight of his remorse. The air between them quivered, charged with the electric tension of wounded hearts tentatively reaching across the void. A cautious willingness flickered within her, a faint light at the end of a tunnel marred by betrayal. Despite the sting of his indiscretions, she found herself contemplating the fragile potential of mending what had been torn apart.

The counsellor, a quiet spectator to this intimate dance of confession and consideration, leaned forward. Her voice, a soothing balm, broke the spell, "John, Sophie, I understand this is immensely difficult. But it's important to remember that healing begins with openness. Share your feelings; let them breathe."

Her empathetic tone wove through the thick atmosphere, inviting honesty to shed its fears. She fostered a safe harbour for their troubles, her office a sanctuary where the tempests of emotion could rage without judgement. The counsellor's words were like a gentle hand guiding them back to a path obscured by shadows, urging them toward a place where understanding might bloom amidst the ruins.

"John, can you tell Sophie what you need from her to begin rebuilding?" the counsellor prompted, her inquiry piercing the fog of uncertainty.

Sophie shifted, her keen intellect attuned to the undercurrents of his response, ready to dissect the sincerity of his words. Yet, there was more than mere analysis in her poise; it was an offering of patience, a tacit agreement to navigate the labyrinth of healing together.

The room, wrapped in dusky hues as the evening light waned, held them in a timeless embrace. In the dimming glow, hope dared to whisper, and two souls grappled with the possibility of redemption through the veil of their intertwined shadows.

John's fingers ceased their nervous dance along the chair's armrest, coming to rest in a clasp that betrayed his inner turmoil. He swallowed hard, feeling the counsellor's words settle upon his shoulders like an invisible mantle. The idea of vulnerability tugged at the barriers he had constructed around his heart, compelling him to allow light to seep through the gaps in his facade.

His gaze found Sophie's, and in her eyes—a stormy sea of blues—he saw the reflection of his own fears. The desire to be the man she deserved wrestled with the spectres of his past indiscretions. It was a silent battle, played out in the theatre of his mind, where every doubt was a dagger and every resolution a shield.

"Vulnerability isn't weakness, John," the counsellor had said, her voice a soothing balm against the sting of exposed secrets. "It's the cornerstone of trust."

He drew in a breath, tasting the stale air of the room, heavy with the scent of antiseptic professionalism and the faintest hint of jasmine from the counsellor's perfume. Each breath was an affirmation, a silent vow to tear down the walls, if not for himself, then for the woman who sat opposite him, her composure as admirable as it was heartbreaking.

"Rebuilding trust..." John started, the words rough from the quarry of his guilt. "It means tearing down the old structures, doesn't it? Starting... starting anew." His voice, though hesitant, carried an undertone of resolve that vibrated through the quiet space between them.

Sophie's hands, previously clenched in her lap, relaxed ever so slightly, the delicate interplay of shadow and light upon her features betraying a cautious optimism. Her lips parted, but no words emerged—only a deep, quivering breath that conveyed the depth of her internal struggle.

The counsellor nodded, her silhouette framed against the window where twilight painted the sky in hues of bruised plum and fading gold. "Yes, John. And it starts with a single step. A choice."

"Then I choose..." John's declaration hung in the air, raw and unpolished, "...to be honest. To be present. To be the partner she deserves." Each commitment etched itself into the silence, a promise seeking purchase in the fertile soil of hope.

Sophie's response was a whisper, fleeting as the last rays of day, "And I choose to believe we can find a way forward—together."

A tentative hope unfurled within the room, its petals fragile yet determined, seeking sustenance in the murky waters of uncertainty. There was no fanfare, no sudden illumination; only the shared acknowledgement of the arduous journey ahead. The lingering tension was palpable—a living entity that coiled around them, binding yet not suffocating.

"Let's continue this path," the counsellor said, her voice echoing the subtle thrum of possibility that resonated within the confines of her office. "Explore it together, and see where it leads."

As they stood to leave, the contours of the room seemed to blur, the boundaries between pain and healing, betrayal and forgiveness, all melding into a landscape ripe with the complexities of human emotion. They were starting a journey filled with heart-wrenching challenges, yet for the first time, a glimmer of hope emerged, suggesting that the map they drew might lead them back to each other.

After leaving the counsellor's office, John lingered on the doorknob, as if reluctant to leave the space that had witnessed his rawest truths. The door clicked shut behind him, sealing away the confessions and promises as sacred artifacts to be revisited in future sessions. He took a deep breath, the cool evening air wrapping around him like an unwelcome embrace after the stifling emotional heat of the room.

The sky was a tapestry of twilight, streaks of mauve and indigo bleeding into each other, heralding the night's approach. The trees lining the path to the parking lot swayed gently, their silhouettes whispering secrets only the wind could understand. John felt their murmurs brush against his skin, carrying the subtle promise of unrest and the allure of the unknown. His footsteps were soft against the gravel, every crunch a reminder of the delicate terrain he was navigating within himself.

As he approached his car, his reflection caught in the darkened window—a man seemingly composed yet haunted by an inner disquiet that refused to be quelled. John ran a hand through his short brown hair, the gesture an attempt to smooth the edges of his thoughts, which fluttered like moths against the lamp of his conscience.

He slipped inside the car, the familiar scent of leather and faint cologne enveloping him. It was the scent of routine, of a life meticulously curated to avoid the pitfalls of chaos. Yet, beneath it lurked the musk of unspoken desires and the bitter tang of regret, an undercurrent that no amount of surface cleanliness could erase.

Resting his forehead against the steering wheel, John allowed himself a moment to absorb the weight of the evening's revelations. The encounter with Sophie, fraught with tension and tender vulnerability, had left him feeling as though he'd traversed the expanse of their shared history—every misstep and missed opportunity laid bare.

The engine hummed to life at the turn of the key, a low growl that spoke of power and potential. As he pulled out of the lot, the orange glow of the streetlights cast long shadows across the dashboard, dancing like spectres of doubt over his clenched hands.

However, a thread of resolve, woven from the very fibres of his being, weaved through the uncertainty. He would confront the spectral figures of fear and longing that stalked the corridors of his heart. He would delve into the labyrinth of his soul, facing down the Minotaur's complacency and evasion that had held sway for too long.

With each mile that passed, the contours of his resolution grew sharper, edged with a newfound clarity. He sought more than existence—the depths of connection and richness of experience he had so carelessly chased in another's arms.

The road ahead stretched into darkness, a void where headlights dared to sketch only the briefest of paths. But within John Hawthorne flickered a flame, feeble yet defiant, fuelled by the tentative hope that he and Sophie might navigate this nocturne together, forging a future neither could yet see but both yearned to believe in.

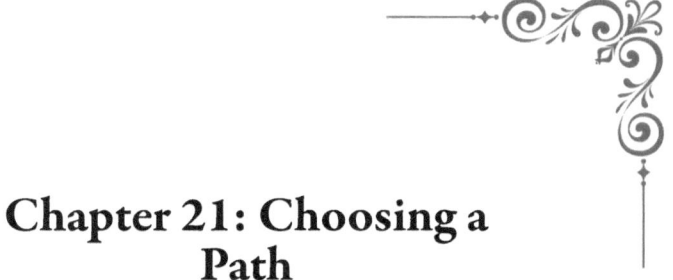

Chapter 21: Choosing a Path

John stood motionless at his bedroom window, the soft morning light seeping through the semi-drawn curtains and casting a warm glow on his contemplative face. The neighbourhood was waking up; sunlight teased the edges of well-manicured lawns, and dewdrops sparkled on the petals of azaleas, like remnants of an evening's secret tears. He watched as the world outside stretched and unfurled in the day's embrace, while inside, his chest felt tight with an array of conflicting emotions.

The chime of his phone sliced through the stillness of the room, a discordant note that set his pulse racing with unfamiliar urgency. It was a message from Jessica Sterling—the woman whose very name stirred a cyclone of desire and doubt within him.

"Meet me at the pool?" The words glowed on the screen, simple yet charged with a silent power that seemed to pull him magnetically toward the source.

John's thumb hovered over the keypad, hesitation creasing his brow. The community pool – a public space transformed into a private theatre where the play of memories danced vividly in his mind. Each memory was a brushstroke of colour, painting a picture of Jessica in her element: the water glistening on her skin, her laughter mingling with the sound of splashing, her eyes reflecting the depth of summer skies.

With a deep breath that did little to steady his racing heart, John typed a response. "I'll be there."

As he sent the message, the atmosphere around him felt charged with the electricity of imminent storms. The decision to go brought no relief. He stepped away from the window, leaving behind the comforting light of morning for the uncertain journey ahead.

John's footsteps were a soft patter against the sun-warmed concrete as he made his way to the community pool. The familiar route unspooled before him like a reel of silent film, each house a set piece from a life scripted by habit. The rhythmic clacking of a sprinkler punctuated the hush of mid-morning, casting a fine mist that settled on his skin like a whisper.

He passed by the Jenkins' manicured lawn, the scent of freshly cut grass flirting with his senses, and it was there, beneath the broad canopy of an ancient oak tree, that John's mind slipped into the past. He remembered the first time he saw Jessica at the pool, sunlight haloing her chestnut hair as she emerged from the water like some ethereal creature from a dream. The spark that ignited between them had been immediate—a magnetic pull as undeniable as gravity that drew him into her orbit.

The memory carried him onwards, through streets alive with the susurrus of leaves and the distant laughter of children. Each step seemed to echo with the palpable tension of that initial encounter, the air thick with the promise of something forbidden and intoxicating.

Upon reaching the pool, John's gaze found Jessica instantly. She stood at the water's edge, the sun casting her figure in a golden glow that seemed to highlight the contours of her body through her sundress. Her emerald eyes met his, and for a moment, the world around them dimmed, reduced to mere background noise.

"John," Jessica's voice was a melody laced with excitement and vulnerability as she stepped closer. "I've been thinking about us, about what we could be." Her words curled into the air, mingling with the scent of chlorine and sunscreen. "There's so much out there waiting for us—adventure, passion, a life that breaks away from all this," she gestured expansively, encompassing the boundaries of their well-ordered lives.

She leaned in, her breath a caress against his cheek, her presence a gravitational force tugging at the edges of his restraint. "Can't you feel it, too? That hunger for something more?" She searched his face, seeking affirmation, her own yearning laid bare in the space between them.

As Jessica spoke, John felt the weight of her vision settle upon him, heavy with possibility and fraught with the peril of desire. Here, in the charged silence of the community pool, the future loomed large, its seductive enchantments woven through her every word.

John's heart thrummed a chaotic rhythm as Jessica's plea hung in the air, her vision of a life unrestrained by convention pulsing through his veins like a siren's call. His gaze lingered on her, tracing the earnest contours of her face and the undulating fabric of her dress that whispered secrets with every breath of wind.

The allure of her proposition, ripe with the sweet tang of forbidden fruit, clashed violently against the image of Sophie—her steady blue eyes, the quiet strength of their shared history. He felt himself teetering on an invisible precipice, each path suffused with its own peril and promise.

"Jessica," he began, his voice a low murmur wrestling with the cacophony within, "this... it's not just about adventure. It's about loyalty, commitment." The words tasted like ash, a bitter testament to the turmoil that carved through him. Her offer was a tempestuous sea, and he, a vessel caught in its merciless grasp, tugged toward the depths where light could not reach.

She reached out, her fingertips barely grazing his arm, sending ripples of heat cascading beneath his skin. The contact was fleeting, but it seared a memory into his flesh—a branding of what might be if he dared to leap.

"Think about it, John," she whispered, her voice a velvet laced with steel. "We could be extraordinary."

With that, she turned away, leaving him adrift in the swell of possibilities that threatened to drown the life he knew. John observed her retreating figure, sensing a subtle shift in the atmosphere, as if the world had slightly shifted.

He left the pool, the water's surface mirroring the tumult in his soul, Jessica's words echoing in the chambers of his mind. Each step towards his old patio was laden with the gravity of unspoken choices and the ghosts of laughter that once filled those summer nights.

The patio greeted him with a deceptive calm, the slats of wood cool beneath his feet, a stark contrast to the inferno that blazed within him. He stood there, amidst the remnants of evenings spent enshrouded in the intoxicating scent of night-blooming jasmine and the warmth of shared confidences.

His hands brushed against the back of the chair where Jessica had sat, her laughter spilling into the night like a melody that promised joy untethered by the mundane. The memories were vivid and visceral—a tableau of passion that flickered in the fading light of what was and could never be again.

In the silence, John wrestled with the shards of longing that pricked at his conscience, the seductive dance of what-ifs and maybes that Jessica had awakened. The patio, once a haven of intimacy, now served as a crucible for his indecision, its empty spaces a reflection of the chasm that yawned before him.

The soft clink of wine glasses resonated in John's memory as he traced the etched contours of the empty bottle left on the patio table. A ghostly echo of laughter, Jessica's laughter, wove through the silence, entwining with the whispers of wind through the trellis. The scent of the rich Merlot they had shared lingered in the air, mingling with the earthy aroma of damp soil from the garden beds nearby.

John closed his eyes, allowing himself to sink into the tapestry of recollections. Flashes of Jessica, her chestnut hair glinting in the moonlight, her emerald eyes reflecting the stars above, played across his mind. There was a freedom in those nights, an electric current that surged through their veins and pulsed with the promise of uncharted tomorrows.

A shiver ran down his spine as the warmth of those memories clashed with the cool breeze that swept across his skin. The joy they had found in each other's company was undeniable, yet it was a joy laced with the forbidden—a flame that could all too easily consume everything in its path.

With a heavy sigh, John turned away from the patio, the theatre of lost evenings and lingering desires. He stepped through the door into the quiet sanctuary of his old home. The transition felt like moving between worlds, from the realm of dreams into the stark light of reality.

Sophie was there, seated at the kitchen table, her silhouette defined by the soft glow of the lamp. Her eyes met his, blue pools of still water veiling an undercurrent of hurt. In her gaze, there was both resignation and resolve, a testament to the strength of her character.

"John," she began, her voice steady but tinged with vulnerability, "I've been thinking... about us." She paused, searching for the words that could bridge the chasm between them. "I know things have been strained, but I believe we can find our way back if we're willing to try."

Her offer hung in the air, a lifeline extended across the tempest of his emotions. The stability she spoke of was a comfort to the chaos within him, yet it also anchored him to a shore he wasn't sure he wanted to claim.

In that moment, the house seemed to hold its breath, waiting for John's response. The shadows cast by the fading light played upon the walls, hinting at the complexity of choices yet made, the interplay of loyalty and desire, comfort and risk.

John stood motionless, caught in the gravitational pull of Sophie's earnest plea. His heart, a battleground of warring affections, ached with the weight of impending decisions. The silence stretched between them, fraught with the echoes of past promises and the murmur of uncertain futures.

As he looked at Sophie, her composed expression masking the turmoil beneath, John knew that whatever path he chose, it would be one paved with profound consequences—for all that had been and all that might yet be.

John nodded, a gesture as fragile as the peace hanging in their shared silence. Sophie's words, sincere and unwavering, reverberated through the chambers of his heart. The life they had meticulously constructed together rose up around him—walls adorned with shared memories, foundations rooted in mutual respect, a ceiling that sheltered but also confined. Her love, steadfast as the oak in their backyard, promised sanctuary. Yet, beneath the tranquil surface, John felt the undercurrents of his restlessness pulling at him.

"Thank you, Sophie," he murmured, his voice a blend of gratitude and sorrow. His eyes lingered on her face, tracing the lines of loyalty etched there. In her gaze, he saw the reflection of a life he was familiar with—safe havens amidst chaos. However, the echoes of another laugh, the spectre of a different touch, whispered of unexplored waters, tempting him with the seductive song of what might be.

Turning away from Sophie's hopeful eyes, John reached for the door. He needed air—the kind of air that filled his lungs when he was alone, unanchored by expectations or past vows. The door clicked shut behind him, a soft punctuation to the silent discourse between husband and wife.

The evening wrapped around him as he walked, the streets of the neighbourhood unfurling like the pages of a well-thumbed novel. Each house, each tree bore witness to moments suspended in time—some steeped in the warmth of companionship, others tinged with the heat of forbidden encounters.

He passed the cafe where he and Sophie had shared countless Sunday brunches, the clink of coffee cups a steady rhythm to their weekend routine. Next, he strolled by the park where Jessica's laughter had once intertwined with the rustling leaves, an impromptu picnic igniting flames that danced too close to the edge.

The contrast was stark—asphalt and grass, coffee and wine, tranquillity and tempest. With each step, John delved deeper into the duality of his desires— the contrast of a heart divided. He tasted the sweetness of his wife's unwavering affection, yet inhaled the intoxicating allure of a passion that refused to be tamed.

A breeze stirred, carrying the faint scent of roses from someone's garden, mingling with the promise of rain. It was as if nature itself conspired to mirror his inner storm, the atmosphere dense with the electricity of his indecision.

John paused at the bridge overlooking the creek, where water flowed beneath him, indifferent to human plight. Here, suspended between land and sky, he allowed himself a moment of vulnerability. The memories cascaded through him—a torrent of tenderness, thrill, loyalty, and longing.

In the end, it was not just a choice between two women—it was a choice between two versions of himself. There was the man who cherished the gentle cadence of marital vows, and the one who yearned to leap into the abyss, chasing the ephemeral joy that came with risk.

John let out a sigh, seemingly burdened by the weight of his world, and turned back towards his path home. The journey was solitary; the road ahead shrouded in the twilight of his own making. His decision lay heavy within him, a secret not yet ready to be spoken, a truth that shimmered like the fading day—elusive, beguiling, and achingly real.

The sun began its slow descent, casting elongated shadows across the pavement like dark fingers stretching out to touch the world. John walked through them, his own silhouette distorted and frayed at the edges, much like the thoughts tangled in his mind. The orange glow of twilight bled into the blue canvas of the day, painting a picture of time slipping away—each second pulling him closer to a precipice he wasn't sure he was ready to face.

His footsteps were soundless, absorbed by the cushioned earth of the park that had become both sanctuary and prison. The familiar sounds of the neighbourhood—the distant bark of a dog, the rustling leaves whispering secrets to one another—seemed muted, as if the world held its breath waiting for John's decision. He could almost feel the pulse of the evening, throbbing with the same restless energy that coursed through his veins.

He arrived at the quiet park bench etched with initials and memories, its wooden slats worn smooth by countless reflections. This had been his retreat, where ideas took shape and decisions found their footing. But never before had the weight of such a choice pressed so heavily upon him. He sat, the wood cool beneath him, and felt the solitude envelope him like a shroud.

The air was rich with the scent of damp soil, a harbinger of nightfall. John closed his eyes, inhaling deeply, seeking solace in the fragrance of the earth. He listened to the soft lullaby of crickets beginning their nocturnal serenade, harmonising with the last calls of birds bidding the day farewell. It was in these moments of sensory surrender that the gravity of his situation became most acute.

John thought of Sophie—her steady presence, her unwavering commitment. Their history was etched into the very fabric of his being, a tapestry of shared experiences that could not simply be unravelled without consequence. And then there was Jessica, who beckoned him into the unexplored realm of his desires, offering him horizons tinged with the unknown.

A leaf spiralled down from an overhead branch, twirling in the air before landing gently on his knee. Despite its insignificant size, the leaf served as a reminder of the delicate balance of life and the multitude of paths that a single decision could change.

The park around him deepened into shades of indigo and grey, the transition from day to night almost imperceptible until darkness claimed its dominion. John remained still, a figure carved from the very essence of contemplation, his heart waging wars no passerby could fathom.

John found himself standing at the threshold of a future painted with strokes of passion, stability, adventure, comfort, uncertainty, and truth. He let out a breath he didn't realize he'd been holding, the sound swallowed by the encroaching night.

With the heaviness of his heart matched only by the dusk enveloping him, he rose from the bench. His movements were deliberate, a testament to the inner resolve that was solidifying with each passing moment. The choices he faced were not just about the women in his life but about the man he wished to become.

In the silent communion with the twilight, John acknowledged the inexorable change within him. It was here, in this hallowed space between light and shadow, that he would gather the shards of his courage and step forward into the life he was meant to claim.

John watched the day's end with an intensity that mirrored the burning sphere's final descent. In the waning light, his features were etched with the weight of impending change, the slow demise of daylight reflecting the close of one life chapter and the anxious tremor of another's inception.

He could feel the ache—a tangible entity—in his chest as he acknowledged the truth of what lay ahead. John's hand grazed the roughened wood beside him, the tactile memory of countless evenings spent pondering life's curious twists. His fingers traced the grains, each line a roadmap of choices past, each splinter a reminder of potential paths yet untaken.

The world around him grew hushed as if nature herself held her breath, awaiting the verdict of his heart's tribunal. In the shadowed half-light, he rose. He moved with the certainty of a man deeply rooted in his decision. There was no fanfare, no grand gesture to mark the gravity of the moment—only the quiet assurance of his footsteps as he turned back toward the home that had cradled his past.

The path ahead stretched before him, shrouded in the ambiguity of twilight. It meandered through the neighbourhood, a serpentine trail of possibilities that beckoned with both promise and peril. Each step served as a silent testament to the path he had chosen, and each breath whispered the life he would soon embrace.

John's jaw set against the building crescendo of his resolve, his eyes fixed on the dimming path. The night's embrace was near, yet within him burned a light no darkness could quell—a flame kindled by the fervour of his own beating heart.

John wove through the quiet streets, his footsteps a soft cadence against the hush of twilight. Houses stood as silent sentinels, their windows flickering with the first touch of evening light, casting long shadows that stretched across the pavement like dark fingers.

The scent of jasmine hung heavy, its perfume seeping from gardens he passed, ensnaring him in a web of nostalgia. It reminded him of times lost, of whispers shared in the sultry embrace of night. This dusky interlude seemed to suspend the world, teetering on the brink of revelation, yet cloaked in the velvet shroud of secrecy.

John's gaze swept over the familiar landscape, each contour of the neighbourhood etched into his memory, each tree and lamppost a mute witness to the tumult churning within him. A dog barked in the distance, the sound muffled and far away, as if it too respected the sanctity of his solitary pilgrimage.

He took a deep breath, the cool air filling his lungs, tinged with the distant aroma of woodsmoke from someone's fireplace. His heart beat a rhythm that seemed to echo the uncertainty of the shifting hues overhead, where the last vestiges of sunlight fought a losing battle against the encroaching darkness.

As John walked on, the neighbourhood settled into a gentle hush, a quietude that mirrored the stillness he sought to find within himself. It was a silence not devoid of life but brimming with the murmurs of countless untold stories— of secrets kept and promises broken.

His silhouette, now just a shade among shades, began to merge with the night. The contours of his figure blurred, edges softened by the dimming light, as he became part of the fabric of the evening itself. To any onlooker, he was a man alone, wrapped in contemplation, his presence a fleeting imprint on the cusp of nightfall.

With each step toward the threshold of his home, John carried with him the weight of decisions unspoken. Yet there was a resolve in his stride—a silent declaration of intent that needed no words. The path before him remained uncertain, shrouded in the enigma of dusk, but he pressed forward, drawn by the inexorable pull of destiny.

Chapter 22: Rebuilding Trust

John Hawthorne stood motionless in the centre of his well-ordered living room, a tableau of suburban serenity belying the tumult churning within him. His gaze lingered on the familiar comforts: the plush throw pillows neatly arrayed on the couch, the mantel lined with smiling family portraits. Yet all these trappings felt like a veneer, a cover for the raw and restless craving that simmered beneath the surface of his existence.

He inhaled deeply, tasting the stillness of the air, redolent with the faint scent of lemon-scented polish from the morning's chores. The weight of his decision pressed down upon his shoulders, an invisible yet oppressive force that demanded reckoning. With each breath, he steeled himself against the inevitable—the conversation that loomed over him like an oncoming storm.

As he walked by, his hand caressed the smooth fabric of the couch, an absent gesture that sought solace in a place where none existed. John stepped through the threshold of his front door, leaving behind the sanctuary of predictability, and ventured into the uncertain morning.

With every step towards Jessica Sterling's house, his footsteps fell deliberate and heavy upon the concrete path, as if he were walking through molasses, each stride a battle against the inertia of his own indecision.

The short journey seemed an odyssey, fraught with the kind of anticipation one feels at the precipice of irrevocable change. The air around him thickened, charged with the electric tang of an impending tempest.

As John approached the door of her home, the world seemed to sharpen into focus, each detail imprinted with vivid clarity. The rustle of leaves whispered secrets in the breeze, and the distant bark of a dog fractured the morning's calm.

At her doorstep, he paused, his heart pounding fiercely against his chest, a drumbeat announcing the forthcoming confessions. The tension in the air was almost corporeal, a shroud woven from threads of anticipation and the chilling thrill of what lay just beyond the wooden barrier before him. John raised his hand, poised to knock.

John's knuckles rapped against the door, a sharp counterpoint to the chaotic rhythm of his pulse. He could feel the vibration through his hand and up his arm, as if the wood itself held a current that connected him to her even before she answered.

The door swung open, and there they were—caught in the silent vacuum of each other's gaze. Jessica's emerald eyes bore into his with an intensity that seemed to hold the world at bay; they spoke of shared secrets and smouldering memories in the absence of words. For a heartbeat, or perhaps an eternity, neither moved nor spoke, the air between them thick with the ghosts of whispered promises and clandestine encounters.

"Jessica," John began, his voice betraying the tremor he so desperately wanted to conceal, "I've come to say something important."

She leaned against the doorframe, arms crossed, yet her posture did nothing to mask the vulnerability flickering in her eyes. Her silence was an invitation for him to continue, a silent beckoning laced with both fear and resignation.

"Look, I..." His voice faltered, and he swallowed hard. "I'm sorry, truly sorry for the hurt I've caused you. This...what we had, it was never fair to you—or to Sophie." The name of his wife tasted like betrayal on his tongue.

A shadow passed over Jessica's face, a cloud dimming the sunlit warmth of her features. "John," she said, her voice smooth but edged with the shards of her broken expectations, "we both knew what this was. Or at least, we thought we did."

"I got lost," he admitted, searching her face for absolution. "Lost in the thrill of you, in the escape. But it wasn't real—not really. Not like my life with Sophie has to be."

"Has to be?" she echoed, a wry smile tugging at the corner of her lips, though her eyes remained pools of unshed sorrow. "Or wants to be?"

"Both," John said, mustering the conviction that had spurred him to her threshold. "I want to rebuild the trust I've shattered. With her. With myself."

Jessica pushed off from the doorframe, her movements languid yet deliberate. "Then go," she uttered softly, the single word a release and a condemnation all at once. "Go and be the man you want to be, John Hawthorne. Just remember that some things, once broken..."

"Can't be mended," he finished for her, the understanding passing between them like the last flicker of flame before darkness claims the embers.

"Exactly," Jessica whispered, stepping back to close the door. "Goodbye, John."

A hush draped over them, thick and suffocating, as John lingered on the threshold. He could see the struggle painted in stark relief across Jessica's features—the way her eyes glistened with a sheen of unshed tears, how her lips trembled ever so slightly.

"Jess," he began, his voice a mere whisper, but it was enough to draw her closer, a moth to the dying ember of their connection. "I never wanted to hurt you. You brought something into my life I didn't even know I was missing. And for that," he paused, swallowed by the gravity of his own words, "I am eternally grateful."

The room seemed to contract with the weight of his confession, the walls pressing in as if to bear witness to this final act of their drama. She took a wavering breath, and he heard it—the softest of sobs caught in her throat. "Grateful," she echoed, her voice laced with a bitter edge that cut through the tension between them.

"More than you can imagine." John reached out, tentative fingers brushing against the cool skin of her arm, leaving a trail of goosebumps in their wake. "You deserve happiness, Jess. Happiness that doesn't hide in shadows or whispers."

Her laugh was short, a melancholy sound that tugged at the frayed edges of his resolve. "We both sought refuge in those shadows, didn't we?" she murmured, stepping back from his touch with a grace that belied her turmoil. "But now, daylight calls you home."

The air between them was charged with an energy that spoke of endings and beginnings, of love and loss intertwining like lovers' limbs. A finality loomed over them.

"Goodbye, John Hawthorne," Jessica said, each syllable a note in the elegy of their affair. Her hand reached for his, a fleeting connection that sent a jolt through him—a reminder of what had been.

"Goodbye, Jessica Sterling," he replied, the taste of her name bittersweet on his tongue. Their hands parted, the space expanding into a chasm filled with the echoes of their past.

She stood framed in the doorway, a vision of allure and heartbreak, the perfect embodiment of the tempest they'd weathered together. And then she stepped back, retreating into the sanctuary of her home, the click of the door punctuating the silence.

John turned away, the ghost of her touch lingering on his skin like the memory of a forbidden kiss. As he walked next door to his old home, the morning breeze whispered through the leaves, carrying with it the scent of jasmine and the faintest hint of regret.

He crossed the threshold into the quiet familiarity of home. The walls, which once echoed with laughter, now stood mute, absorbing the weight of his heavy heart. His footsteps, a measured cadence against the wooden floor, were testament to the quiet resolve that had settled in his bones—a man determined to mend the fractures in his life.

He found Sophie in the living room. She was the picture of serenity, a stark contrast to the storm of emotions churning within him. Her blonde hair fell around her face in gentle waves, and she looked up from her book with those perceptive blue eyes that seemed to pierce through his facade.

"John?" She spoke the word with a cautious tenderness, the timbre of her voice wrapping around him in an almost tangible caress.

He cleared his throat, finding his voice in the stillness. "Sophie, we need to talk." His words hung between them like a delicate veil, trembling at the prospect of being torn away.

A frown creased her smooth brow, and she closed her book, setting it aside. She motioned for him to sit, her movements graceful yet fraught with an instinctive wariness. He took his place on the couch beside her, close enough to feel the warmth radiating from her skin but impossibly distant all the same.

"Nothing has been okay for a while now," John began, his tone hushed as if in reverence to the truth he was about to unveil. He met her gaze, his own eyes raw with sincerity. "I've made mistakes, terrible ones. And I've hurt you without even realizing how deep the wounds went."

Shock painted her features, a silent tableau of confusion and dawning realisation. Yet beneath the initial jolt there was something else—a guarded flicker of hope that dared not fully ignite.

"Sophie, I've been lost," John continued, each confession carving out pieces of his soul. "But I don't want to lose you. You are the compass that guides me back when I stray too far from who I am, from who we are together."

Her hands clenched into fists, then she relaxed, a visual echo of her internal struggle. It was as though she was grappling with the desire to reach out and the instinct to protect herself from further harm.

"John, what are you saying?" The question was whispered, a plea for clarity amidst the shadows of doubt.

"I'm saying that I want to rebuild us. I want to earn back your trust, piece by painstaking piece." His voice echoed with the unspoken promise to repair the damage.

They sat there, two souls caught in a dance of vulnerability and longing, the silence stretching out like a bridge over troubled waters. The air was thick with the scent of the blooming jasmine from their garden, its fragrance a bittersweet reminder of promises once whispered under the stars.

Sophie reached out tentatively, her fingertips brushing against his hand. It was a gesture so fraught with uncertainty yet filled with a latent yearning, a silent acknowledgement of the love that still lingered, defiant in the face of pain.

"Tell me everything, John," she said at last, her voice a mixture of steel and silk, commanding yet vulnerable. "And maybe... just maybe, we can find our way back to each other."

John turned the worn pages of the marriage counselling brochure. The paper felt thin and fragile under his fingertips, much like the current state of his relationship with Sophie. He cleared his throat, the sound more for fortifying his own courage than to catch her attention.

"Marriage counselling," he began, his voice threading through the quiet of the room like tentative steps across a frozen pond, "I think we need to for the next few months." His eyes sought hers, searching for a flicker of acceptance in the cool blue depths.

Sophie sat across from him, her body language an origami of cautious interest, each fold creasing her expression with both hope and scepticism. The air between them was tinged with the scent of jasmine, laced with the muskier note of impending spring, a blend that spoke of change and the passage of time.

"Transparency," John continued, gently laying the brochure on the coffee table—a symbolic offering between them. "That's my promise to you. No more secrets. No more shadows hiding our truths."

Her gaze lingered on the brochure, as though she could read the subtext hidden within its lines—the silent plea for redemption and the blueprint for rebuilding their fractured bond.

"Okay," Sophie said after a pause heavy with consideration. "We'll give it a try." Her voice weaved a delicate thread through the dense layers of their past mistakes.

Over the next few weeks, they navigated the process of reestablishing their connection, akin to two strangers learning an unfamiliar dance. Each conversation was a delicate probe into the tender flesh of their wounds. Laughter was a rare gem unearthed in the mineshaft of their interactions, glinting with the possibility of what might be rediscovered.

John watched one evening as Sophie absently twirled a lock of her short blonde hair around her finger, a habit he'd always found endearing. It was during these small, unguarded moments that he glimpsed the woman he fell in love with, still there beneath the layers of hurt.

"Remember when we got caught in the rain at the park?" he ventured, the memory surfacing like a lifeboat in a stormy sea. "You laughed so hard, and your hair was plastered to your face..."

A smile cracked the stoic facade Sophie had been wearing like armour, a momentary lapse that allowed the warmth of nostalgia to seep through. "We looked like a pair of drowned rats," she admitted, and for a fleeting second, her eyes danced with the ghost of that day.

Sharing such memories gave them brief breaks from the constant tension. Each story acted as a salve, easing the sting of their recent history.

Gradually, the space between John and Sophie shrank, their evenings filled with the soft murmurs and the clink of cutlery against plates as they shared meals once again. They were tentative steps on a long path of healing, each one a testament to their willingness to mend the tapestry of their union.

And as night wrapped its velvet arms around the world outside, inside, the Hawthorns sat side by side, their hands nearly touching on the sofa's armrest. The distance that remained was a silent acknowledgement of the journey ahead, but also a recognition of the ground already covered.

With each passing day, the air in their home grew less charged, the undercurrents of emotion less turbulent. A sense of equilibrium began to return, fragile yet tenacious, like the first green shoots after a devastating fire. Their shared determination to reignite the spark in their relationship was the kindling for a new beginning, and slowly, almost imperceptibly, the embers of their connection began to glow once more.

John lifted the corner of the Afghan draped across the back of the couch, his fingers brushing against Sophie's as he pulled it over their laps. The slight touch, almost accidental, held the weight of a thousand conversations, apologies, and promises. Under the woven threads, their hands tentatively met, tentative at first, then with purpose, intertwining like roots seeking nourishment in the same patch of soil.

Sophie's laughter, a sound that had become scarce in their home, bubbled up unexpectedly at some old sitcom rerun, filling the room with echoes of simpler times. John watched her, the crinkles around her eyes, and felt something shift inside him—a cautious optimism, like the first glimpse of dawn after an endless night.

"Remember when we tried to reenact this scene?" he asked, voice laced with affectionate humour.

"Disastrous," she replied, her hand giving his a gentle squeeze, "but fun."

The shared memory hung between them, a fragile bridge over the chasm they'd been navigating. It was a small yet significant breakthrough—the kind of moment that could change the course if given enough attention and care.

Later, when the TV's glow had faded and the night pressed against the windows with its cool breath, John stood and offered his hand to Sophie. "Walk with me?"

The words were an invitation, a chance to step outside the confines of their home and into the vastness of the world, where anything might happen. She took his hand, her grip strong and sure, and together they stepped out into the neighbourhood.

With their hands clasped, their unhurried walk conveyed a silent solidarity that left a lasting impression. The evening air was cool, carrying with it the scent of jasmine and freshly cut grass—the familiar aromas of suburban life. Distant sounds—children's laughter from a backyard, the rhythmic bark of a dog, the soft hum of cars in the distance—merged into a symphony of normalcy, a backdrop to their tentative steps towards healing.

Streetlights cast pools of amber light onto the pavement, each one a beacon as they passed from one to the next. Shadows danced around them, hinting at the mysteries of the night, yet within the circle of their joined hands, a warmth held back the darkness.

With every step, John felt the solid ground beneath them, the resilience of the earth mirroring the resolve in their hearts. They walked through the neighbourhood, not as two people lost but as explorers rediscovering a once-familiar terrain.

Sophie's hair caught the light of the moon, a shimmering halo that made her seem ethereal, otherworldly. But her presence was grounding, pulling John back from the edge of his thoughts, back to the here and now—to the woman beside him who still wore his ring, who still walked by his side.

Their journey was far from over, with the path ahead uncertain and rife with the risk of reverting to old patterns. Yet, for the first time in a long while, there was a sense of movement— of progress. Hand in hand, they ventured forward, each step a silent vow to continue— to fight for the love that had once seemed unshakeable and could be so again. Amidst the whispers of the night a delicate and new hope sprang to life.

The evening air wrapped around John and Sophie like a whispering shawl, cool and secretive, as they continued their walk through the quiet neighbourhood. The gentle rustle of leaves beneath their feet spoke of change, of things shed and new paths taken. The stars above blinking one by one signalled that even in darkness there is a pattern to follow.

Their hands remained entwined, fingers laced with the familiarity of years and the tentative pressure of newfound understanding. They exchanged no words, finding them unnecessary. Their silence spoke volumes, a language of pauses and breaths that said more than any confession.

With every step, the subtle scent of night-blooming jasmine seemed to rise from the gardens they passed, infusing the air with a fragrance that was at once comforting and intoxicating. It served as a reminder of nature's ability to endure, to bloom even when shrouded in twilight.

John glanced sideways at Sophie, taking in the soft curve of her cheek illuminated by the ambient glow of street lamps. Her eyes held a reflective sheen, pools of liquid resolve that mirrored his own determination. They shared a journey fraught with missteps and wrong turns, yet here they were, pacing toward a future they dared to mend together.

A dog barked in the distance; its echoes are a testament to life stirring within the calm expanse of suburbia. The sound symbolized their personal awakening, the stirrings of hope fluttering against the confines of past hurts, yearning for release.

As they turned a corner, a gust of wind tousled their hair, an impish reminder of the world's unpredictable nature. In this moment, they found comfort in unpredictability and knowing they could weather it together. The world might spin on its axis, but they had each other to steady the roll.

They stopped at the crest of a small hill, where the road dipped down toward their shared home. From this vantage point, they could see the outlines of their life together, etched against the backdrop of suburban serenity. There stood their house, a beacon of continuity amidst the shifting landscape of their relationship.

John squeezed Sophie's hand, a silent promise etched in the gesture. She returned the pressure, her thumb brushing against his skin in a caress that spoke volumes. A cautious optimism tethered them to the present, a buoyant thread weaving through the fabric of their bond.

With a collective inhale that seemed to draw in the very essence of the night, they stepped forward, descending the hill toward the light that beckoned them home. This was no grand finale, no sweeping resolution. Instead, it was the beginning of many tomorrows, the first brushstroke on a canvas that awaited the colours of their renewed commitment.

And as they moved into the embrace of shadows cast by their front porch, the unspoken understanding between them solidified into something tangible, a cornerstone upon which they would rebuild. Their journey toward healing had truly begun.

Don't miss out!

Visit the website below and you can sign up to receive emails whenever Amanda Burrows publishes a new book. There's no charge and no obligation.

https://books2read.com/r/B-A-BJDBD-DZMMF

BOOKS 2 READ

Connecting independent readers to independent writers.